A CUP OF WANDERLUST

A CUP OF SERIES BOOK 2

ALEXIS GORGUN

To everyone who has big dreams but is too scared to make that first step, this one is for you.

To my lovitas: for all the love, joy, and endless happiness you bring into my life.

Published by Alexis Gorgun

Copyright © Alexis Gorgun

All rights reserved.

2023

Cover Design: www.rejenne.com

Developmental and line edits: Lizzie Bell

Proof reading: Paula at LilyPadLit

No part of this book may be reproduced in any form or by an electronic or mechanical means, including information storage and retrieval systems, without written permission from the author, except for the use of brief quotations in a book review. To obtain permission to excerpt portions of the text, please contact the author on her website.

All names, characters, places, and incidents in this book are fiction and figments of the author's imagination. Any resemblance to actual persons, living or dead, business establishments, events, or locales is entirely coincidental.

www.alexisgorgun.com

CHAPTER 1

REE

ANDREW PARKER. Twelve letters in his name. Twelve chances to be a decent boyfriend. Too bad he failed that test within the first month.

Any guy with boyfriend potential gets the honor of having their full name saved in my phone. Anytime I'm not treated properly, I remove a letter from their name. If they lose all of their letters, I ditch them. It's become a tried-and-true way to filter out the weeds.

No one's made it past two months. Which isn't a surprise. Why would a boyfriend be different if my father couldn't last longer than a few years with me? When I was sixteen, I dated someone I actually liked, and I'm still scared by that experience. Since then, I've developed a rule—I don't date people I like. It's much easier to keep sex and feelings completely separate. Pretty sure this qualifies me as a genius.

Sure, it'd be nice to be proven wrong, but that's a fantasy. And that's what makes my letter docking system the most perfect system ever. It keeps me grounded in real life and gives me a concrete reason to move on.

If a man doesn't hold the door open for me, I'll dock a letter. Or if he puts the toilet paper roll upside down, sorry bro, it's another letter lost. For larger infractions, like passive aggressiveness or gaslighting, I'll remove multiple letters.

A couple of hours ago, Andrew lost his last letter while we were at a party for his friend. Turns out, they weren't *just* friends. So, I snuck into an Uber without a goodbye, removed his last letter from my phone, and that was that. But in the silence of my apartment, the itch to travel begged me to listen.

And listen I did. There's nothing like booking an impulsive getaway trip.

I settle into the black faux-leather airport seats with a bottle of wine in hand. A quick trip to the duty-free store brought my buzz back. I unscrew the cap and take a long pull. My half-full backpack lays between my feet. Whatever Drunk Me packed will have to last for however long of a trip I've booked. Given the half-full status, I doubt I packed correctly.

I can always buy stuff when I land, but I'd prefer not to waste precious funds on something so basic as clothes. On the plus side, though, the wine bottle will easily fit inside.

My phone rings and I smile when I see who it is.

"Heyyyy," I say, dragging the word out because I know my sister, Jules, hates it.

"Where are you? Andrew messaged me on Insta saying you disappeared from the party?"

"Oh, you know, the usual."

She snorts. "He lost the last letter?"

"Affirmative."

"I'll block him."

Jules gets me. I always block them once they lose all their letters.

"We still on for brunch tomorrow?" she asks.

"About that…"

"Not again." She sighs in the way only a big sister can, full of disappointment but also admiration. "Where are you going this time?"

I open my passport and scan the boarding pass nestled inside.

"Istanbul," I say.

Oh shit, Drunk Bree. Worst decision *ever*.

The wine I just drank threatens to come back up. My hand shakes, and I grip the phone tighter to make it stop.

"Seriously?" she asks.

"As a heart attack."

"Not funny. Are you going there for Bilet?"

Bilet is the stray dog Mom became obsessed with during her recovery. The street dog with a name that means *ticket* in Turkish. Apparently, they named him that because he has a penchant for traveling around the city on the public transport. The people of Istanbul love him. There's even an Instagram hashtag dedicated to him and his whereabouts within the city.

I only know this because Mom regularly sends updates to Jules and me about his comings and goings. I hate she clutters our group chat with such nonsense. Nonsense I refuse to open. Mom acts like we all live in Turkey and not Seattle.

"No," I say harshly. "Bilet has nothing to do with it."

He has everything to do with it, but I'm too angry at myself for booking this trip, to be honest. Out of all the places in the world I could've chosen while drunk, I chose Istanbul.

Is this karma biting me in the ass? Stalking Bilet isn't going to magically heal me or change the past. Well, I'm not sure if it's considered stalking, if it's an animal. The dictionary really needs to add qualifiers to their definitions.

I take another sip of wine. And another. My regrets about this trip are a problem for another time. Like when I arrive in Turkey. I already paid for the ticket, so it's not like I can back out now.

"How long will you be there?" Jules asks.

My boarding pass has no information on my return, so I click on my confirmation email and scan the dates.

"Ten days," I say.

"Ten days," she sputters. "Bree—"

"I'm sorry, okay? I know I'll miss the family dinner you planned, but what's done is done. You can always join me?" I invite her every time I do something like this—which is more than I care to admit—and she always responds in the same way.

"You know I can't. Not only do I have the kids, but I have a job. One I can't do from home."

4

I mouth the words along with her. Her reaction is now like a knee-jerk reaction to my question at this point.

"Because you chose to not follow your passion," I say. "You—"

"Can we get back on track and focus on the fact you're going on another impromptu trip? You're gone practically all the time. And now you're missing dinners you promised to attend. This is getting out of hand."

I rub my temples to stave off the building headache. "Or maybe I'm just living my best life?"

"You keep running away."

"I am not. I'm enjoying life."

"Ever since Mom—"

"Oops," I say, "going through a tunnel. You're breaking up."

"You're at an airport. Don't you dare hang—"

"Love you. I'll call when I arrive."

"Leaving won't stop you from feeling!" She shouts it in a rush, the words melding into one long one.

I ignore them, and say, "Byeeeeee."

I love Jules to death, but I can't stand when she turns on her "mom mode" with me, as if being six years older gives her the right. Or maybe it became natural for her when she had to step into that role to help Mom. Either way, it's become a permanent wiring in her brain.

And it's annoying.

I want her to be my sister, and only my sister. To have fun with me. But I can't remember the last time she let loose and freed herself of responsibility. Her kids and job kind of cramp her style and make it difficult, but still.

I wish she'd try.

5

For me.

Traveling has become part of my personality. It's a total vibe, and one I enjoy rocking. If only she'd join me, she'd finally get it. She'd finally understand why I do it.

"Good evening, everyone," a voice says over the speakers. "We'll now begin our boarding process for flight TR210, our nonstop service from Seattle to Istanbul. Passengers requiring extra assistance may board at this time, followed by…"

I tune out the rest of the announcement as almost everyone stands at once and scrambles to be first in line. Like we don't all have assigned seats.

Amateurs.

I prefer to be one of the last to enter. The aisles are clear, and I don't have to wait for people to realize they've passed the row they're supposed to be sitting in. I hate having to do that awkward dance of shoving my ass into the person already seated and trying to make space for them to pass.

My ass is big enough to make it a thing. When that's added to my five-foot-eleven stature, it's even more awkward since I'm taller than most people.

When the line dwindles, I pack the wine bottle in my backpack and take my place in line. A scan of my boarding pass, a check of my passport, and I'm on my way to row twenty-nine, seat B. It's a middle seat, but that's no problem. Sleeping is my superpower and I plan to wield it on this flight.

There's an older woman already sitting by the window. She's got a movie going as well as noise-canceling headphones on. The woman doesn't glance up when I sit down, and that makes her the perfect seat partner. I slide my backpack under my seat, place my headphones on, and take out my iPad to avoid any potential conversation.

The seat next to me, the aisle seat, is free. My hope that it'll remain that way, and I can steal it for myself, rises when only a few stragglers bypass me on the way to their seat.

But just when I think boarding is complete, *he* arrives.

The gorgeous man towers over the flight attendant that's right on his heels, talking nonstop. He somehow glides down the aisle like it's a runway. His tan loafers complement the navy trousers that are the perfect length to show a little ankle. Never thought ankles could be sexy, but oh how wrong I've been. He's paired everything with a short-sleeved cream sweater that looks softer than cashmere.

My oh my, this guy looks so out of place back here in economy. He'd fit more on a private plane, or at least in first class.

As he approaches, he doesn't constantly look at his boarding pass. Props to him for memorizing one number and one letter.

His shortish brown hair has a perfectly messy look to it, and I can't help but notice his overall symmetric features. He has a straight nose and light scruff that coats his chiseled jaw as if he forgot to shave the past day or two.

But his eyes... they're a work of art. The vibrant color stands out against his tanned skin. Amber and chestnut weave together into a unique pattern that's utterly fascinating.

My fingers itch to draw, to capture the beauty, but I focus on my current doodle, refusing to give into the temptation. I can do that later, in the privacy of my nonexistent hotel room.

Out of all the people on this plane, I'd be down for him to be my seatmate. It'll give me some eye candy on this twelve-hour flight. However, I'm going to have to rethink my nap plan if he sits next to me. I can sleep when I'm dead if this man graces me with his presence.

I pray to every deity I can think of that he'll sit next to me.

When he stops right in front of me and deposits a brown leather bag in the overhead bin, I'm giddy with excitement.

He settles next to me and a citrusy wave of bergamot swirls around me. I close my eyes and inhale the fresh and addictive scent.

Thank the travel gods he smells amazing. If he didn't, it would've put a damper on this whole fantasy I've got going on in my head.

He glances at me, and our eyes meet because I'm already openly staring at him.

Whoops.

But getting hit with the full force of his gaze is heart stopping. Literally heart stopping if the squeeze in my chest is any indication of it.

I rub at my sternum, trying to bring life back to my body. He doesn't break our stare, and it's like I'm teetering on the edge of a boundless chasm, a bottomless well of tawny warmth that threatens to engulf me.

A force tugs at the very fabric of my being, inviting me to leap into the unknown. And I'm already halfway tumbling into those eyes of his.

He glances away, and it's like a slap of reality. I snap back to my senses, utterly confused.

What in the unholy abyss is this? Is he a hypnotist? Because I've never been put in a trance, and yet it feels like I was just in one.

CHAPTER 2

$\mathcal{H}$AYDEN

TWO HOURS BEFORE

Today has been a disaster from the moment I woke up. Adrien, my boss, is up my ass nonstop. Traffic to the airport was horrendous. And then I find out they booked all legs of my flight for economy class and not business.

I can't deal with much more. And I certainly can't deal with this never-ending line at airport security. My gold card for the airline doesn't help speed up the process. Neither does my expired Global Entry card. I'll add renewing it to my never-ending to-do list when I return to the US.

My patience is paper thin. I have too much to do before the flight takes off to waste my time here in line. And the couple in front of me seem to be unaware of the world around them. They're chatting and giggling as if they're at a party and not at an airport security checkpoint. I glance at my watch again, my irritation growing with every second that passes.

The woman rifles through her enormous tote bag, pulling out what looks like an endless stream of miniature shampoo bottles and electronic devices. What the hell? How many iPads do these people have?

Her companion is still wearing his belt and doesn't seem to realize that it needs to come off, along with his shoes. He must've missed all the signs and announcements while in line for the past thirty minutes.

I grit my teeth and fidget with my boarding pass. The couple finally places their things into the plastic bins, but they're moving at a glacial pace.

"Come on," I mutter under my breath, frustration bubbling up. I've still got to call my new assistant and figure out what the hell happened to my flight.

After, I'll have to return Adrien's calls and answer some of the fifty work emails I've received in the past two hours. The thought of having to deal with all the problems at NomNom causes all the energy from my body to evaporate. My motivation to handle any of these work problems is officially at zero.

I'm so tired of it all. Tired of Adrien and his demands. Tired of my ideas being blocked all the time. That's why I planned my vacation in the first place. After the constant nagging from my family to take one, I finally booked it. And yet, work is still on my mind.

The woman finally places all her items in the security bins, but then drops her boarding pass. It flutters to the floor. I watch in exasperation as she bends down to retrieve it, causing even more delay. Anger, hot and uncomfortable, fills my chest.

I'm seconds away from losing it.

When it's finally my turn, I throw my shoes and laptop into the bins, determined to make up for lost time.

The second I've collected all my belongings, I call my new assistant. She's a friend of Mom's who needed a job after her husband died. I hired her to help, but now I'm regretting that decision if she messed up this bad on her first task.

"Hi," she answers on the second ring.

"Hi. There's a problem with my flights. They're all booked for economy and not business."

"Oh my goodness. I'm so sorry. I—"

"It's fine." It's not fine, but I don't have time for her excuses. "I need you to check if there's another flight out today from Seattle. If not, I need the return changed to the appropriate class. I have to arrive in Istanbul by tomorrow at noon for my meeting with Deniz." I've canceled on Deniz too many times in the past months, and I refuse to delay it anymore.

"Sure thing. I'll call you in a few."

I hang up and check the latest message from Adrien. It's a news article about our biggest competitor, Table-Ease, announcing their expansion into Europe.

I don't have the energy to deal with him, but if I don't call him back, he'll continue messaging and calling me until I respond. Boundaries aren't part of his vocabulary.

"Finally," he says. "Why didn't you call me sooner?"

"I'm at the airport. Remember? I'm taking two weeks off."

"I don't care where you are. When I message you, I expect you to respond."

I roll my eyes. What a prick.

"The news from TableEase isn't a surprise," I say. "We discussed expanding into Europe last year and decided against it."

I use "we" for the sake of politeness, although he ultimately decided against it. From day one, he's consistently rejected my ideas for growth. It's been this way ever since my brothers and I sold NomNom to Adrien nearly three years ago, and when I stepped into the role of CEO. He's on the board of directors, along with his two best friends. Which means they'll go along with whatever Adrien wants.

"Well," he says, "you were wrong back then, and now we're late to the European market. Let's not even talk about the market share we're hemorrhaging to them in Asia. What kind of CEO are you?"

Outrage ignites within me as he dares to blame me for his mistakes and then questions my ability to be a CEO. The audacity of this man is unreal. And I've officially had enough.

I'm tired... of everything.

Tired of working for someone else.

Tired of constantly refusing to move to Singapore because I don't want to miss out on time with my family.

Tired of working on something I've lost my passion for.

I've only got two months left on my contract, and it's two months too long to be dealing with this asshole. TableEase started to aggressively target our market share six months ago. And the past six months have been brutal because of it. Twelve overseas trips within six months can do that to a person. Adrien's trying to squeeze out every bit of life I have in me before I leave them.

"Adrien," I say, already over this conversation. "I'm about to board my flight. And then I'm officially on vacation for the next two weeks. There's nothing that can be done about TableEase expanding. I can resend you the proposal discussed a year ago about the expansion into Europe. Why don't you look it over and we can talk about it when I get back?"

"No. That's not acceptable. You can't just take a vacation in the middle of this shitshow. You need to cancel it and come to Singapore immediately."

"This is my first vacation in five years." This trip to Istanbul is my desperate attempt to get away, to recharge. Sure, I have a few meetings with Deniz, but that's for my passion project, not my work with Adrien. Istanbul is my favorite city, one filled with great memories and most of my firsts in life. My first love, my first heartbreak, my first time connecting to a place we lived in.

"I don't care," Adrien says. "I need you back in Singapore now."

"That will not happen. My flight's about to board. I'll speak to you in two weeks."

"You can't do this—"

"I informed you months ago about my plans. I'll see you in a couple of weeks."

I hang up, refusing to listen to his response.

Fuck, I need a drink.

Or five.

* * *

In Seattle, I listen to the voicemail from my assistant informing me there are no other flights. But she spoke to the airline and says they'll take care of me on the flight.

Whatever that means.

There's a woman holding up a sign with my name on it after the gangway. I approach her.

She smiles and says, "Follow me. I'll escort you to your gate. Your connection is tight, and I was informed that you can't miss the flight."

"Thank you," I say, getting into the golf cart.

When we're on our way, I pull up the group chat with my brothers and read the messages they sent while I was on the plane.

Theo: Where are you off to now, asshole?

Anders: Have you seen the TableEase news?

Me: Istanbul and of course I saw it.

Anders: All okay?

Me: I've got it under control. You know I live for challenges like this.

THE LIE CAUSES my insides to swarm, but they don't know how much I hate my job. I downplay it all the time. Like pretending to love flying to Singapore every other week and living in a constant state of jet lag. By saying that I only work ten-hour days. Or how I enjoy working with Adrien. Or that I party all the time while traveling, but in reality, I work nonstop.

And the worst part is, I can't quit. Not without violating the terms of the contract we made when we sold NomNom to Adrien. I signed on to be CEO for three years, and I refuse to back out.

NomNom is the first time I ever applied myself to something meaningful. It's also how I contribute to my family. Me being the CEO is what allows my brothers to work on their passions and our parents to live in their dream home.

Anders: How's Adrien taking the news?

Me: Really well, actually. I was already planning to expand to Europe, so we won't be too far behind them.

Theo: Aren't you the CEO with the most-est.

Anders: He's definitely the best CEO out of all of us.

THIS IS why I can't tell them I hate my job. They're proud of me. I'm finally their equal and not just their youngest brother who never applied himself.

Theo: Well, don't be butthurt over TableEase getting the drop on you. I should make you a plaque saying "Hayden is the best CEO in the world."

Me: Plaques are old school, old man. But I wouldn't mind a coffee cup with that on it.

Theo: Fuck off. I'm not that much older than you. And a coffee cup? What are you? A dad?

I CHUCKLE. Man, I miss my brothers.

Me: Throw in a tie and it'd be on dad level.

Anders: Now I know what to get you for Christmas.

Me: I'm about to board. I'll write when I'm in Istanbul.

THE GOLF CART rolls to a stop, and at the door of the plane is a flight attendant.

"Welcome, Mr. Watson," she says. "I'm so sorry there was a mix-up with your seats, but please rest assured I'll be taking good care of you on the flight."

I glance at her name tag. "Thanks, Mindy, but I don't need any special treatment. It was a mistake on my end."

"Either way, it would be my pleasure to ensure you have a smooth trip."

She's going above and beyond, but I'm too tired to appreciate it.

Mindy reaches for my bag, but I insist on carrying it myself. I lead the way to my seat, not needing an escort, but there's no way to shake her.

When I'm a few steps away from my row, I finally notice the bombshell that's sitting in the middle seat. Right next to where I'm supposed to be. Red hair that reminds me of Autumn leaves and creamy skin stand out in a sea of mundane.

Our gazes collide, and for a timeless instant the noise of the cabin fades into a distant hum. And the chaos within my mind quiets. In this fleeting moment, it's like our souls brush against each other in greeting.

Her lips curve into a subtle, enigmatic smile. There's a hint of adventure within the smile, and promise. I can't help but be drawn to her. Huh, maybe sitting in economy won't be so bad with her next to me.

I look away and quickly settle into the seat. An announcement states that boarding is complete and flight attendants move down the aisles to do a final check of the overhead bins.

Feeling my seatmate watching me, and unable to resist

getting another look at her, I turn my head in her direction.

She holds my gaze, not at all ashamed I caught her staring.

Tiny flecks of gold burst through the forest green of her eyes. She continues to hold my gaze, almost daring me to break contact first. Electricity races across my skin at the challenge she throws down.

We stare at each other for a few more beats before Mindy interrupts by handing me a glass of champagne.

My seatmate gazes at the glass with longing before she unzips her backpack and pulls out a full-sized bottle of wine.

What in the world?

She unscrews the cap and lifts the bottle in my direction in salute before drinking deeply. I chug my champagne in solidarity. I can't look away as she wipes her mouth with the back of her hand, recaps the bottle and re-zips it inside her backpack.

I have so many questions, but the most important one is what else does she have in her bag?

She goes back to doodling on her iPad as if nothing happened. I glance at her screen. She's drawing what appears to be a version of the Loch Ness Monster. Her Nessie has huge, fake eyelashes, and she's doing her lipstick in a mirror. My seatmate scrawls the words "you have to believe in yourself" above Nessie before drawing what looks like the beginnings of a mermaid next to it.

I snort and she glances at me. I give a pointed look at her headphones and there's no light on. She smirks in response before continuing to work on her drawing.

Who doesn't activate the noise canceling abilities on the headphones if they're wearing them? Curiosity blooms inside me, unexpected and vibrant. I haven't felt much beyond annoyance and numbness this year. But with her, there's something there.

Mindy returns to take my empty glass and offers me a cup of coffee. I gladly take it and she says, "I'll return when we start our food service."

I give her my thanks and glance at my seatmate from the corner of my eye.

This time, she scowls at my coffee as if it personally offended her. Now I'm even more curious about what she's thinking.

CHAPTER 3

REE

We've been in the air for forty-five minutes and all Mr. Hottie has done is open his tray table and place his half-drunk cup of coffee on it.

I've kept up my doodling to keep my hands busy and to pass the time. When the flight attendants came down the aisle with drinks some minutes ago, I ordered a mini wine bottle and I've already finished it. I debate if I should bring out the bottle in my backpack again, but I hold off. I don't want Mr. Hottie to think I'm an alcoholic, even though I've got no buzz going on.

But I need a distraction from the fact that I booked this trip and alcohol isn't working.

And my seatmate? Now that's a good distraction because I can't figure out what he's doing. He hasn't started a movie. Or taken something out to work on like a tablet or a laptop. He also doesn't take out a book.

Or anything.

He just sits there with his cup of coffee and stares at something in the distance. I keep waiting for him to do something more, so I'll get a clue as to what is going on.

But I'm left with nothing. Nada. Zilch.

Only him drinking coffee every once in a while, even though it must be cold by now.

Maybe he doesn't realize that drinking coffee on a flight is a no-no? They don't use bottled water to make it, and that's just gross.

After another ten minutes of him just sitting there, I can't take it anymore.

"Excuse me," I say, pulling down my headphones.

He turns to me.

"You realize this is a twelve-hour flight?" I ask.

"I'm aware. The pilot even made an announcement about it." His tone is deadpan, and I can't help but be captivated by his voice.

It's perfection, especially when it's not filtered through my headphones. Gravely and deep, he sounds like the perfect narrator for a smutty audio book. I'd buy it and listen to it nonstop. Ohhh, maybe that's his job. Or maybe he's a sex phone operator.

"Are you a sex phone operator?" I ask and immediately laugh at the bewildered expression on his face.

"What?" he asks, clearly confused.

"Your voice is hot and then it got me thinking about sex phone operators and if they're a thing still and… here we are."

"I don't think they exist anymore."

"Shame," I say. "You could've made a killing."

"I'll be sure to add that tidbit to my resume."

"Good idea. And while you're at it, you should add that you like to sit on long-haul flights with nothing for entertainment but a cup of black coffee." I say coffee like it's a sin.

He chuckles. "Not a fan?"

"Of airplane coffee? Ew, no. And you shouldn't be one either."

"I like that you've been watching me." If possible, his voice dips lower, becoming sexier.

"Don't read too much into it. I'm bored."

He makes some sort of sound, like a cross between amusement and laughter.

"So… inquiring minds want to know," I say. "Are you planning on spending this entire flight looking off into space?"

"I'm not staring off into space. I'm watching other people watch movies."

I blink at him and then blink some more. Did I hear him right? Because that's so cool.

"Which one are you watching?" I ask, scanning the screens I can see.

"Other side of the aisle, one row in front of us. Super-hero movie."

I lean partially into his seat so I can see too. I rub against his sweater, and I can confirm it's softer than anything I ever dreamed of.

"You ever watch it?" I ask.

"Who hasn't watched the latest *Batman*?"

23

I grin. "So why re-watch it, then?"

"It's fascinating to see which movies people choose to watch. It says a lot about them as a person and it's more fun this way."

"What does watching a superhero movie say about someone? That they like to rescue people?"

"Nah, they're the egomaniacs and the mansplainers of the world."

I laugh, because yeah, I can see where he's coming from. I gaze between the gaps in the seats in front of us.

"What about them?" I nod toward the gap. "It's a war movie. What does that mean?"

"They're adrenaline junkies who like destruction."

"Sounds like my kind of people." I laugh.

He stares at me with an unreadable expression. I have no clue what it means, and it bothers me. I want him to be dazzled by me. To be amused by me as much as I am by him. If nothing else, for pure entertainment's sake. But I wouldn't be opposed to joining the Mile High Club with him.

"Which movie would you watch?" I tap on the screen in front of him. "If you turned it on."

"I like to remain mysterious, so I'd never be caught dead watching a movie on a plane."

"But you'll drink the coffee and risk getting E. coli. Good to know where your priorities are."

"If it's a choice of getting diarrhea or letting a stranger get a glimpse at my personal preferences, I'll choose diarrhea every time."

Hello mile-long red flag list with that sentence alone. But somehow, I'm here for it. He's mysterious and fascinating and I'm just bored enough to be entertained instead of turned off.

"You must be shitting your pants all the time then," I say.

"Something like that."

"Charming."

"I try."

But he doesn't have to try. He's got a personality that would draw most people in and a sly sense of humor to keep them hanging around. I couldn't have asked for better seatmates than him on my right and Silent Susan on my left. Not sure which deity is shining down on me, but I'll take it. This must be the karmic balance to Andrew losing the last letter in his name.

The cute flight attendant that gave him his coffee comes back around with what appears to be a menu in hand.

"I'll return to take your order in a few minutes," she says, giving him a winning smile.

He nods and looks over the menu.

I lean into him again, our arms brushing against each other. I need a better look at this menu and what they're offering him.

"Why in the world do you get a business class menu back here?" I ask.

"No reason."

"No reason, my ass. Whose dick do I have to suck to get this kind of VIP treatment?"

He chokes on his cold coffee and faces me.

"Are you implying I sucked a dick?" he asks with a curious tone rather than an offended one.

"I mean, that'd be hot, and I'd totally pay money to see it. But it's the best explanation I've got since someone is now being a Closed-lip Clarissa."

"My assistant accidentally booked me in economy class and the airline is trying to make it up to me."

"Meh, I like my version of events better."

He huffs out a laugh.

"If it was a mistake," I say, "you sitting back here, then why not take your private plane instead?"

"That's wasteful and bad for the environment."

"Wait, I was joking. You have a private plane?"

He glances at me before refocusing on the menu.

That's a *yes* if I ever heard someone not say it. Who is this man? I reach out and tilt his hand so I can get a better view of the menu.

"What are you doing?" he asks, glancing at me out of the corner of his eye.

"Reading the menu with you. It's like watching people watch movies."

"I've created a monster."

"There are some good choices here." Grilled lamb with rosemary jus and rice. Salmon on a bed of spinach and potatoes. Eggplant pasta. Damn, this is better than the normal pasta or chicken options in economy. "You should get the lamb."

"Why?" he asks.

"So I can try it too."

He doesn't even blink at my request and instead nods along. I like that. I like that more than I care to admit. Few people can keep up with my humor and crazy ideas. I have a feeling he may be the exception to that.

"With some red wine?" he asks.

"Obvi. They've got to have better stuff in business than back here."

"And what about the wine in your backpack?"

I snort. "It'd be better than that one, for sure."

He grins and closes the menu. The flight attendant must've been watching him because the second it's closed, she reappears. Hell, I don't blame her. I'd make him a priority if I were in her shoes.

"What can I get for you, Mr. Watson?" she asks.

"I'll take the lamb with your best red wine as well as the salmon and a glass of white wine."

"You want to eat *two* dishes?" Her penciled eyebrows rise to her hairline.

"I'm hungry." He says it in a tone that melts her on the spot. One she's helpless to resist and again, I don't blame her one bit, because I'm right there with her melting into my seat.

I adjust the air vent and blast myself with cold air, needing to calm my overheated body down. Whew, that's a potent smile right there.

"Okay, I'll see what I can do," she says before leaving.

"Two?" I ask.

"Well, I can't have you eating my entire dinner. Worst case, they say no, but they should have enough."

"Or more like you want to keep me on my toes and not know which dish you really want."

His lips twitch and I know I'm right. We go back to watching other people watch movies before I ask, "So, Mr. Watson, is Istanbul your final destination?"

"It is, Ms. ..." He waits for me to finish the sentence with my name.

"Adler. Bree Adler."

"That was a very James Bond introduction of you."

"You just dated yourself, Mr. No Name Watson."

"It's Hayden." He huffs and I'll consider it to be a partial laugh. "Are you staying in Istanbul?"

"Yup, for ten days."

"I wonder if we're on the same return flight, because I'm also returning in ten days."

"Probably, but you'll be up in business class because there's no way you'd be back here. They wouldn't let you, not after ordering *two* dinners. You're probably now on an extra special priority list, so they don't lose money thanks to you."

"Or I might get blacklisted and banned from flying after getting so much food." He grins. "Thanks to you."

"What can I say? I'm a bad influence." Which, according to Jules, is spot on. She hates it when I give her kids brownies for breakfast or shower them with gifts.

"We're a match made in heaven."

Why those words turn my insides to mush and make me swoon, I'll never know. But they do, and in that moment, while we gaze at each other in the middle of a crowded flight with a baby screaming in the background, I realize I could like him.

And that's... new.

My letter removal system doesn't make room for feelings. It's a countdown until I move on from someone. It's easy and works well for me.

But Hayden Watson... I like his humor and wit. I like

that he gives me shit back. Good thing we only have this flight together before we part ways. There's no chance I could fall for him for real in twelve hours.

The same flight attendant returns with two trays in hand, and another attendant stands behind her carrying two full wine glasses.

"Here you go, Mr. Watson," the flight attendant says, passing the trays to him.

Hayden hands me a tray, as well as a drink, before taking his own. The flight attendants look back and forth between Hayden and me a few times, clearly confused.

"I can't fit everything on my tray table." Hayden smiles his melting smile again at the attendants. "Thank you so much for making this happen."

"Any time," she says. "If you need anything else, let me know." The flight attendant removes the tops on both of our dishes and leaves.

I rub my hands together in glee.

"You're drooling," Hayden says.

"I'm about to make these chops my bitch."

He lifts his wine glass to mine. "Cheers to that."

We dig in and I can't help the moan that slips out. This is way better than some pasta dish. Drunk Bree didn't pack any snacks or think it was a good idea to load up on some in the airport, so this is heaven.

"Keep moaning like that," he says giving me a long and heated look, "and I'll keep you stocked with any food you want."

"Careful. That sounded an awful lot like you're going to see me again after this flight."

"And who's saying we won't?"

"We're going to be in a city of fifteen million people."

"It's not like we're going to play 'Where's Waldo?' in the city," he says.

"That would make for an interesting trip."

"Where are you staying?" he asks.

"Why?"

"So I can cheat on the whole 'Where's Bree?' game."

"So, funny thing… I don't actually have a place to stay." Drunk Bree shouldn't be allowed access to my credit card anymore. I should put a reminder somewhere for her to book a hotel or some shit next time this happens.

He stills and looks me up and down. "What do you mean?"

"Well, you see, this was a last-minute trip. And I didn't have time to book accommodations before I boarded the flight."

"How last-minute?"

"Like a couple of hours before the flight took off."

"Huh." He says it like his brain can't compute the concept.

"I'll figure something out." I lift my shoulder, the picture of nonchalance. "I always do." And I do, eventually.

"So, this isn't the first time you've just forgotten to book accommodations somewhere?"

"Nope, and it probably won't be the last. Where are you staying?"

"At a place in Bebek."

"Is Bebek in Istanbul?"

He nods. "First time in the city?"

"Yeah."

"What brings you to Istanbul?"

"A dog," I say.

"A... dog?"

"Yup. You?"

"Work," he says.

"Care to elaborate?"

"Not really, but it deals with animals too. Are you a vet?"

"Yikes, no," I say. "I don't even like animals." Mom may like Bilet, but I think dogs are dangerous and disease-ridden pests. I had an idea one night, months ago, that if I could follow Bilet around, perhaps I could understand why people love dogs so much.

And if I understood that... maybe I could heal. Bilet helped Mom heal, and I hope maybe it will work for me too. But now that I'm on my way to Istanbul, I'm not sure if I'm ready for that.

"But you're here to see a dog?" he asks.

"Yup."

"Interesting," he says.

"You keep saying that."

"Because you just might be the most interesting person I've met recently."

"That better be a compliment," I say.

"It is. Trust me."

I down the rest of the wine.

"You've got"—he brushes his thumb underneath my lip—"some wine here."

The slight contact of his thumb against my skin is enough to turn me on. Huh, that's new. I blame my reaction on the mediocre orgasms Andrew gave me.

"I… thanks." I clear my throat. "I'm stuffed, but I wonder if they'll serve you dessert."

"And let me guess, you want some?"

"I have a normal-food stomach and a dessert stomach. My normal-food stomach is full, but my dessert one is empty."

He grins before saying, "I'll see what I can do."

CHAPTER 4

$\mathcal{H}$AYDEN

NORMALLY I'M indifferent to flights. They're just a means to an end. A temporary place I must endure before reaching my destination. And a way to disconnect from the constant demands Adrien has.

But this flight?

I wish it would last for days, weeks even.

All thanks to Bree. I'm feeling something for the first time in years—interest. And not just for a quick fuck. It's so different from the normal numbness that's been plaguing me that I almost don't trust my response to her.

What is it about her?

When she gets up to stretch and walk around for a bit, I bite back my groan at the perfection that is her ass. It's begging for someone to bite it, to slap it, to enjoy it. She has the type of beauty that makes people take notice, but paired with her model height, curves, and confidence… she's striking. Multiple heads turn when she walks down the aisle. And I'm right there with them.

She asked me questions about myself, but I've kept everything vague. The details don't matter, not when she's a temporary moment in my life. A moment that'll last the flight, and perhaps spill over into the city. It will undoubtedly be full of fun, but it'll still be a moment.

No one ever keeps in touch with me. I learned that through my entire childhood, moving to a new country every few years for my dad's job. Friends promised to call, but they didn't. They promised to visit, but it never happened. My ex-girlfriend promised to try long-distance, but it only took her a month before she cheated on me.

So, I'll enjoy this moment with her, or even a handful of them, but then we'll part ways. There's always an expiration date. And no one has proven me wrong yet, not in almost thirty years.

Even if it's selfish, I want to lean into her anyway. To hold on to how she makes me feel. Maybe a holiday fling will get me out of my head and infuse life back into the hollow chambers of my heart. And maybe it'll be enough to sustain me for… who knows how long until I feel something like this again?

Damn, that's the most depressing thought in the world.

When she returns to her seat, she places the iPad back on her tray table.

"Are you an artist?" I ask, not able to help myself from knowing more about her.

"Noticed that, huh?"

Her answer is full of sass, and I grin. "Can you show me?"

She shrugs and passes the device to me. There are multiple logo designs, all creative, and some sketches like the Nessie she was drawing earlier, all with something funny written on them.

She's talented, but halfway down the photo roll, I come across something truly amazing. There are paintings where she took inspiration from a famous painter and put her own spin on it. There's one of Seattle's skyline done in the style of van Gogh's *Starry Night*. A jungle, but in the style of Picasso. A beautiful house melting like in Dali's clock.

I stare at the details of the jungle and zoom in to different parts. "These are gorgeous. Why are there only a few of the mashups?"

"They started as a joke, and only commissioned by my sister for her friends."

"And the logos?"

"My full-time job. It gives me the flexibility to work from anywhere in the world."

"Impressive."

She shrugs like it's not that big of a deal. But starting a business, building up clientele, and earning enough money to live on takes hard work.

I trace my finger over her screen. Maybe I could use this as a way to see her while we're in Istanbul, before we part for good once we return to the US. Maybe I could use her skills to create a logo for Deniz's business in

Istanbul. It'd give me a reason to meet up with Bree while we're in the city.

"Do you have a business card?" I ask.

She laughs with her entire being, and it's addictive. Too addictive.

"I packed while drunk a few hours before the flight, and I'm pretty sure I forgot to pack essentials," she says. "You really think I remembered to bring a business card?"

She's the embodiment of spontaneous chaos. I always thought I was spontaneous, but she's taking it to another level. I've never taken a trip without booking accommodations or packing properly.

"What essentials?" I ask.

"Everything you're thinking about." Her voice drops to a whisper and all I can picture is her naked in my bed. Her red hair fanning across my pillow while I cherish her body.

I shift in my seat, trying to ease the tightness in my pants, and she grins in response. She knows exactly what she's doing to me.

"Then," I say, "I guess I'll have to find you the old-fashioned way."

She nods, sagely. "Not sure where you'll find a carrier pigeon, but I'd like to see you try."

And just like that, she steals a genuine laugh from me. A laugh unlike the one I force around my family to hide how not okay I am.

"I meant Googling you," I say, "and finding your website."

"What are we, in the year 2005? I expect you to be more resourceful than that. There's social media these days if you haven't heard. And you have my full name. I mean, I basically already gave you everything you need."

I snort. She doesn't hold back.

"Let's skip all that and get to the real question," I say. "Can I have your number?"

That way, we can meet up during our time here.

"Yeah, no."

"No?" I ask, surprised.

"First…" She holds up a finger. "You book your flights in the wrong class."

"That wasn't me—"

"Doesn't matter. Second…" She holds up another finger. "You can't do basic internet stalking. I mean, that's an ick if I ever heard one."

"An ick? Wouldn't that be a green flag? Or a beige one at the minimum?"

"Not in my book."

"Interesting," I say. "And is there anything else to add to this list of icks?"

She thinks for a minute and says, "Not yet. But we've still got many hours left, so you never know."

"Just to be clear, there's no chance for me to get your number?"

"Eh, not really," she says. "That ship has sailed, and we've only got eight hours left on the flight."

"Then that just means I've got eight hours to change your mind."

"You can try." She laughs. "But just to let you know, the chance of that happening is zero."

* * *

SIX HOURS TO go and she begins another doodle on her iPad. I watch as she draws a cute dinosaur with a meteorite coming right for it. I'm so entranced that I keep staring. She writes the words "maybe I should make a wish" above the dinosaur's body and I laugh.

She glances at me out of the corner of her eye. "I see you like to watch other people draw, but have you ever read a book while someone reads?"

"Can't say that I have. I'm normally not close enough to another person to do it."

She chuckles and changes the app she's in. She turns the iPad toward herself, hiding it from me. When she's done clicking around a bit, she places the device back down where it's half on my tray table and half on hers.

"You're welcome to read aloud," she says with mischief brimming in her gaze.

I've never been one to back down from a dare, so I clear my throat and say loudly, "One of his long, hard tentacles pushes into me, teasing my pussy. Testing if it'll fit."

She snickers as a few people turn my way.

"Hey." I glare at the onlookers. "Don't yuck someone's yum."

They roll their eyes and give me a strange look as Bree laughs harder.

"So you're into tentacle porn?" I glance at her. "I think finding out about this is second date material."

"Don't yuck someone's yum," she parrots back to me, grinning.

She moves to grab the iPad, but I take the device and read the rest of the scene. Tentacle porn exists, and I'm fascinated. I take note of how the creature pleasures the woman. I mean, I could use some of these moves.

"Had your fill?" she asks after another few minutes. "Did I turn you into a fan?"

"I've got so many questions. Like why is this on your iPad? But more importantly, I need to know what the name of this is so I can download it. Now I need your number because I need the name of this."

"The name is on the top, so you don't need my number." She laughs and taps the top of the screen.

* * *

FOUR HOURS TO GO, and we've moved onto a drinking game. Every time the cart rolls down the aisle, we have to take a sip of our wine. Every time we can guess the name of the movie on a screen we can see, the other person has to take a sip.

"I know this great little wine bar in Istanbul," I say, still angling to get her number. To get a date. When I'm with her, I forget about all my problems. Like my normal self is trying to dip a toe back into life, past all the bullshit plaguing me. I haven't thought once about work, or Adrien, since boarding. And that's a first.

"Nope," she says.

"Aren't you curious? Just a tiny bit? They also do food pairings. If you thought airplane lamb was good, just wait. It'll blow your mind."

"All this talk of food is just going to make me hungry. I highly doubt Mindy is going to give you two meals again."

"Let me take you out when we arrive. You won't regret it."

She smiles so wide, it's blinding. "It's still a no."

* * *

Two hours to go, and I'm getting antsy. She's still not budging.

"Let's play truth or truth," I say.

"Don't you mean truth or dare?"

"Nope. Truth or truth."

She chuckles. "You're ridiculous."

"It'll be fun."

"I'm not sure if I'd call truth or truth fun," she says.

"Come on, live a little."

"Fine." She grins. "But only for two minutes. And if we don't want to answer, we drink."

"Fine. I'll take it. Ready?"

She nods and places her hand on her plastic cup. I set a timer on my phone and place it on her tray table.

I press start and ask, "When was the last time you cried?"

"Six months ago. You?"

"Last week," I say. "I watched a sad movie."

"Aww, that's cute."

I grin. "Are you single?"

"Yes, are you?"

"Yes."

To say I'm relieved is an understatement. Even though I'm attracted to her, I wouldn't touch her if she were taken.

"Best date you've ever been on?" I ask, trying to see what she's into.

"I haven't had a good one."

Before I can ask a follow up question to that loaded statement, she asks, "When's the last time you lied?"

"Before I got on the flight."

"To whom?" she asks.

"You're going out of turn."

"You can go twice if you answer," she says.

"My brothers."

She raises an eyebrow at me.

"They weren't ready to hear the truth," I say with a shrug. "What will it take for me to get your number?"

She takes a sip of her drink.

Shit.

"Can I take you out?" I ask.

She opens her mouth to answer, but the timer goes off. She glances at it with a grin, but I scowl at it. It just interrupted the most important question I asked. And it appears like she has no desire to tell me the answer now that the game is done.

Double shit.

* * *

BREE'S the most stubborn person I've ever met. I'm using all my negotiation tactics on her, and she's immune to every one of them.

It's been eight hours of me trying… and failing.

And I'm now obsessed with her. Obsessed with

winning her over and getting her number. It's become my new goal in life.

I realize this isn't a normal reaction or healthy, but I don't care. Not when I'm having too much fun.

I'm not sure how one flight can change my entire focus in life. But here we are.

The challenge she presents is addictive as fuck. Paired with her personality and beauty, she's the most irresistible person I've ever met.

I've laughed more in the past twelve hours than I have all year, even when I include all my forced laughs with my family.

She's exactly what I need in my life—fun.

We have ten days in Istanbul, and I need to spend every second with her. To soak her up until I'm filled to the brim. This is our only chance to have fun together. She won't keep in touch when we leave. No one ever does.

We land before I'm ready, before I'm able to convince her to give me her number. The doors open and everyone in the plane impatiently waits as others grab their bags.

I'd normally be like them, but not now.

Not when I've got Bree standing next to me. We walk down the gangway, and I'm racking my mind, trying to think of a way to keep in touch. To meet up while we're here. To not have this be the end, not yet.

Twelve hours wasn't close to enough.

She slows her pace and I slow mine to match. The other passengers push past us, in a hurry to leave.

"This looks like goodbye for us." She adjusts the backpack on her shoulder and sticks her hand out for me to shake. "Until we meet again Hayden Watson."

I take her hand in mine, but don't let go after a quick shake. I hold on and run my fingers over her silky skin. "Let me give you a ride to Bebek," I say. "At least it'll get you into the city before you figure out where you'll stay."

"You do realize all the advice for women who travel alone is to be in full-on stranger-danger mode?"

"I can provide references if you need them. Or you can Google me now?"

"I wouldn't read the references." She laughs. "You sure you're famous enough to be on Google?"

I nod.

"I've got to see this." She takes out her phone and types on it. She holds it up to me and looks between me and the phone a few times. "You're hotter in person."

"Good to know." I grin.

"I'm going to send your info to my sister. If I turn up dead, you'll be blamed."

"I can live with that. Come." I place my hand on her lower back. "Your chariot awaits."

CHAPTER 5

REE

I'M IN TROUBLE. Deep, disastrous trouble. More than not knowing where I'll stay. More than being in Bilet's hometown and still unsure about how I'm going to handle it.

No, it's worse than all of that.

Because I like Hayden. More than in a you're-hot-let-me-be-your-sex-slave kind of way. Which, to be fair, is more than I'd normally feel toward someone. But I like him in the I-think-we-could-be-friends kind of way.

And that's too scary to even consider deeply.

As I grappled with these unsettling emotions on the flight, I kept myself distracted by playing ridiculous games with him and drinking. But the most thrilling diversion of all has become my phone number. Who would've thought we'd be so invested in this and that he'd try to convince me with an intensity that defies all reason?

It's been a test of endurance, and a challenge that pushed me to the limit. His ceaseless pleas, his artful negotiations, and his puppy dog eyes are all weapons he wielded in his relentless pursuit, testing my resolve.

I came close to giving in to him so many times. I never would've guessed how powerful I'd feel, how wanted it'd make me feel, by playing this game with him. It's exactly what I needed after Andrew and his wandering eye.

But now the flight is over, and I agreed to be in a car with him because I'm not ready for it all to end. Even if I don't have sex with people I like. Even though I'm at risk of breaking that little rule if we take this further.

He's kept his hand on my lower back as we walk through the airport and to passport control. It's remained there while we wait for his luggage while I rock just a backpack.

The Turkish language flows like music around me. It's a melody that speaks of a rich and diverse culture, but all I can focus on is his hand. The firmness, the confidence in his guidance. I'm so turned on and the blast of warm air and sun when we step outside doesn't help the situation.

Cars honking, people shouting here and there to get the attention of a nearby person, and the engines of idling buses and taxis fill my senses. It's already so vibrant here, and we haven't even left the airport.

Hayden guides us to a sleek, black SUV. A driver opens the door, and Hayden indicates I should go in first. He greets the driver in a low tone before getting in himself.

My face is glued to the window as I stare at the

modern roads, grassy embankments, and compare the utilitarian architecture of the houses in the city outskirts to the houses back home in Seattle.

"Do you have any ideas about where you want to stay?" Hayden asks after some minutes.

"Not really." I pull myself away from the window and look at him. "I planned on stopping by a coffee shop and doing some research. Why?"

"What if you stay with me?"

"Why in the world would I do that?"

He snorts. "Because you need somewhere to stay. And I have a house with plenty of room."

"You sure you can afford a house if you were flying in economy?" I joke. When I Googled him to verify his identity, the words multi-millionaire jumped out at me.

"There's only one way to find out," he says.

"You're right. I should Google you again, obviously."

He grins and I turn on my mobile data. I mean, I could use a free place to stay. But if I stay with him, I have to either find a way to not like him or to not have sex with him.

I tilt my phone away from him and read everything I can on his Wikipedia page. It says his first startup, NomNom, is a joint project with his brothers. It's a hugely successful reservation platform for restaurants in Asia, including reviews, menus, and allergy information in multiple languages.

Apparently, they sold it for one hundred million a few years ago, but he's still the CEO. Interesting. He was mysterious on the flight about his work. And it was a total vibe. But thanks to Google, I now have the tea. I scroll down to personal life and there's no mention of a girl-friend or wife. Hopefully he was telling the truth about that.

He's going to expect an answer to his question about staying with him and I'm not sure what kind of safety net I can put in place to protect my heart.

I glance at Hayden, and he's still staring at me.

"And?" he asks.

"You need a better photo on Wiki."

"I'll take that into consideration." He grins. "But I meant about staying with me."

"Only if we make a deal," I say, spitballing it. One thing is for certain, I need a distraction from the dog I came here to stalk. And Hayden provided that relief on the flight. We had the most fun when we played our games, particularly for my phone number. If we were to play a game that pushes our self-restraint to the limit, maybe I wouldn't even have time to think about Bilet.

"I'm listening," he says.

"I'll stay with you, but sex is off the table."

"For the entire time?" His eyes widen.

"Of course not." Hmm, what kind of test can I make here? Either way, I'm going to fuck him. That much is clear. He has six letters in his last name. If he loses all six in a few days, I'll fuck him and leave him. But if he keeps them all, and the sex is amazing, then I'd be willing to break my rule of hooking up with people I actually like. It's only for ten days. I'm sure I won't get too attached in that short amount of time. It's not every day someone who looks like Hayden drops into my lap, and I'm all about living life to the max.

"For the next five days," I say. "I've got to make sure you're decent."

"Three," he counters. "Promise I can prove I'm great in that time."

"Four, and that's my final offer."

"What happens if one of us gives in before the deadline?"

"You don't think you can manage some self-control?" I ask.

"Around you? Definitely not."

I grin, pleased. "Then we need some sort of penalty."

"If you lose, I want a custom piece of art from you."

"Okay, and I'd like the same from you."

"Fair warning." He grins. "You won't want to keep my picture. I'm not an artist. But how about I throw in a massage? Now that, I'm excellent at."

I can't help but look at his hands. Yeah, I bet he'd be amazing at giving a massage.

"Sounds good."

"Perfect," he says. "I have just one condition to add."

"By all means."

"We end everything between us in ten days once we return to the US."

"Obvi." I thought that much was obvious. "Oh, I'm excited. I've never had a vacation fling before."

He laughs and holds his hand out for me to shake. I grasp his in mine and he pulls me closer to him. "I have a feeling I'm going to enjoy this deal of ours."

Truer words have never been said.

* * *

"We're here." Hayden strokes my shoulder, and I blink awake.

Oh wow, okay. My superpower of sleep activated without my control. I shake off my power nap and take in the house in front of me.

Hello, mansion.

Nestled into the hillside, it has a commanding presence with its two-story stone façade that exudes a sleek and sharp sophistication.

I scramble out of the car, curious about the inside of the place I'll call home for the next week. I spin in a circle at the entrance, taking in the foyer. It's illuminated by a dazzling crystal chandelier cascading from the soaring ceiling.

Leaving my shoes by the front door, I walk on bare feet over the cool and polished marble floors. The home is decorated in rich creams and browns. It looks and feels like a professional decorated it. A subtle floral scent hangs in the air, and there are plants in strategic locations, soulless artwork on the walls, and tailored sculptures and decorations throughout.

A gigantic cream and red Turkish rug adds a splash of color and comfort in the living room. Hayden leads me upstairs and shows me my room. My bed has a fluffy white duvet and a shitload of pillows. I resist the urge to jump into it because that's going to have to wait. I refuse to touch the bed without first washing off all the travel grime on me. At least I have my own bathroom.

He points across the hallway. "That's my room."

"Convenient."

He grins and leads me downstairs again. The entire

back of the house is full of windows. He opens the sliding door off the gorgeous kitchen and a blast of hot air hits us. The pool glistens in the sun. A few lounge chairs sit next to it, but the best part of this entire place is the view of some sort of river.

"What's the river called?" I ask.

"That's the Bosphorus, and it's actually a sea strait between the Black Sea and the Sea of Marmara. It separates the Asian and European sides of the city."

"It's beautiful."

The hillside is littered with houses, one on top of each other. And yet, I can't see his neighbors to either side or above us, because there are tall bushes on all sides except for the one facing the Bosphorus.

"The kitchen is fully stocked. I need to run to a meeting but make yourself at home while I'm gone. Can I have your number now?"

"Nope," I say with a grin. "But you can give me the Wi-Fi password."

He smirks and passes me a piece of paper with the info already written on it. "I'll be back by noon. When I get back, we can go to my favorite brunch place and walk around if you want."

"Sounds good. Thanks again for letting me stay here."

"No problem." He checks his watch. "I need to get going."

"Toodles."

He disappears, and the roar of the car engine rumbles through the home. I take a quick shower and wrap myself in the plush white robe hanging in the bathroom. My stomach growls, so I grab my iPad and phone and bring everything to the kitchen.

I make myself a plate of crackers, cheese, and fruit to hold me over until he comes back.

I connect to the Wi-Fi and send Jules a text and a photo of the view.

Me: You should've become a hacker instead of a dentist.

Jules: Why are you writing me this in the middle of the night?

Me: It's morning here. And I thought you should know because I could totally use your skills. I've arrived in Istanbul and I'm staying at Hayden Watson's house. (Write this down in case I die.) Google only takes me so far, hence my need for your nonexistent skills.

Jules: I'll be sure to get right on that.

Me: Right? It shouldn't take longer than a few hours to learn.

Jules: Wait. I just Googled him. Who meets a millionaire in economy?

Me: Trust me, it was unexpected. You sure you don't want to join me?

Jules: And who'd watch the kids?

Me: Mom?

Jules: You know I can't do that.

Me: You're right. Sorry.

I GRIMACE. She's right. Mom wouldn't be up for watching them longer than a couple of hours. Not since the accident. And Jules hasn't been away from the kids for longer than a few hours. Since her divorce, she's made them a priority, and I get it. I do. But they're five and seven now. Even when her ex has them for a night or two, she still won't leave Seattle or have a night out. It's time she lives for herself and not just for them.

Jules: No need to be. I've got to go. I need sleep. Have fun and do everything I'd never be brave enough to do.

Me: I promise.

Jules: And promise to call Mom.

Me: Oh, come on. I'm on vacation.

Jules: Bree…

Me: Fine, love you.

Jules: Love you too.

AT LEAST I didn't promise when I'd call Mom, just that I'd call her. I'll wait until I'm back in Seattle to do it. It's not easy to spend time with her, and even though I definitely win the award for the worst daughter of the year, I'm doing the best I can. Jules doesn't believe me and expects me to do more. But I'm tapped out.

I head back to my room to unpack. And by unpack, I mean finally open my backpack and see what I brought. Other than the wine bottle. That pool is calling my name, and I need to know what I'm working with.

I settle onto the carpet and reach inside the bag. The wine comes out first, and then my hand connects with something long and ribbed. When I pull it out, I stare at my hot pink vibrator in disbelief.

At least my drunken self knew I'd need some relief while abroad. And to be so close to Hayden and not jump him? Yeah, this is going to get a workout.

I pull out the rest of the items and place them on the bed to take stock.

Okay, I've got one shirt, one thong, a hot pink vibrator, a summer dress, and sandals.

That's it.

I laugh. For ten days, I've got one dress and the outfit I wore on the plane. But I can make it work. There's a laundry machine here, and I can run a load a day and alternate between my outfits. I can buy a bathing suit, or another bra and underwear set, and I'll be good to go.

I hang the dress and throw the rest of my stuff in the top dresser drawer. The bed calls to me for a nap, but I want to get on the new time zone as soon as I can.

I put my clean thong on, grab a towel, and head outside with my phone and iPad. There's nothing like a beautiful surrounding to inspire creativity.

I pull the lounge chair into the sun and stretch the towel atop it. No one's around, so it doesn't matter if I'm practically naked.

My latest client needs a logo for a new Irish pub they're opening. From their brief, they want a mix of modern and classic as well as using the colors typically associated with Irish pubs, so browns, golds, and greens. Their name is Irish Tap, and I have an idea to incorporate a tap pouring a beer into a Guinness glass within the letters.

I play around in Illustrator until I have three design options and send it off to my client for feedback. Sweat drips down the back of my neck. I've been out here for over an hour, but I've been too busy to notice.

That's my favorite part of my job, getting so caught up in a project where time becomes meaningless.

I stretch my neck and roll my shoulders before placing the devices on the chair and approaching the pool. Without checking the temperature, I dive in, and the cool water refreshes my overheated body. I lay on my back and float, enjoying the sun on my skin and the fresh air. The faint noise of cars and horns makes it into this oasis, but only if I focus on it.

Hayden needs to buy a float or five for this pool. Oh, maybe a unicorn float. That'd fit the aesthetic perfectly. I giggle and randomly move my arms and legs, not caring if I bump into the wall.

A throat clears and I open one eye to find Hayden by the edge. His intense gaze thoroughly surveys me, and I bask in his attention.

"How long have you been there?" I ask. I make no

move to cover myself. He's already seen it anyway, and my body is the one thing I'm confident about. I like how I look. I like the curve of my ass and boobs and my stomach that's kind of flattish but has some meat on the sides.

"Not nearly long enough," he says, voice strangled. "Forget to pack a bathing suit?"

"Aren't you observant? Do you have a unicorn float by chance?"

He laughs. "I could get one for you. On both accounts."

"Why? Do my breasts offend you?"

He makes a choking sound. "Offend is the last word I'd use."

His words make me smile. But it's the look in his eyes that causes an inferno to flare inside my body. They're famished, and I wouldn't mind if he took a bite, or twenty. But it's day one of our little game, and I refuse to lose already.

But perhaps... I can make him lose.

I grin and swim to the edge closest to me. Hayden's there with an outstretched hand. I grab onto it, and he pulls me fully out as if I weigh ten pounds.

The move is so unexpected that I grasp onto his biceps to keep me steady. He wraps an arm around my waist and pulls me into his body.

Holy shit. The amount of strength he has to pull me out in one move is unbelievably hot, especially for someone like me, who's not one hundred pounds.

This man is something else.

I tilt my head back, our gazes lock and hold. Time slows as I breathe him in. His stare burns in the best way possible. It doesn't matter that I'm dripping wet, in more ways than one, and that he's fully clothed.

He's tall enough and muscular enough to make me feel small. Something I don't feel often... or ever. We don't move apart. If anything, I lean closer.

He grips me firmer and pulls me into his body just a fraction more. His belt digs into my abdomen. We're a perfect fit.

The longer he stares at me, the more my chest feels like a swarm of butterflies ready to take flight. My heart jumps forward, backward, and pulls to the side before fumbling around for the next few beats, trying to return to its natural rhythm.

It's the most intense moment of my life, being in his arms practically naked. His stare unwavering. Who knew eye contact could be so intimate?

His thumb swipes back and forth against my hip, and I shudder. My nipples pebble and he pulls back slightly and looks down at them as if they called out for him.

"Cold?" he asks, voice gruff.

"Not at all."

He stares at my nipples for an inappropriate amount of time. So much time that I'm a turned-on mess the longer he looks. I need his mouth on me, on them, like I need food. I'll die if he doesn't touch me, kiss me, do... something.

Shit, I need to stop this inferno inside me. So, I do the only thing I can do.

I push him into the pool.

He shouts in surprise and falls in. I laugh. Now *this* was a good idea.

When he surfaces, he says, "You play dirty."

"I have no idea what you mean." I lift my chin high in the air.

"I see how it is now. Aren't you going to help me out?"

"If I did that," I say, "I'd count it as another ick."

He laughs and pushes himself out. He strides to me and brushes the back of his hand oh so lightly across my nipple.

I shiver in response.

"What are you doing?" I whisper. Is he ready to call an end to the game?

"You had some water there." He grins.

I open my mouth to tell him off, because he's just playing with me, when his phone rings from his pant pocket.

I snap my mouth shut, surprised it's still working.

"Good thing my phone is waterproof," he says. He pulls it out without taking his gaze off me and answers with a curt, "Hello."

Not wanting to stand there like a fool, I walk on unsteady legs to the chair and my towel. His gaze burns into my ass like a physical touch. But I don't hurry to my things. No, I walk slower, testing my own restraint. I'm so close to turning around and jumping him, phone call or not. Bet or not. But I refuse to. Not on the first day.

"Worst timing ever, asshole," he says and then laughs at whatever the person on the other line says.

He mumbles something too low for me to hear. I grab my items from the chair and throw the towel over my shoulder before heading inside. There's no need to cover up, not when he's seen me practically naked already. And not when I'm caring less and less about my rule as long as he cracks first.

I was so close to offering my body to him like a sacrifice to an ancient god. Whew, if I didn't push him in when I did, I might've done something rash.

I open the fridge and find a bottle of champagne there. This better be enough to cool me down.

I pop the cork and place my lips around the bottle, sucking back as much as I can without suffocating myself. Notes of vanilla and cream tingle on my tongue. It's so good, so smooth, it probably costs a month's worth of rent per bottle. Which is all well and good, but it does nothing for my overheated insides. Or for my pulsing core.

"Thirsty?" he asks, coming to my side.

I make some sort of humming noise and offer the bottle to him. "Want some?"

He takes it from me without breaking my gaze and drinks deeply.

I can't help but imagine him licking and sucking my tits with those oh so sensual lips. It takes everything in me to not moan. His gaze flicks down to my still bare breasts, and I need a distraction. Again. He's too tempting for his own good and I'm not sure if suggesting this game was the best decision I've made recently... or the worst.

"You wanted to take me out, right?" I ask.

He nods but says nothing.

"Perfect. I'll shower first," I say. "Give me twenty." I rethink that because I'll need some time with my vibrator in order to function today. "Actually, make that thirty."

He places the bottle back into my hands. "Does your

thirty minutes mean thirty or does it mean an hour?"

I take another swig of champagne. "Guess you'll have to wait and see."

"So mysterious." He grins. "I like it."

I salute him with the bottle before taking it with me up to my room. The second I close the door, I run for the drawer housing my vibrator and bring it into the bathroom. I won't even have to insert it to come.

With the shower running, I grab a towel and use it to cover my mouth with one hand and press the ON button with the other.

I jump when the vibrations hit my clit. My body is wound so tight, and I'm so sensitive, it'll take one minute to come. I think about Hayden and that's it. I'm done for.

I try to muffle my scream into the towel, but who knows if it's enough. I've never been one to keep quiet in the bedroom.

My legs shake after my orgasm. I'd go for another round, but I want to keep him on his toes concerning how long it takes for me to get ready. I quickly shower and wash my hair before donning my bra and dress. A quick application of makeup, a messy bun, and I'm good to go.

I finish in fifteen minutes, speeding through everything to throw Hayden off his game. Nothing like keeping a guy guessing to shake things up.

He looks at his watch when I reappear and raises an eyebrow. "Interesting."

He's in a new outfit, this time with khakis and a white linen shirt with the top three buttons undone.

Hello, sexy tanned chest.

"Surprise." I make jazz hands and he laughs.

A drop of water trails down my neck from my wet hair, and he tracks the movement.

"Come," he says, stepping forward and brushing the water away. "Let me show you the neighborhood."

He guides me out of the house, and we bypass his car and walk down the steep driveway that connects to a smaller road. One so narrow, two cars wouldn't be able to fit. There's no hard shoulder on the road, just a drop. I'm glad I was asleep when his driver brought us here because this is nerve-wracking and we're just walking.

"Istanbul is best seen on foot," he says.

"Says who?"

"Says me."

"Have you even been here before?"

"I take offense to your doubt. I'll have you know, I used to live here. I know these streets better than the back of my hand."

"Those are lofty words, you know. And I'm going to have to hold you to them. Congratulations, you've been upgraded to a probationary fling plus tour guide while we're here."

"Looking forward to it. Just remember…" He brings his lips to my ear before whispering, "Tips don't have to be monetary. I'll accept any kind of reward."

My thighs clench together. Come on body, get it together. All he did was whisper in my ear. There's no need for such an overreaction. And yet my puss disagrees.

Traitor.

Hayden grins as if he knows exactly what he's doing to me.

Asshole.

CHAPTER 6

$\mathcal{H}$AYDEN

Traffic was horrible, and it took twice as long as it should've taken to get to my meeting with Deniz and back. But seeing Bree practically naked made all the stress from the drive disappear.

My head pounds with lack of sleep and food, but I push on. This is the shitty part of traveling along with jet lag.

"Have you ever had a Turkish breakfast before?" I ask her as we walk along the road.

"Nope." She glances at me out of the corner of her eye. "Are you going to pop my cherry?"

"Yes." I stare at her plump lips. "And I'll enjoy every second."

She stumbles and I grip her elbow to steady her. She laughs and corrects the strap on her emerald boho dress.

I adjust my grip and link her arm in mine. She doesn't pull away, not even when we arrive at the main promenade next to the Bosphorus. Boats bob in the water, the fronts tied up along the walkway. I love this area. It's large enough to fit at least five people side by side, and it allows me to walk next to Bree without blocking anyone.

The water is busy with shipping vessels full of containers, million-dollar yachts, and a mixture of tourist and recreational boats. It never gets old, watching the hustle and bustle of the Bosphorus. It's why I insisted on buying a house with an unobstructed view of it. It took over a year to find the perfect place, and I lucked out. My agent approached his friend and enticed him to sell it to me.

It's how things work here. Turkey is flexible, and I love countries like this. Where anything is possible if you know how to ask. Where convenience is part of life. There's always someone available to do something, to help.

There's a flip side to it, of course there is, but it's worth it.

My phone rings in my pocket. I take it out and glance at the screen. Surprise, surprise. It's Adrien. Even though I told him I'm taking two weeks off, it doesn't appear like he's taking that message to heart.

I hit ignore and continue walking. I can't deal with him now. My phone buzzes again, indicating a voicemail.

Of course, it does.

I guide Bree along the walkway, dodging stray cats and dogs. They walk freely throughout the city and the people of Istanbul are kind to them.

In coffee shops, it's not abnormal for a couple of stray dogs to lie in the middle of the floor while stray cats weave between people's legs.

One of the dogs we come across flops down in the middle of the promenade, as if it wants to sun itself. It's huge and must weigh over one hundred pounds. Bree stiffens and grips my arm tighter. She leans into me, trying to get as far away from it as possible. She pulls me to the farthest side of the path and almost onto the grass.

I'm not sure she's going to like the city if she doesn't like dogs. She'll soon discover that strays are synonymous with Istanbul. It's part of life here and why I want to work with Deniz and her organization.

"Why are there so many strays?" Bree leans further into me as we skirt around a dog trotting down the promenade.

"There are a few theories. Dogs and cats have been part of the city for centuries, but now most are abandoned by their owners when it becomes too much of a burden to care for them."

I stare at Bree's profile, and she doesn't appear affected by that news. Behind her, a couple of cats lie near a bench and meow for attention. An older woman throws some bread their way, and a young man drops some meat from his sandwich next to a dog near him.

"They seem to be doing just fine on the street," she says, a hardness to her voice I don't understand.

"Yeah, the city comes together to care for them, but it's not enough."

She glances at me, face unreadable. "What do you mean? They seem fine."

"They're strays. They don't live a long life."

Deniz's company plans to focus on training, vaccinating, sterilizing, and confirming the health of stray dogs before putting them up for adoption. Potential owners will need to jump through some hoops to ensure they'll be good owners and not dump their dog.

"Hmm." It's all she says, and I don't know what it means.

She mentioned before she doesn't like animals, but she's here for a dog. It doesn't make sense, but Bree is a conundrum and reacts differently than I expect at every turn.

I lead her up the stairs to the hidden gem of a restaurant that has a perfect view of the city and the Bosphorus. It's light and airy, full of white walls. The scent of freshly baked simit makes my mouth water every time I'm here.

The hostess brings us straight to our table on the awning covered balcony. I made sure Ela, my local assistant while here in Turkey, made a reservation to ensure we got the best table.

"Wow," Bree says, her gaze glued to the view. "This is gorgeous."

Pride fills my chest. I love sharing my favorite places with people and seeing them enjoy it. And Bree does more than enjoy, it's like she immerses herself in it. Her face becomes so expressive and easy to read when she's like this.

"So," she says, "what's so amazing about a Turkish breakfast?"

"You'll have to wait and see." I have a feeling Bree likes to be surprised when it comes to food and life.

She pouts, her kissable lips getting bigger and providing more temptation. "I'm so hungry, I could eat my hand."

I laugh, completely in agreement, and motion to the waitress. "I'll order for us."

The waitress lifts a finger, indicating she'll be a minute.

Bree shifts and the strap of her dress dips down her shoulder. Without thinking, I reach across the table and push it back into place. I brush my hand down her arm and she gives my hand a pointed look.

I can't help but touch her. All I want to do is worship her, drown in her, but I need to hold back for a few days. Then I can have my way with her. She insisted on this game, this test, between us. But the challenge and distraction she's providing me with is a nice reprieve from Adrien and all the work waiting for me. It's perfect for a vacation fling.

I chug my water, as if that'll calm me when in reality it just makes me wish my mouth were busy with something else. Something involving part of Bree's body.

The server approaches and I order for both of us before turning my attention back to Bree.

She stares at me with an adorable expression. Wide eyes, open mouth. "You speak Turkish?"

"Yeah, I learned it in high school when I was living here."

"That's impressive you still remember the language."

"Are you implying I'm old?"

She shrugs. "I mean, if the shoe fits."

"I'm only twenty-nine."

"Really? I would've thought you were older."

"Ouch." I clutch my heart. "You wound me."

"I somehow doubt that." She laughs.

"How old are you then?"

"How old do you think I am?" she asks.

"Nope, I'm not taking the bait for that trap."

"You already did. So, let's hear it." She leans closer into the table. "How old am I?"

I look her over, from her creamy skin to the dress she's got on that perfectly encompasses her personality—flirty, fun, a bit wild.

"You're old enough to drink," I say, "but not old enough to be a grandma. So, I'll say you're the perfect age."

"Good to know where your standards are." She laughs. "But I'll help you out, I'm twenty-six."

The server places two Turkish teas in front of us.

"Hold it from the very top or you'll burn your fingers," I say. "They use sugar cubes, but they don't drink tea with milk here."

"I'll drink it straight." She carefully grabs the hourglass shaped cup and takes a sip. "Oh, this is good. I'm going to need one of these bad boys every day while I'm here."

"I can make that happen," I take a sip of my own tea, relishing the slightly bitter taste of black tea. "Do you have any other plans while you're here, apart from drinking tea? You mentioned a dog?"

"Hmm. I did, didn't I?"

I wait her out, curious about her caginess.

She stares at the view. "I plan to find the dog that takes all the public transport. Bilet."

Interesting that she knows about him. It's a well-known fact here, but outside Turkey? Not so much.

"Why?" I ask.

Her gaze snaps back to mine. "That's the million-dollar question, right? Because now that I'm here, I'm not so sure."

"Before you got on the flight, what was it about the dog that made you fly halfway across the world?"

"My mom loves him, and I was curious. About him. About the people who love him."

It doesn't feel like the full story, but I won't push her for more. Not now, not when I've just gotten her to agree to stay with me.

"There's an Instagram hashtag dedicated to him," I say.

"Yeah, I plan to use it tomorrow to find out where he is."

"I could have my driver take you."

"No need," she says. "I'll act like a local and use the same public transport the dog uses."

"Let me take you. After my morning meetings."

"Is this going to become a habit?" She raises an eyebrow. "Me waiting for you to finish your mysterious work stuff before you take me out?"

"Do you want it to become a habit?"

She lifts her shoulder. "I'm not sure."

"I only have two more meetings, and I'll be free for the rest of the trip. I'm supposed to be on vacation for the remainder of my time here." I could've finished my meeting with Deniz today, but when I planned my vacation here, ten days of nothingness was too much to handle. Meeting with Deniz and working on her nonprofit gave me something to do, and it helps that I'm passionate about the cause.

"At least let me take you the first time," I say. "Help you get around and get used to the transportation system here. If nothing else, you can use me as a translator."

"Do you always pimp out your translation services?"

I wink. "Only for special women."

"Ugh, fine. You can take me. But on one condition."

I wave a hand at her to continue. "Go on."

"You tell me what you're really doing here."

"Why?"

"Because you're too cagey about it, and it makes me think it's something illegal."

"Fair enough," I say. "I'm meeting with a nonprofit to fund them and help them create an expansion plan. They want to save the strays from a life on the street."

"Really?" She shifts in her seat and has a look of pure disgust on her face.

"Really." I say it slowly, trying to figure out her reaction.

"I'll be right back." She stands so fast, the table rattles before she hurries inside the restaurant.

Any other woman would fawn over me for helping animals, but Bree is… disgusted?

What just happened?

 REE

I RUN cold water from the bathroom sink over my wrists. Deep breath in, hold, and out.

I don't understand why I'm getting triggered this much by Hayden's words. There were so many opportunities to get triggered on the walk over, with all the feral dogs lying around. But I didn't have a panic attack, and I was damn proud of myself. It helped to have Hayden's arm through mine, guiding me around. His presence offered more comfort than I thought possible.

But finding out he wants to save the animals? The same kind of dogs that can turn on anyone at any moment and attack?

For some reason, that's too much.

I close my eyes and focus on the water hitting my

wrists. After another minute, I shut the faucet off and dry myself with a towel.

I grab my phone and open my message thread with Jules.

> Me: He loves animals. I think I'm going to be sick.

HAYDEN'S probably the type of person who cries during war movies when the horse dies, instead of over the thousands of people being blown up left and right.

To be honest, I've never been an animal person. And since January, that opinion's now solidified into a firm belief.

> Jules: You're waking me up again? What the hell is your problem?

> Me: Turn your phone off if you don't want messages to come through.

> Jules: Thanks for that oh so helpful advice.

> Me: I'm sorry I'm waking you up again. I'm all screwed up on what time it is. But now that you're awake... help!

> Jules: You're being ridiculous. He can love animals and still be a good person.

Me: No, he can't. He's choosing to fund a nonprofit to save the strays. He could choose anything to fund, like something for people. But he's chosen that. He's getting a letter removed because of it.

Jules: Oh no, he's kind. What a terrible flaw to have. I guess that makes him human, just like the rest of us.

Me: There's no room for your sarcasm in this conversation.

Jules: Is there room for some tough love?

Me: Nope, not that either.

Jules: Too bad. If you ever showed up to the therapy sessions, you'd understand your reaction is normal, but also skewed.

Me: Oops, losing connection. Got to run.

Jules: Don't you dare. I'm awake a second time because of you. So now you have to hear me out.

Me: Ugh, fine. What wisdom do you want to impart on me?

Jules: Why not use this as an opportunity to understand his love for animals?

Me: Ew, why would I do that?

Jules: Because dogs aren't the enemy. Just because—

I JUMP out of our message thread and toggle off my mobile data aggressively. I refuse to read anything more. She doesn't get to write anything about dogs. Dogs *are* the enemy. How could she, out of all people, say otherwise? She wasn't there for the attack, but she was there for the aftermath.

For me. For Mom.

That should be enough for her to agree with my statement. It feels like she's turning on me by saying that, and I'm regretting my decision to come here even more. What made Drunk Me think this would be a good idea? Finding Bilet will not solve anything. Understanding why people love him won't heal me. And I'm doubtful I'll even be able to see him without having a panic attack. Hayden only talked about dogs, and it triggered one.

Ugh, I'm such a mess.

I run my hands through my hair and pull when I reach the ends. It was a stupid idea to come here. To cling to some silly hope.

Jules thinks I blew off therapy because I couldn't be bothered. But I tried, even though she doesn't know that.

I just couldn't.

I'd make it as far as my car, but I couldn't turn it on. Or if I did, I would drive in the opposite direction of the therapist's office.

What happened is always in the back of my mind. Even when I'm doing other things, it's still there. Talking about it won't help that, especially talking to the same therapist that's seeing Mom.

The same mom who saved me but paid for it dearly. I

was the one who should've paid the price, not her. And now I can't even bring myself to call her to say hi.

I'm the worst daughter in the world.

Guilt's already poisoned my blood. It's just a matter of time before it seeps in deeper and consumes me fully.

I need a distraction.

I can't deal with this right now.

When I get like this, I normally book a trip somewhere, but I'm already abroad. Walking around the neighborhood won't cut it. Especially not with all the strays roaming around. No, I need something to distract me from the guilt and anger that still swirls through my insides.

I need something extra to take the edge off.

My stomach cramps with hunger pains.

Okay, food first. Then, distraction.

But before I leave the bathroom, I input Hayden's full name into my phone and leave the number part blank since I don't have it. I then remove the "N" in his last name so it's down to WATSO. I shove the phone back into the pocket of my dress and breathe out a sigh of relief.

That small act makes me feel enormously better. I'm in control, and I've got this. I can walk back out there and pretend like nothing happened. It's not like I haven't got months of practice doing just that.

I exit the bathroom and return to the table.

"Sorry about that," I say.

"Are you okay?"

"Sure." I grab my water with shaking hands and chug it.

The waitress saves me from further questions by

placing piles and piles of food on the table. The metal circular containers hold what looks like a version of scrambled eggs, cheeses, honey, jams, breads, tomato and cucumber slices, olives, and sausages. It's beautiful, and I snap a picture of everything to send to Jules later.

"Do you have any allergies?" Hayden asks.

"Nope."

"Can I put a bit of everything on your plate for you to try?"

"Knock yourself out."

He passes me the plate after putting a sample of each thing on it.

"What's that?" I point to the reddish egg mixture.

"Menemen. Scrambled eggs with tomato and a mixture of different peppers." He points to a flaky pastry. "That's börek, it's phyllo filled with different things. But this one is cheese."

I do a happy dance after tasting the slightly spicy eggs. They're amazing, and I don't think I'll be able to eat eggs any other way from this moment onwards. The breads are fresh and melt in your mouth and everything pairs so well together.

I'm in food heaven.

Hayden remains silent as we eat, but he keeps shooting me strange looks. Clearly wondering why I disappeared for five minutes after he told me he's philanthropic.

"Are we going to pretend what happened... didn't happen?" he finally asks.

"Obvi."

He nods once. "Fine, keep your secrets. For now."

"Oh, I plan on it. We made an agreement to have fun together, but we said nothing about sharing secrets."

"You're right. Perhaps I should negotiate to include that."

"Be my guest, but so far you've lost every time we play a game, Mr. I-still-don't-have-Bree's-phone-number."

"Those be fighting words."

I grin. This is what I need, to banter with Hayden and use him and our game as a distraction. First and foremost, I'm here to have fun—with a side of dick while tackling some trauma. Well... the trauma thing is still up for debate. But the dick and fun part? Yes, please.

And I know the perfect place to have some fun. A place with no dogs at all—a boat.

"Do you have a boat as well as a plane, Mr. Billionaire?" I ask.

"That depends on who's asking."

I grin. "I'd like to go on a boat ride when we're done here."

"Sure, but on the way home, we're buying you a bathing suit." He holds up his hand when I open my mouth to make a quip about him being offended by my boobs again. "Because you'll need it. For later."

"Well, when you put it that way, fine. But let's hurry and eat. Life's not going to wait for us."

CHAPTER 8

$\mathcal{H}$AYDEN

BREE JUST LAID down the makings of a new challenge. A truth challenge, and somehow, someway, I'm going to make that happen before our time together ends.

I have no right to Bree's secrets, but I'd like access to them. And why not? Our games are the most fun I've had in ages.

I text Ela to arrange for a boat ride once we're finished eating. She responds minutes later with a confirmation.

"The boat will be ready in an hour," I say as I guide Bree toward the main shopping street. "Do you want to go shopping now? Kill some time?"

"I knew you had a boat," Bree murmurs before saying louder, "Sure, let's go shopping."

When we step inside the first air-conditioned boutique we see, it's a relief from the heat outside. Bright colors fill the space, as well as palm fronds interspersed on the walls. There's a distinct scent of coconut in the air, and it matches the beach theme they've got going on.

Bree frowns as her gaze darts around the store.

"What's wrong?" I ask.

"I doubt they'll have my size here. The ones on the wall look three sizes too small."

When a woman from the shop approaches, I ask if she can help Bree find her size. The lady approaches Bree and asks in broken English for her size. Bree shoots me a glance, and I stride to the other side of the room to give her some privacy. I stare at the palm frond on the wall I'm facing. It's much safer to look at it than imagining Bree in all the sexy bathing suits here.

"Next time I travel somewhere," Bree says, coming to my side, "I should remember to pack proper things. This might be one of those countries where finding my size is a challenge."

"Has this happened before?"

She shrugs and I take it as a yes.

"If they don't have the right things," I say, "I'll have something made for you."

She pats my chest as if she thinks I'm joking. "You do that."

The saleswoman returns and motions for Bree to go to the changing room. We head back together, and I wait outside the door.

Bree laughs from inside the room.

"What's so funny?"

"They're the completely wrong size," she says. "I asked for a twelve US and it's a twelve UK."

"That means nothing to me. Can I see?"

"Why?" she asks.

"Maybe it's not as bad as you're thinking."

"Oh, it's bad." She laughs again.

Now, I'm too curious not to see it. Is it too big or too small?

"It's not like I haven't seen—"

She opens the door and everything else I was going to say dries up in my throat. The triangles barely cover her nipples, and the rest of her perfect tits are on display. She grabs me by the front of the shirt and pulls me inside before closing the door again.

"I don't want to offend anyone out there with my nips," she says.

I look down at said nips, hints of dusty pink peeking out. They're perfect like this. Straining to break free of the material. Her creamy skin stands out against the navy of the bathing suit top.

"Hmm," I say, "your nipples do seem to want to join the party here."

She huffs out a laugh, her hand still tangled with my shirt. I take a step closer, unable to resist her. Bree's gaze tracks from my eyes to my lips and back to my eyes.

I fist my hands to avoid touching her. I'm stronger than this. I agreed to this challenge, and I don't plan on losing. I chant the words in my head, hoping the more I remind myself of this fact that I'll start to believe it.

"Two of you can't be in there," a saleswoman shouts in Turkish.

"I'm just helping her tie the top," I reply, keeping my tone even to not give us away.

"Problem?" Bree asks, staring at me. I shudder as she flattens her hand and caresses my chest.

I lean closer to her ear, unable to resist her vanilla scent. It's addictive, just like her. I rub my nose along her neck and whisper, "What's your plan here?"

"What do you mean?" Her words are breathy. It reminds me of silk sheets and fucking all night long.

"They think I'm in here to fuck you against the wall." I pull back to get a look at her face, at her expression. To gauge where she's at.

Her breaths speed up and her pupils dilate. Her lips part, and it takes everything in me to not lean in. To not steal a kiss.

"You're... you..." she says, dazed.

I like that she reacts to me. More than like it. I crave it. It's a dangerous game, us teasing each other like this. And it's just a matter of time before one of us breaks. But the moment we do? It's going to be mind-blowing.

Leaning into her, she gasps, but I reach for the bathing suits on the wall behind her and take them off the peg.

"Let's give these back," I say, still pressed up against her. "But we're buying the one you're wearing."

"I don't think this is appropriate for the public."

"You're right. This is only for me." I run my finger along the strap, starting from her neck, down to her chest. She arches into my hand and swallows hard.

I pull away before I can get my hands on her gorgeous tits.

She huffs in annoyance. "You're cruel."

"Might I remind you that you're the one who pushed me into the pool?"

"I can officially say payback is a bitch."

"Well, you could always tap out now. I'd be more than happy to get on my knees for you. Sink my tongue into your dripping, wet pussy. Swirl it like—"

She slaps her hand over my mouth. "I think we're even now."

I laugh and kiss her palm. "Let's go before someone breaks down the door. We've been in here long enough. But I really can get someone to come to the house, take your measurements and make something for you."

"You were serious?" she asks, shocked. "There's no need for that. This is only the first place we've visited. I'm sure there's somewhere else with the right size."

"I insist," I say. "Time is our most valuable asset and I refuse to waste it searching for something that works." I also can't handle seeing her in anymore bathing suits without doing something I'll regret. Like having my way with her against the wall in a changing room.

"Well, okay, sugar daddy. Custom clothes it is."

I grin and leave her to redress. I shoot a text to Ela to find someone who can make clothes. Ela recommends a seamstress and a personal shopper. She explains they can adapt already made clothes to Bree's body much easier in the time frame. I agree, and she promises to send someone over today.

When Bree returns with her swimsuit in hand, I pay for it.

"Hey, I can afford a bathing suit," she says. "Let me get it."

"I'm sure you can. But since it's for me, I'll do the honors."

She rolls her eyes and goes outside while I pay. I reemerge onto the street and spot Bree on the other side.

"O.M.G. look at these," she says, holding up a neon-colored fanny pack. "Aren't they adorable?"

I cross the street and take the neon bag from her hands. "Adorable isn't a word I'd use." I move to put it back on the display, but she swipes it from me and holds it up to my face.

"I think this is your color," she says.

"Eh, I see myself as more of a pink guy."

She grins and snatches two pink ones. She pays for them before I can even grab my wallet. I'm left dumbfounded that she actually wanted this thing. After extending the strap, she fastens it across her chest as if it were a cross-body fanny pack.

She hands me mine and motions for me to put it on.

"You didn't have to do that," I say. "Let me pay for both of ours." I dig in my wallet for some cash to reimburse her.

She puts her hand on mine to stop me. "Don't be cringe," she says. "Accept the gift with a thank you."

"Are you sure?" I ask.

Women don't buy me things, it's always the other way around. I've also never been with someone long enough to celebrate an anniversary, a holiday, or a birthday. This is new, and I'm not sure how to feel about it. I fasten the silly purse around my waist to cover my reaction.

"Definitely," she says. "I don't need your money, but I needed some sort of purse. And this is way better, don't you think? Also, on the plus side, there's no chance you'll lose me in a crowd with this thing on."

"As if you're a toddler at risk of running off?"

"I mean, you never know." She laughs. "I'm easily distracted."

"Maybe I need to attach a leash to the back of that thing, then."

"Oh, great idea. But first, can we get some ice cream?" she asks.

"Spoken like a true toddler." I laugh.

"But what is life without dessert?"

CHAPTER 9

REE

HAYDEN MISSPOKE when he said boat. What he meant was a private yacht that's staffed with two waiters and a captain.

I take a video and send it to Jules. She won't believe it unless she sees the evidence. The main deck has a U-shaped couch with a table in the middle. On the right are stairs that go to the captain's area and in front of me is a cabin. Inside, I open all the doors and find a kitchen, bath-room, and bedroom.

"Can we sit out on the front?" I don't know what the place where people with yachts sunbathe on is called, but I've got to soak up the rays while I'm here.

I'm tempted to change into the bathing suit he bought me, but he said it was only for him. I'd be lying if I said I didn't like that.

"Sure," he says.

Hayden says something to the crew in Turkish before grabbing my hand and leading me along the edge of the boat. In the front, the yacht has a cushioned area that's big enough to fit three people comfortably.

I lie down on the cushions, and Hayden settles in next to me. Close, but not close enough to touch. Within minutes of the boat moving, a waiter brings out a dish of nuts, grapes, crackers, and cheese. And he has a bottle of champagne. Now this is the best distraction.

Hayden pours us each a glass and we remain silent as the yacht glides through the water. I absorb everything around us—the gorgeous buildings, the architecture, the boats passing by. Hayden remains quiet, as if sensing my desire to soak up this once-in-a-lifetime experience. I periodically glance at him to see what he's doing, but he's always staring at me when I look. I smile and he returns it with one of his own before I turn away.

"There's the Galata Tower," Hayden says, suddenly sitting up and brushing my arm with his. He points to a stone tower with a band of arches circling the tower toward the top. "Legend says if a couple climbs the tower for the first time together, they'll be destined to marry."

"Have you climbed it before?" I ask.

"Nope. I'll only do it with the woman I'd like to spend the rest of my life with."

"Well, when you finally find her, I hope for your sake she can make it up the steps."

He grins. "It's only one hundred and forty-six steps."

"But what if she only has one leg?" I ask.

"Then I'd support her the entire way."

"And what if she couldn't walk at all?"

"I'd carry her," he responds instantly, not having to think about it. "I wouldn't let anything get in the way."

He would, and I can't help but envy a woman I've never met. Someone he hasn't even met, but he's already made future plans with. No man has ever made future plans with me, not for more than a few weeks. And Hayden already has plans with some woman, and I... don't.

Sure, I use the men I sleep with as much as they use me. They were a way to keep the loneliness of life away at best, and an easy fuck at worst. But imagining someone loving me enough to want to take me up that tower pokes at a secret part of me. One begging for someone to want a future with me. For a man to not only win me over, but to be convinced to keep me.

Maybe if I meet the right someone, they'll keep me grounded and tie my loose strings back to Seattle. Strings that snapped back in January.

A queasiness rolls through me at the thought of January, but I chug the champagne to keep it at bay. I refuse to think about any of that now, not when I can dwell on it endlessly once I return home.

"Well," I say, "whoever she is, she'll be lucky to have someone so determined. You'd make a good partner."

"I would be the best husband." He grins before growing serious. "But I'm not sure if I'll ever meet someone who will accept my lifestyle."

"And what lifestyle is that?"

"I travel for my job nonstop. I'm never home. I work all the time. Those aren't qualities people line up for."

Listening to him is like listening to myself. I hate being home, and I work all the time if I'm not traveling. But like it or not, I'm stuck in Seattle. Mom sacrificed too much for me to leave her for more than my trips. She's still not healed and sometimes I wonder if she will ever be. If I'll ever be.

"What about you?" he asks.

"What about me?"

"Do you want to get married one day?"

"I'm not sure. Right now, I'm focused on other things." Like figuring out how to overcome some trauma and repair the relationship with my mom. Basic things.

"Like what?" he asks.

"Figuring out the future of my business."

"*Hayden Bey*," a voice calls from the bottom of the stairs.

The voice strings together some words before Hayden responds, and I break our eye contact.

"What did he say?" I ask.

"He asked if we'd like more food or drinks."

"I'm good. But what else am I looking at?" I point to the buildings on the side of the strait.

"Well, that right there is the Topkapi Palace." He points to the huge white palace with spires and domes. "A bit further up is the Hagia Sophia." He gestures to the domed structure with four spires around it. "Do you want the history for each?"

"Hmm. Well, you see, I'm not interested in the history

of famous landmarks. That stuff is easy to find online. If I have a tour guide, I want you to show me the real Istanbul. The stuff I can only experience with a local, or with someone who's lived here for years."

The famous landmarks were my original plan between stalking Bilet, but not anymore. Hayden claims to know this city, and I'd love to have a different experience on this vacation.

"Making me earn my keep, huh?" He smirks.

"Perhaps." I lift my shoulder, and he tracks the movement.

He has a gleam in his eye when he says, "Challenge accepted."

"Good, but fair warning. If you're a boring tour guide, I'm known to fall asleep in random places."

"Well, we can't have that happen, can we?" He laughs.

"It is a superpower, one that I'm still mastering."

"A superpower, huh?"

"Yeah, I'm special like that," I say.

"I have one too."

I raise an eyebrow. "Do tell."

"I don't think I will."

"Rude." I gape at him. "You can't say that and then not tell me."

"I'll tell you… eventually."

"You're annoying," I huff.

"Not as annoying as my brothers."

"How many brothers do you have?"

"Two."

"Your poor mom."

He laughs and takes a bite of a grape. "My dad would agree with you there. Is your sister older or younger?"

"Older."

"And your parents?"

"Never knew my dad. Mom... she lives in Seattle near my sister and me."

"My parents, brothers, and I all have homes in Portland. We like to stay close too."

"Yeah..."

I clam up after that statement. Mom, Jules, and I live in Seattle because that's the city Mom had us in. When I was young, I used to dream about living somewhere else. Just for a change. But Mom loved the city, and I learned to love it too. It's been my home my entire life. But not anymore. Not when it's now tainted.

I'm lost in thought for the rest of the ride, and Hayden again remains silent, which I'm grateful for.

"You okay?" he asks as we walk back to his house. "Do you feel sick from the boat?"

"I'm fine. I think the jetlag is hitting," I lie.

I'm wrapped up in thoughts of Mom and Seattle, thoughts full of thorns that cut deep. The boat ride was supposed to help me escape, but it's not working like it usually does. Instead, the weight of my thoughts is too much. All I want to do is sleep. Tomorrow, I might face Bilet and I'll need to mentally prepare myself for that.

"Are you up to get measured for the clothes? They'll be at the house in around an hour."

"Sounds good," I say. "But when they're done, I think I'll crash for the rest of the night."

"I'll have food delivered while they're working with you."

"Can you order Turkish food?"

"I've got the perfect thing for you," he says with a smirk.

Oh, I'm sure he does.

CHAPTER 10

$\mathcal{H}$AYDEN

HAVING a man touch Bree where I can't is a form of torture I didn't think was possible.

Phone in hand, I flip it over and over again. I need something to distract myself from her being measured. Of picturing my hands on her instead of theirs. I pull up the group chat with my brothers. They're always a good distraction.

> Me: Did you pop the question yet, Anders? Or did you chicken out?

> Anders: Fuck off. I'm doing it in two days.

> Theo: As if he'd let Zoey leave Finland without a ring on her finger.

Anders: Damn right. How's Istanbul?

Theo: More importantly, who or what was I interrupting when I called earlier?

Me: You have the worst timing ever, asshole.

Theo: It's my specialty, but way to avoid the question.

Theo: You had that tone, the one that says you're about to fuck someone.

Me: Disgusting that you know what I sound like when I'm about to fuck someone.

Theo: Aha! You don't deny it.

Anders: Who is she?

Me: It's a long story, but I'm having fun.

AND I AM. It would be even better if Theo and Anders were here. I miss them and our parents. It's been months since we've all been together for more than a hurried meal here or there. Months too long, but right now Anders is only a short flight away. I type without thought, words I'd normally never say.

Me: Anders, why don't you and Zoey come to Istanbul after you propose?

Theo: Are you okay?

Anders: What's going on?

THEY TEXT at the same time, and I roll my eyes. They're both so dramatic.

Me: Nothing, why?

Theo: You've never asked anyone to join you on one of your trips.

Me: That's not true.

I'M SO USED to lying to them that my contradiction comes without thought. Of course, it's true. I took on the traveling role because I used to like it. I get this itch when I'm in one place too long. I need to travel, to experience something different. It's probably because we moved around so much as kids, and it's been ingrained that home isn't a place. It's the people you're with.

My family.

It feels like I haven't been home for any length of time since Christmas. And I won't get enough time to see them until I'm free from my contract as CEO for NomNom. I can't quit early, not when I've spent the past few years trying to prove to my family that I'm reliable. That they can trust me with this. That all the jokes and pranks I make aren't the only facets to my personality.

Our startup was built from nothing more than my insistence that we should go into business as a family. My brothers were reluctant at first, and I don't blame them. I almost failed out of school and took nothing seriously. But now I've proven that I can be serious and smart with business. And it worked. They're all proud of me.

Powering through these last two months are important. It'll show them I'm not a quitter, that I can see something through until the very end.

I just need a break, then I'll be refreshed and ready to face these next two months. It's not like Anders and Theo can help me. They're too busy with their own lives. I'm the one who insisted on taking on this role, and I need to see it through.

> Anders: I'll talk to Zoey, but maybe we can come toward the end of your trip? For a day, at least. If nothing else, to meet this mysterious woman of yours.

> Me: Sounds good. Text me if it works out.

THE DOORBELL RINGS and I collect the food from the delivery driver. It's the perfect excuse to talk to Bree. She loves food and hopefully it'll cheer her up. She's so full of life, but there was a moment on the boat when it seemed like her exuberance was sucked out of her. All that was left was a husk of a person.

I'm not sure what set her off, or where she went, but I hate to see her shutdown like that. Hopefully, the promise of new clothes and food will bring her back.

I knock on her door, and the personal shopper opens it. He steps aside to reveal Bree standing with her arms out, and wearing what looks like a version of a man's shirt. The seamstress pulls and pins things into place.

Bree looks up with a strained smile. "Hey, we're almost done."

"Good, because the food just arrived."

Bree fidgets the entire time the seamstress works. It's not until the seamstress picks up an iPad that Bree relaxes. The seamstress shows the screen to Bree. The shopper and Bree take turns writing things on the screen. They go back and forth for a bit before curiosity gets the best of me.

"May I?" I ask and hold my hand out for the iPad.

Bree passes it to me and chews on her lip while I look at the screen. There's a photo of a bathing suit with a plunging neckline and a buckle at the bottom of the V with some sort of coverup next to it. Handwritten notes of the belt placement and her measurements line the side of the screen. I swipe to the left and there's a photo of a skin-tight dress for a night on the town, and another day dress that looks like a men's shirt with a belt wrapped around the waist. That explains what she's got on now.

"Is it okay to request those things?" she asks.

I glance at her. "This isn't enough. It won't last you all week. Order more."

"No, I don't need more. This is more than enough."

"What about bras and underwear? Pajamas?"

"You've got a washing machine. I can make do," she says.

I pass the iPad back to her, confused. Any other woman would be jumping at the chance to get a whole new wardrobe. But she's not, just getting the minimum needed for the next days. And she seems super uncomfortable with the entire idea. Shit, I thought I was helping her out, but maybe I overstepped?

"If that's what you want," I say.

While Bree changes back into her own clothes in the bathroom, I talk to the seamstress in Turkish to make sure she has everything she needs. I promise to pay double if she can finish it by tomorrow evening. She agrees and I show them out.

Once the door's closed, I head to the kitchen to find Bree.

"I hope that wasn't too horrible," I say.

"It was fine. It's just weird to have someone spend so much time measuring my body. Thanks for organizing that, though."

"Drink?" I ask.

"Just water."

"Still feeling tired?"

"Yeah… and hungry. What did you get?"

"Just some simple but amazing things. First up is a wet burger." I pass it to her. "It's doused with a tomato and garlic sauce and stored in a steam box."

She opens the wrapping and takes a deep breath. "It smells amazing."

"And here are sarma which are stuffed grape leaves." I open the next container to reveal the green wrapped deliciousness about the size of a finger. I could have these every day for the rest of my life and die a happy man. "This one has rice and meat."

She makes grabby hands and says, "Give me."

The tension in my body bleeds out. Good, she's happy again.

She picks up a sarma and bites into it without hesitation. "Oh, wow, these are amazing."

I watch as she licks her lips and takes a bite of the burger. I'm too fascinated watching her enjoy everything to want to eat my food just yet.

"You're staring," she says.

"I know."

"Nothing awkward about that," she quips.

"Nothing awkward about it at all." I laugh and grab a bottle of water for each of us.

We both remain standing and devour the food.

"I should be finished tomorrow around noon again," I say. "Then we can find Bilet and after that, I'll show you the real Istanbul."

I've thought about where to take her, and I'm making a list on my phone. I love she wants to see a different side of the city, and not the places I've visited hundreds of times with friends or family.

"Perfect."

"I know you weren't willing to give me your number, but can I have it now?" I ask. "Just in case anything changes tomorrow, I'll have a way to contact you."

"Okay, fine. I guess you deserve it after buying me new clothes."

I hand her my phone and wait until she finishes inputting her number before grinning so widely my cheeks hurt.

"Why are you smiling like that?" she asks. "It's creepy."

"Because I won. I finally got your number. You sure you're going to win our current challenge? I think a custom art piece would go perfect right there." I point to a random wall.

"Pfft, you didn't win my number. That challenge ended once we left the plane."

"Semantics." I laugh.

"You cheater."

"Only when it counts," I say. "But I do have something that'll ease the sting of losing for you."

"I'm listening."

I open a container full of baklava and pass it to her.

She grabs a piece and points it at me. "This isn't over."

"How optimistic of you."

She glares at me, and I laugh. We only have ten days together, and they're going to be the best days with her around.

CHAPTER 11

REE

I CAN DO THIS. *I can do this.*

I. Can. Do. This.

The past three months, I've spent time at a dog adoption center trying to desensitize myself. And by spending time, I mean driving by the place and pretending I'm inside. But that's totally training in my book. And now I'm about to put it to the test.

If Hayden wasn't next to me, I'd have canceled this little adventure by now. I never would've made it to Taksim or the historic train line Bilet's riding today. But I can't back out now, not without explaining everything, and that's definitely not going to happen.

My three panic attacks while Hayden was at work are why I never went through with booking the trip here.

What was Drunk Me thinking?

Hayden doesn't comment on the fact that I'm a sweaty mess on our journey. Thankfully, it's hot outside. Maybe that's how I'm getting away with my body's stupid reaction to facing this dog.

I talk the entire way as we change trains and walk down the street. Words that are nonsense based on the strange looks Hayden keeps shooting at me. But I ignore him and plow on with my verbal diarrhea. My brain is too full—too stressed—to care about Hayden and what he thinks about me right now. It's full of Bilet and trying to stop clocking every single stray on the street.

To the right of me, five lie scattered on the sidewalk. To the left, a few roam down the street in a pack. I keep us more to the right. At least those dogs aren't looking for trouble if they're sunbathing.

In Taksim, Hayden directs us to the stop where a single car tram arrives. We climb up the stairs, and even if I'm not ready, I have to be. Because Bilet's here.

Luckily, the cart is busy, so I don't even see him. I just know he's in the middle row since it's the only seat without people. As people exit, I force myself to take a step closer to him, my heart racing with every inch I gain.

Most people go about their business. They aren't fazed there's a famous dog riding alongside them. Hayden places a hand on my back and guides me one step closer until I can see Bilet with no one obstructing my view.

Thanks to my mom, I know he's an Anatolian Shepard mix and is estimated to weigh over one hundred and fifty pounds.

Floppy ears, tan in coloring, with a hint of black on the tip of the ears. He has black spots, almost like beauty marks, on both cheeks. They're almost where dimples would be on a person.

But most interesting of all is his eyes.

Maybe that's why he's so popular.

He has four distinct wrinkles between his brown eyes, making him look like an old man. But his eyes are so expressive, as if they're telling a story. One just out of grasp.

"He's beautiful," Hayden says.

"Hmm." Bilet is unique, but I wouldn't call him beautiful.

"Do you want to pet him?"

"Nope." I don't elaborate.

"It's okay," a woman says in heavily accented English. "Bilet doesn't mind if people touch him."

I turn to the woman seated in the row across from Bilet. She appears to be twice my age, with gray-streaked brown hair resting on her collarbones.

"How do you know?" I ask. It's a ridiculous question, but I need a distraction or else I'm going to pee and shit my pants at the same time.

"It's a well-known fact. Also, I follow him around."

Huh, I didn't think I'd meet a seasoned Bilet stalker.

"Why?" I ask. Is it for the same reason as me? Or does she actually like animals?

She lifts her shoulder. "It gives me something to do since my husband died."

"I'm sorry for your loss."

"Thank you. There's too much time in a day to waste when you lose your purpose in life. Bilet gave me a purpose again."

Goosebumps spread across my arms. I've never related more to someone's words than now. There *is* too much time in a day to fill when you're lost. I didn't lose my purpose like she did, but I've been adrift for months, years even. All trying to fill this void inside me.

A void that's been my constant companion for too long.

I glance at Bilet.

But how can a dog, especially a street dog, help with that? What's so special about him?

Bilet stares at me, as if he knows I'm thinking about him. That I'm weighing and measuring his character to determine his worth. My body trembles and sweat dots my hairline the longer I look at him. I turn sharply away from him, not able to stand his interest in me.

Hayden remains silent behind me, but I can feel his questioning gaze as I pay more attention to a woman than the dog I came here for.

This woman is exactly what I need, more than Bilet himself, to understand why people like dogs.

"Were you always a dog lover?" I ask.

"Yes, but I never had one."

"How long have you been following Bilet?" I ask.

"About a year now. You?"

"I came all the way from America for him," I say.

"Good for you. Bilet needs all the love he can get."

"Why do you say that?" I ask. "He's the most beloved street dog there is."

"Maybe, but I think he travels on trains to be around people, searching for a home."

Talk about projection. It seems like this woman sees

what she wants in Bilet and projects her own experience on him. Is her love for him even real, if that's the case?

Do people love animals because they project their own issues onto them and then feel empathy toward that version of themselves? If that's the case, did Mom get over everything by projecting her issues onto Bilet?

I turn to Hayden and say, "Shall we get off on the next stop?"

"So soon?"

"Yup."

I glance one more time at Bilet, whose eyes are now closed. On the plus side, I didn't have a panic attack in front of Hayden.

When the tram stops again, we get off. I let out a long breath, and Hayden looks at me with a strange expression on his face.

"What?" I ask.

"Oh, just busy doing some mental gymnastics, trying to make it make sense."

"Make what make sense?"

"You."

"Good luck with that." I laugh. "Let me know if you crack the code."

"Will do." He smirks. "Got to say, my first go at stalking Bilet was anticlimactic."

"Disappointed I cut it short?"

"Maybe," he says with a wink.

"I like to keep you on your toes."

"Well, you're definitely accomplishing it."

"Good."

Cigarette smoke is a nonstop companion as Hayden

grabs my hand and guides me through the street. Almost everyone smokes here, which is so different from back home. But it's all part of the experience, all part of this ancient city with history running deep through its foundation.

The streets are so crowded it's hard to walk. Good news is, I can't see the dogs. The bad news is, I don't see them until we're practically on top of them. If I could jump on Hayden's back and have him carry me around, I would. I'm constantly on alert, waiting for a dog to appear.

Horns blare as cars weave in and out of traffic. Taxis and minibuses honk in a short beep, politely asking if anyone needs them. And it all causes my nerves to ratchet up. I'm a jumpy mess by the time Hayden guides me down a side street and onto another one. The scent of cooked meat drifts in when we pass by sporadic stands. I'm surrounded by food, food, and more food. And that's way better than dogs, dogs, and more dogs.

We end up at a cafe with some small tables and chairs outside it. A few more cafes are scattered on the street, and it's super cute.

Once we sit on the wooden chairs, a server approaches. Hayden orders something for us before taking off his sunglasses and placing them on the table.

"So..." he says.

"So..." I mimic.

He laughs. The server brings a Turkish tea, along with a small glass of water, a saucer containing an empty coffee cup, and a small bronze pot with a lip and long handle. I've never seen coffee come in something like that.

The server places down a plate with a few cubes of… something… on it. Hayden thanks them and pours coffee so thick a spoon could stand up in it.

"That"—he points to the cubes—"is lokum, or Turkish delight."

I lift the coffee cup and take a sip. It's like tasting coffee on steroids. "It's so strong."

"It is. That's why you have the lokum and water."

I take a bite of the lokum, the powder sugar leaving a small dusting on my fingers. It's pistachio flavored and perfectly balanced in sweetness. Nothing like the kind they sell in America.

Hayden turns the coffee cup and drinks from the same spot I did. He holds my gaze the entire time, and wow. Who knew sharing a drink could be so sexy? He smiles his melty smile at me, and it has a hint of smugness to it.

I've got no clue what kind of challenge he's trying to throw down, but I'm sure as hell going to pick it up and run with it.

I grab the cup again and place my lips in the exact location he just had his. We trade off on drinking from the cup, neither of us straying from that one place. I set the cup in front of him the wrong way, trying to confuse the spot, but he has a knack for where it is.

At the bottom of the empty cup is a glob of grinds. I tilt the cup left and right, fascinated that they're there.

"Some people learn to read the coffee grinds and predict the future," he says.

"Did you ever learn?"

"No, but I should make Anders do it. He's one of my brothers and owns a coffee shop. His customers would eat that shit up and he'd hate every minute." He has an evil grin on his face and pulls out his phone. "I need to write that idea down. Theo would love it."

"Theo's your other brother?" I ask.

"Yeah. Theo owns a cocktail bar and Anders a coffee shop."

"And what about you? Do you own a restaurant or something?"

"Nope. I just have a passion for good food and drinks."

"Then it sounds like we're a lot alike." I pick up the tea and take a sip, careful to hold it at the tippy top, just like he showed me. "I like eating and drinking, and did I mention eating?"

He takes the tea from me, drinking from the spot I just drank from. "I don't think you mentioned it. Eating you say? Would've shocked me Ms. Order-a-meal-from-business-class-for-me-too-because-the-food-is-better."

"Priorities, Hayden, priorities." I laugh.

He grins. "What does your sister do?"

"Jules is a dentist, but she doesn't like it much anymore. It's more a means to an end."

"And what end is that?"

"To provide for her kids," I say. "Her ex is a deadbeat, and she's keeping it together. Somehow."

"That's tough."

"Yeah. Do your brothers have any kids?"

"No. Anders is about to get engaged to his girlfriend," he says. "And Theo... Theo's in love with someone who doesn't view him like that."

"Poor Theo."

"Yeah..." He takes another sip of tea. "Has Jules ever met a boyfriend of yours?"

"Yikes, no. I don't introduce anyone I date to my family." It's easier that way when they fail my letter removal test. "What about you? Has your family ever met an ex?"

"No, I haven't really dated since I was eighteen. And it was here in Istanbul before I moved to the UK for college."

"Wait... you haven't had a girlfriend since you were eighteen?" I don't believe that for one second. He's rich, handsome, and successful. There's no way that can be true.

"I've dated, but nothing serious. My entire life, we moved to another country every few years. And no has ever followed me or kept in touch. Now I'm too busy to even imagine making room for one."

His condition for us to end when we return to the US makes more sense.

"Are you close with your family?" I ask, steering the conversation back to safer topics.

"Yeah, they're amazing. They've always been there for me."

"Must be nice," I murmur.

"But you and your sister sound close?"

"We are."

"But not your mom?"

"It's complicated." And we're definitely not like how we used to be, all because of me.

"Why?" he asks.

"Anyone ever tell you that you're a nosy bastard?"

"Who me?" He grins and bats his eyes. "I'm an angel.

But if you ever meet Theo, you'll rethink that statement. He's the nosy one."

I laugh, and he lifts the last piece of lokum toward me. But he's not offering it to me to take. No, he lifts that shit right to my mouth. I close my lips around the piece, catching his fingers in the process.

I chew, swallow, and lick my lips free of powdered sugar. He tracks the movement with intensity.

"You've got some sugar here." He lifts his hand and rubs the bottom of my lip. Then he licks his finger clean, holding my gaze.

Hot damn. I must be on the verge of getting sunstroke because holy shit. How could I have thought sharing the same spot on a cup was sexy when there's *this*? It's so hot, I'm about to combust on the spot. The digit disappearing between his lips. The pop when he removes it. Can he just suck my clit and get it over with?

Why in the hell did I take sex off the table?

I open my mouth to say something embarrassing, like that we need to renegotiate the terms and the time frame of our challenge, but growls and barks fill the air. I freeze and scan the alleyway for the source of the commotion. Two snarling street dogs circle each other, their growls so deep and menacing I'm thrown back to six months ago.

A few people watch the dogs from the side, not daring to get closer. The black one lunges toward the white one and in an instant they're full-on attacking one another.

I need to get out of here. I can't stay here for a single second longer. But I'm paralyzed with a deep fear, as memories overtake my senses.

I gulp down air and squeeze my eyes shut.

Mom and I in the park, doing our weekly "jog." We always used that word, even though we'd devolve into fits of laughter each time. The closest we got to a jog was when we'd embrace in the beginning. She'd always jog to me and engulf me in a hug so strong it felt like she could tie us together if she hugged me hard enough. She's the type of person who would greet someone as if she hadn't seen them in years, even if had only been a few days.

I push away the memory and try to focus on something, anything. But the dogs are still going at it. A few shop owners yell something at them, but the dogs don't care.

My chest tightens.

No. No. No. I can't have a panic attack.

Not here.

Not now.

The tightness builds until it feels like a vice is wrapped around my body. Every inch of me trembles and I'm frozen.

"Bree?" Hayden asks.

It takes all my energy to meet his worried gaze. He throws money on the table and stands abruptly, flipping his chair over.

It would be funny, if I could move. If I wasn't stuck.

He lifts me into his arms and jogs out of the alleyway. Jogs as if carrying me isn't a big deal. People give us weird looks, but he doesn't seem to care because he doesn't stop. He turns left and right and right again down some streets and only stops when he finds a wall low enough to sit on. There aren't as many people around us as he deposits me on it and presses my head between my legs.

He calls out something to a person and the sound of their flip-flops hitting the pavement fills the air. I focus on that as Hayden crouches next to me.

"Take a deep breath, hold it, and let it out slowly," he says.

I try to do as he instructs, but my body rebels. My breathing ratchets up and spots dot my vision.

He grips my face in his hands, and I look at him. "I'm here. You're going to be okay. Take a breath through your nose."

I take a breath through my mouth.

His lips quirk. "Your other nose." I snort and he says, "Good."

I take my first full breath in minutes.

"Good. Breathe out through your mouth."

Flip-flops pound the pavement again, and he looks away from me before standing and exchanging words with someone. The stranger hands Hayden a water bottle before walking away. Hayden places it on the back of my neck. The coldness grounds me, and his other hand rubs circles on my back.

Minutes later, I feel semi-normal. Well, I can at least breathe again, so that's a win. I straighten, and he passes me the bottle.

I take a long drink and pass it back to him.

"Better?" he asks.

"Yeah."

"It was the dogs, wasn't it?"

I glance at him "I…"

"You're scared of dogs." He says it like a fact, and it is. "Were you attacked?"

I can't speak, so I give a jerky nod as a response. It's more than I would give anyone else, but he helped me. Saved me. If he hadn't moved me, I might've gotten completely lost in the memories.

"Thank you... for helping me," I rasp.

He's being too kind, too caring. No man has gone this far out of their way to help me. My exes wouldn't have even noticed I was having a problem.

But Hayden did.

"Let me call my driver. He can take us home." He pulls out his phone, but I grab his arm.

"No, please. I'm fine, and I don't want to cut our day short."

"Are you sure?"

"Yeah, give me a few more minutes and a cocktail, and I'll be good to go."

He tucks a piece of hair behind my ear. "Surprised you said cocktail and not ice cream."

"I mean, both are possible. Right?"

"I'll see what I can do."

CHAPTER 12

$\mathcal{H}$AYDEN

BREE INSISTS SHE'S FINE, and maybe she is. But I'm not okay.

I can't stop picturing the way she froze. Only her eyes moved, and they were begging me for help. I was scared, not knowing what was causing it, but needing to help her.

Now we're in a random bar, and I'm still wound up.

"You don't need to treat me with kid gloves," she says, drinking her third cocktail.

"I'm not."

"You are. You haven't stopped staring at me since my little panic attack. It's embarrassing."

"Do they happen often? The panic attacks?"

"Nope." She says it quickly, too quickly.

It's making sense. Her disgust at my work with Deniz, how she gives the stray dogs a wide berth.

I still don't understand how Bilet fits into this, and why she came to Istanbul for him when she's scared of dogs. But I'd prefer to be there if she sees him again. To make sure she's okay.

She confirmed she was attacked, but I don't remember seeing any scars on her by the pool or in the changing room. Then again, I was too enthralled with her breasts to even notice.

Either way, she clearly wants to act like it never happened. I can do that.

"What's the plan for dinner?" she asks as she pulls her red hair up into a ponytail but then lets it loose again when she realizes she doesn't have a hair tie.

"It's a surprise," I say, "but we need to get going soon to make it in time."

She accepts my answer with ease and jumps out of her stool. "Lead the way, tour guide."

As we weave our way through the streets, a lanky man approaches us with a flower bouquet.

"Flower?" The man shoves a rose into her face, and she takes it from him.

"No, thanks," I say in Turkish, taking the flower from Bree to give back to him. I dislike the pushy behavior of the sellers, and it often makes me feel as though we could be at risk of pickpocketing if we engage with them.

Bree swipes it out of my hand and asks the seller, "How much?"

"Ten lira," he says.

She digs into her purse and holds out the bill to the man.

He lifts his hands in the air and says, "No, I can't

accept money from you."

The man gives me a meaningful look, and I take my wallet out.

"Why won't he take my money?" Bree whisper-shouts to me as if the man she's talking about isn't standing right there understanding every word. It's adorable.

"Because we're together." I glance at her. "He believes the man should pay."

"That's sexist."

"Not exactly. He's trying to be polite."

She steps away from me and grabs the arm of the man selling flowers. She pulls him about ten steps away and calls out to me, "Problem solved, I'm not with you anymore."

I laugh and stroll toward them.

"Oh no you don't." She points at me. "You can't come near, or else you'll ruin this entire exchange."

The seller grins at the two of us. I stay where I am, curious about what she's going to do next.

She turns her back to me and talks to the seller, gesturing wildly. They talk for a few minutes before Bree takes the entire bouquet from him.

As she walks back to me, the seller has a shocked expression on his face. Bree can barely fit the bouquet in her hands. There must be at least fifty roses.

"When you said you wanted to buy a flower," I say to her, "I never imagined that you'd have a not-so-secret fetish for them."

"There's nothing like rubbing the petals all over my body," she deadpans.

I laugh and she grins.

"Why did you buy them all?" I ask.

"Why not?"

I give her a look that tells her I can see through her bullshit, but she just skips away. I follow her, too curious to resist.

The first woman we pass, Bree offers a pink rose to her. She shakes her head and darts around us. Bree deflates for a moment before turning to me.

"Your translation services are needed," she says. "Can you tell whoever I give the flower to that they're free?"

She's scanning everyone who passes by, as if assessing whether they'd accept the flower.

"I can do that," I say.

The next person we approach is an older woman. I start talking the second she spots us and explain what Bree wants to do. The woman smiles shyly and reaches out for a pink rose.

Bree gives it away with a huge smile on her face and high-fives me when the woman disappears back into the crowd. This pattern repeats, again and again. And the entire time, Bree is full of so much happiness it's contagious.

When she's down to the last flower, I expect her to save it for herself. Instead, she passes it to me.

"No. Keep it for yourself," I say.

"No." She shoves it back at me, and I take it before it falls to the ground.

"When's the last time someone gave you a flower?" she asks.

"I... never?"

"Oh? Did I pop your flower-receiving cherry?"

"I guess you did." I laugh.

"You're welcome."

"Thank you," I say. This is the second gift she's given me. I'm not sure what to make of it, of her. "Why did you really buy them all?" What I really want to ask is why she was so happy while handing them out.

"Because I've always wanted to be a Flower Santa Claus," she says. "And now I can check that off my bucket list."

"Bree..."

"Hayden..."

"Fine. Keep your secrets, you mysterious and enchanting woman."

She grins at that before saying, "I don't know... he must get rejected repeatedly. I'm not even trying to sell them, and it was hard. Who knows if this is his only source of income or if he has someone he needs to support? I felt bad for him."

"You're going to buy all the flowers in Istanbul, aren't you?" I ask.

"Maybeee. But in all honesty, why not? It's not like I have to pay for accommodation anymore."

Why not indeed?

This selflessness is a new facet to Bree's personality. It's refreshing and not something I come across every day. Not when most people I interact with want something from me.

Demand something from me.

But not Bree.

She's completely independent and doesn't need me.

But I am wishing she did.

CHAPTER 13

REE

HAYDEN LEADS me into a building with a ceiling covered in fake flowers. Musicians play Turkish music in the room's V-shaped center.

Hayden chats with the host, and we're led to our table. The other patrons are a mix of people. There's a group of five guys in their thirties at one table, a group of older women at another, and a mixed group of what looks like university students. But most of the tables have pairs who look like they're on a date.

Being here, wherever we are, feels more intimate than us playing our challenge. Not when we're surrounded by people looking for love. The one thing that isn't part of our agreement.

We settle into our chairs and Hayden talks to the

server before a bottle of liquor, water, and plates of appe-tizers appear on the table.

When he leaves, I ask, "What is this place?"

"This is a meyhane. It's like a tavern, but specifically where you drink raki, listen to traditional music, and eat meze."

"What is raki?"

"It's the Turkish national drink." He points to the liquor bottle before pouring the raki into a glass and topping it off with water. When the water touches the alcohol, the contents turn cloudy and white.

It's like watching a magic show. I totally clap in delight.

We raise our glasses.

"To new adventures," I say.

He looks me dead in the eye. "To new adventures." He takes a sip and places his glass on the table.

I sniff the drink and it smells like black liquorish. I don't know anyone who likes the black kind, but I'll deal with the taste if it's part of the culture.

After a tentative sip, I discover it's smoother than I thought it'd be. I could get into this, especially paired with food.

"It's not a shot?" I ask.

"Nope. The purpose of this place is to enjoy. Enjoy the food, the drink, the atmosphere."

He fills a plate of food for me, taking a bit of every-thing from the table for me to try.

Once he passes it to me, he fills his own plate.

"What if I didn't want something?" I ask, just to mess with him.

He pauses. "Sorry, I should've asked. My dad always prepares my mom's plate."

"That's sweet."

"I know." He winks. "But is there something you don't like to eat?"

"Yes, potatoes. The only acceptable form is vodka."

"How can you not like potatoes?" He laughs. "They're so versatile."

"Most vegetables are. But I've never liked them." That's not true. I did like them at one point, like all kids. But then we ate mashed potatoes almost daily for years because it was cheap, and Mom could afford it. I got potatoed-out, but he doesn't need to know that.

I scoop some sort of hummus looking spread onto some bread and take a bite. Oh, wow. Hummus can fuck off. This is smokey and garlic-y and eggplant-y.

"Screw hummus. This stuff slaps," I say.

He laughs. "They should use that as a slogan."

"I could incorporate it into a logo for them."

"And start importing it into America," he says. "It'd be an instant hit."

"Don't tempt me," I say it as a joke, but for a moment I could picture it. Us working together. Sharing this amazingness with the masses.

"In all seriousness, you could do it."

"Yes, I could." I toss my hair over my shoulder, full of sass. "I can do anything. But I'd rope you into it too. None of this hands-off stuff."

"I wouldn't mind," he says. "It's been too long since I've had to do some grunt work."

I take another sip of raki. I don't know him well

enough to determine if he's serious or not. It felt like a joke in the beginning, but now I'm not sure. I can't get a read on him, but surely there's no way he'd be serious.

"Sounds like a plan," I say, testing him. "You can use all your fancy connections to help make it a success."

"Fancy connections, huh?" He leans closer to the table. "How far down Google did you get in the car?"

"I only stayed on Wiki." Which is true, but I did a little more research before bed last night. And I refuse to out myself like that.

"Uh-huh."

"Oh? What's that?" I ask. "A subject change is calling, you say?"

He laughs and I grin.

The hours pass with us bantering back and forth. It's fun, easy. And, dare I say, magical? Throughout the night, the musicians move throughout the space, stopping at every table and playing for them. Some people request specific songs, but most of them consist of the man singing without discernible words while the guitar accompanies him.

When they stop at our table, Hayden requests a song, and they sing it to me as if I'm the only person in the room. I sneak glances at Hayden. His gaze draws me in, and suddenly I can't look away.

I'm helpless to refuse his silent request to look at him. He stares at me with intensity, as if we're picking up right before the dogs attacked each other.

The music swells and reaches a crescendo.

It's like the singer's vocals are rewiring my heart. Untangling the thorns encasing it and allowing for an opening, just a sliver. Large enough for Hayden to sneak in.

The clapping of other people pulls me out of the moment, and Hayden passes money to the band.

I rub my sweaty palms on my dress and excuse myself to the bathroom. I've got to pull myself together. This is just supposed to be fun. A fling and nothing more. It doesn't matter if he'd be a great friend to have. It's not going to happen.

After a quick pep talk, I return to the table. Only to find another table has been added to ours. A group of women, a few years older than me, is now sitting with us.

Hayden smiles and stands when I arrive. "Meet our new friends," he whispers, his lips brushing the shell of my ear. I shiver at the simple contact. He then quietly adds just for me, "It's normal for tables to interact with one another late in the evening. But I know one of them."

He's so excited by this, but I can't help but feel my stomach drop at the news. Was I not entertaining enough?

I scan our new companions, and they're all beautiful. They wave when I sit down, and Hayden informs me they don't speak English.

Great.

I guess I'll just sit here and drink by myself if I can't join in on the conversation. And while Hayden's busy being chatted up by a beautiful woman with curly hair.

She touches his arm while she laughs at something he said. Her gold wedding band catches the light, but she doesn't act like she's married.

Oh, screw her. Does she have to be so obvious?

But what grates the most is that he doesn't stop it. Does he have a wandering eye like Andrew? Or my dad?

Shit. I knew he was too perfect to be true.

Hayden loses another letter over this. I pull out my phone and open his contact info. WATSO now becomes WATS. He only has four more chances before all the letters of his last name are removed.

I open my messaging thread with Jules.

> Me: How are you?

Jules: Busy, way busier than you. And I still had time to see Mom today. Unlike some people I know.

> Me: Bitch, way to call me out like that.

Jules: You promised to call her.

> Me: I'm in a restaurant right now, but I'll text her instead.

Jules: Fine, but please do it now. She misses you.

NOT WHAT I want to do, but I'll take a message to Mom over watching Hayden cozy up with another woman. I copy and paste the basic "how are you" I sent to Jules and send it to Mom.

She replies instantly.

Mom: I'm good. How's Istanbul?

Me: Good, fun.

Mom: Let's meet up for lunch when you're back.

Me: Okay.

Mom: I miss you.

Me: Same.

UGH, I can't even say it back properly. What's wrong with me? This woman saved me, and I can't even tell her I miss her or love her. We both walked away with scars six months ago, just in different ways. The worst part is, underneath all my guilt is anger. Anger at what I had to do to save her. Anger so endless, I don't even know where to begin to let it go.

I blow out a long breath and drink more raki. Getting drunk always makes everything better.

I try to lose myself in my phone, but every time Hayden laughs, I look up. Every time he smiles, I seem to catch it.

Ugh, this is ridiculous.

I've had enough.

"Hey," I say to him. "I'm ready to call it a night. I can grab a taxi back to the house if you'd like to stay."

He frowns before saying, "I'm ready too."

He says something in Turkish to the women, but I don't say goodbye. I just start walking.

Hayden catches up to me and puts his hand on my lower back.

"The car is just up there." He points to an idling SUV down the street.

I pick up the pace, ready to be in bed.

Once we're in the car, and it moves, he turns to me. "Did you really think I would want to stay without you?"

"You seemed so happy. I didn't want to interrupt."

He looks me over. "You didn't have fun."

"I did until the tables were pushed together."

"Because they only spoke Turkish." He swears under his breath. "I'm sorry. I didn't even think about how boring that would be for you. I used to visit meyhanes regularly when I was eighteen and always had a blast. But I forgot about the language barrier."

"Well, you were having fun with that woman anyway."

"She's the older sister of someone I went to high school with. We were just catching up on her life and family and how she's doing now that she's married with kids."

Oh. Well, that does make me feel better that he wasn't trying to pick her up.

"And the person you went to school with? How are they?"

"Mutlu is apparently good. Living her best life." He says it full of sarcasm, as if it annoys him she's doing well.

"And were you friends with Mutlu?"

"We were more. But it didn't last long."

Ahh, an ex. Wait, *the* ex? The one from when he was eighteen.

He doesn't elaborate, and I don't ask for more.

When we return to the house, he walks me to my room, as if I might have forgotten where it was.

"Be ready tomorrow at nine in the morning," he says.

"You don't have to work?" I ask.

"Nope, we get to spend all day together."

My heart leaps at that. "Tsk, tsk. Slacking off."

He grins and leans against the wall, right next to my door. "It's worth it since I get to spend the day with you."

My heart leaps at that statement. Why? Who the hell knows?

"Good night," I whisper.

"Good night."

CHAPTER 14

$\mathcal{H}$AYDEN

My phone buzzes nonstop.

I blink a bleary eye open and check the name on the screen.

Adrien. The boss from hell. The one who holds all the power by being on the board with his best friends.

I hit ignore and try to fall back asleep. But he calls ten more times in a row.

"What?" I demand.

"Finally. Why haven't you been available?"

"As I mentioned before, I'm on vacation."

"That's no excuse to be out of reach," Adrien says. "The TableEase situation is getting out of control."

"And did you look over the proposal I sent you?"

"Briefly, but it's not detailed enough. I need a five-year strategy for NomNom. By this Friday."

His demand doesn't surprise me. He wants me to do his job for him and leave him a roadmap of what to do. It'll make his life easier when my contract's up. But spoon-feeding all my ideas to him doesn't sit right.

"You can get your strategy in a few weeks," I say, "because I'm unavailable for the next two weeks while I enjoy my vacation."

"I don't care if you're on vacation—"

"You should. Because I doubt you want me to make a formal complaint. Your ten missed calls this morning have really helped my case here."

He sputters before saying, "I should've fired you years ago."

"Probably," I agree. He is the owner, and on the board, so he has the power to do it. "I'll be available in two weeks' time. Until then, I won't answer any more of your calls."

I hang up, pissed. I wish every day he'd fire me too.

THE FERRY SLOWS down as we approach Princes' Islands. It's a perfect summer day, hot and sunny, for us to explore the largest island. To me, this is one of the best places in Istanbul and it's only a short boat ride away.

I haven't been here in years, but it was one of my favorite places to go when I used to live here. I'd take the ferry by myself and spend all day on the island. Roaming, soaking in the beauty, and dreaming. It's here I decided Theo, Anders, and I should start a business together. To not let our experience of living in other countries go to waste.

The entire ride over, Bree acts like nothing happened last night. Like she didn't shut down when she thought I was flirting with another woman. Even though I wasn't.

"Come," I say to Bree as our feet hit land again. "Büyükada is best seen by bike."

"Bike?"

"Yeah, there are no cars here. So, it's either bike, foot, or horse-drawn carriage."

"Bike it is."

I glance at her, surprised she didn't insist on a carriage.

"What? I always felt bad for work horses," she says. "It's irrational, I know. They're strong and it's easy for them to pull the carriage, but I feel like a burden every time I take one."

"I think that's the last thing I expected you to say," I say. "Do you dislike all animals or only dogs?"

"Dogs, mainly. Cats aren't my fave, but that's because they're assholes. Not because I'm afraid of them."

"There are strays here, but not as many as on the mainland."

"Thank the stars for small miracles," she murmurs, glancing around as if checking whether I'm telling the truth.

We make our way past shops selling everything from food to souvenirs to get to the bike rental place. Even surrounded by the bustling crowd, she stands out effortlessly. She's in her leggings and crop top from the flight, and it's hard to not openly stare at her ass. Maybe it's her height, or her beauty, or her bright pink fanny pack that make her stand out to others. But no matter the reason, I can't help but keep sneaking glances at her, unable to look away. Even when we're in one of my favorite places in the world.

When we get to the rental place, there are a good thirty options available. Bree picks out a white one with a flower lined basket in the front.

"Hold this for me?" she asks, passing the bike to me.

I take it without comment, curious why she's heading back to the bike jungle. She keeps glancing between the bike I'm holding and the others in front of her.

"Searching for something in particular?" I ask.

"Maybe. I'll know it when I—aha!" She wheels out the exact match to the one I'm holding and hops on. "Ready?"

I look from her to the bike she picked for me and back. There are other bikes, ones without baskets or flowers, but she chose this one to match her own. Just like with the fanny packs.

She arches her eyebrow, as if daring me to say something about it.

"I had my eye on this one," I say, getting on the bike that's too short for me. "Thanks for picking it out for me."

"We're twinsies." She pulls out her phone from her fanny pack and snaps a photo of us, her in front and me in the back.

"We're something alright."

She laughs and takes off as if she's being chased by the police. I speed to catch up to her, but she slows her pace once houses line the streets rather than shops and restaurants. She turns her head from side to side, probably impressed with the unique mansions that are part of this island. When I first saw them, I had the same reaction.

She stops on the side of the street.

"What's up?" I ask.

"It looks like lace." She points at the three-story white home with tons of embellishments on the façade. "I wonder who owns it."

"I used to make up stories about the owners of each house every time I visited here," I say. "There are so many unique, beautiful, and massive homes on the island."

"What story would you give the owners for this one?"

"Hmm." I look over the front of the house. "The owner has a grandma fetish and bought a house that's full of lace on the outside and doilies on the inside to fulfill it."

She grins and walks her bike further up the street.

"Okay, what about that one?" She points to an orange monstrosity halfway hidden behind a gate and bushes. It's got its own tower on the left and wooden rails and terraces around the top.

"The owner is obsessed with Rapunzel and made their own version of her tower. They test their potential girl-friends by role playing their fantasies."

"That sounds like it'd hurt," she says. "I bet the owner only dates blondes."

"Well, they could have a closet full of wigs in case they need it."

She gives me a funny look before saying, "I'm curious."

"About?"

"What your sexual fantasies are. Got to say, I'm a little concerned after hearing your thoughts on those two houses."

I take a step closer to her, my tone dropping, "Baby, you'd love every second of sex with me, regardless of my fantasies. I'd make your dreams… come… true."

Her cheeks flush and I let me gaze trail over the bewitching pink stain.

"Shall we?" I ask, getting on the bike once again.

"Uh-huh." Her voice is breathy. I can't help but picture her saying that with her legs wrapped around my waist while I pump into her.

Well shit, now I'm riding this ridiculous bike with an erection. If my brothers could see me now, I'd never live this down.

We stop at different houses as we slowly work our way through the island. I never know which one will catch Bree's eye next. We take turns making up stories, with a focus on their supposed sordid fantasies. They get wilder with each house we pass on our way to the lookout point at the top. By the time we reach a white house with an unnecessary number of shutters, we're both in agreement the owner has a penis clamping kink. Bree snaps a photo of every house we made up stories for, laughing to herself as she does.

After a brutal hill, so steep we have to walk the bikes toward the top, she stops and looks back down from where we came from.

She glances at me. "Are you ready?"

"For what?"

She licks her lips and leans closer to me. So close that the urge to kiss her is all I can think about.

"To race."

"Seriously?" I ask, blinking out of my daze.

Before I can finish the word, she takes off down the hill.

"Loser buys lunch," she yells back to me.

She whoops and hollers as she descends, and I jump on my bike to give chase. I'm going so fast it's bordering on dangerous. The wind whips through my hair, and my stomach lurches at the speed.

I feel alive.

Free.

Bree's hair flies out behind her as she nears the bottom of this hill. Just when the road evens out, another bike comes out of nowhere. Heading right for her.

"Watch out," I shout in warning.

Bree shrieks, veering sharply to the left, and crashes into a bush.

I pedal faster and skid to a stop next to her. Dumping my bike, I rush to her side.

"Are you okay?" My hands hover over her body. I'm afraid to touch her if she's seriously injured.

She rolls onto her back and laughs. "Yes."

"Are you sure?" My heart rate gradually eases from the frantic pace it had been racing at when she confirms she's okay.

"Of course." She sits up, and I hold out a hand to help her to her feet.

"That was close. I thought you were hurt."

"I'm fine." She shrugs. "We all get hurt sometimes."

She says it so nonchalantly, it's clear she really believes it. What happened to her?

"Do you know what the best part is?" she asks.

"What's that?"

"I won."

"You did… because you cheated."

She gasps. "I did no such thing. I demand a rematch."

"Well, we've got to climb up that hill again first."

"Chop, chop. We don't have all day." She picks up her bike and hops back on to ride it up the hill.

I stay back, absorbing her zest for life. Her carefree attitude. I can't remember the last time I felt like that.

"You coming, slowpoke?" she yells over her shoulder.

I jog with the bike on my shoulder to catch up. She gets off her bike and pushes it the rest of the way up. I use this moment to jog past her with a laugh.

When she makes it to the top, she's breathing heavily. Her cheeks are flushed and her gaze roams from my shoulders to my arms multiple times. I preen like a peacock under her attention.

"You did not just carry a bike while jogging up a ginormous hill like some athlete."

"Impressed?" I ask.

"Maybe, but you know what this means?" She smiles so brightly, my breath catches. "You'll be bringing my bike back up next round."

I'll climb this hill a thousand times if it brings that kind of smile to her face. "Naturally." I position my bike next to hers. "Best two out of three?"

"Agreed," she says. "But only if I win this round."

"It doesn't work like that."

"It does now." She grins and pedals, leaving me in the dust.

Again.

I shake my head at her antics and follow her down, but

I can't catch up with her. Bree jumps off her bike and does a victory dance in the street.

"I win. I win. I win," she chants, not seeming to care that people keep giving her strange looks.

I dump my bike next to hers and slow clap for her.

She bows and asks, "Are you mad I cheated?"

"Nah, I'm impressed. It's something I would've done to my brothers."

"I should take some pictures for Jules. My favorite hobby is making her jealous."

"Give me your phone, and I'll take some."

She digs for a moment in her fanny pack before jerking her head up and gasping. "I lost my phone."

"You had it before we raced down the hill. Let me call you and see if it's around here."

I press her contact name and walk around, hoping we get lucky. Very faintly, there's a vibration in the bushes. The same ones she fell in. I root around in the bush and pick it up.

"Found it," I say, then pause when I see my name on the screen.

"My hero." She bats her eyelashes for a moment before grabbing her phone from me.

"You misspelled my last name. It has an 'o' and 'n' at the end."

She freezes, then tucks a piece of hair behind her ear. "It's not a mistake."

I take in her stiff posture. This right here means something more. And now I have to know what it is. I steal her unlocked phone out of her hands.

"Hey, give that back," she demands.

"Nope." I turn my back to her, and she tries to climb me.

I laugh and spin around, keeping the phone out of her reach.

"You don't play fair," she says.

"Says the one who cheats nonstop."

"Oh, fine." She grins. "Have a look then."

I open her contact list and scroll through the short list. Most of the people have missing letters.

Interesting.

I press a few more buttons and get to her blocked list. All the names are blank.

She must have some sort of system for whatever this is. I have a feeling it's all related to docking letters for some reason.

I've never seen someone organize their phone this way and by the amount of people she has blocked, she's ruthless.

"You have the most interesting way of managing your phone contacts," I say, handing her phone back to her.

She tucks the phone back into her fanny pack and zips it closed. "You say interesting, but I say brilliant."

"Care to let me in on this brilliance?"

"Nope."

"Then tell me how to earn back my letters."

She stares at me, as if trying to read my mind. "How did you know?"

"I'm ancient, remember. But with age comes wisdom."

"Apparently. But if you're so wise, you should already know the answer to that question."

"I'm more curious about what I did to deserve two

docked letters." Why does she remove letters? Does she have criteria? I have too many questions, but she's hiding behind playfulness. Well, okay, I can play this game. "You must've docked me a letter because of that one time I got arrested in Amsterdam."

A laugh bursts out of her. "What did you do to get arrested?"

"I'll only tell you if you tell me. Fair's fair."

"Hm, tempting. But I'll pass."

I grin, not at all deterred. Playing with her is too fun. "I accept your challenge to find out. But I need to let you in on a little secret."

"Oh?" She leans closer to me. "What's that?"

"I never lose."

 REE

IF I WASN'T ALREADY MELTING in this heat, I'd melt after hearing those words.

He shouldn't be allowed out of the house. He's a danger to all women with his looks, personality, panty-dropping smiles, and voice.

Ugh, I've got to get it together.

"I'm getting hungry." In more ways than one, but I'm going to let him win the last word with that because I've got no comeback that doesn't begin with "fuck" and end with "me."

"We're almost to the top. Let's climb this hill first and then we can get food."

"Fine." I pass my bike to him. "Then use those muscles of yours for good."

"Noticed them, huh?"

"You'd have to be blind to not notice them."

He puffs out his chest and lifts both bikes on his shoulder. "Race you to the top?"

"Hell yeah."

I take off, but halfway up I'm dying. Huffing and puffing like I forgot to breathe, with sweat dripping down my face. And he keeps going, as if he runs up hills for fun. I might have to dock another letter if he does that, because I'm not into hiking up hills. When he reaches the top, he watches with a smirk as I force myself to put one foot in front of the other.

When I finally make it, I stumble to a grassy patch and lie down.

"I hate hills," I groan, staring at the sky.

He settles next to me. "Or more like you hate re-climbing the same hill ten times."

"Or that." I turn my head to face him. "You wouldn't happen to have the superpower of teleportation?"

"I wish, but I've got good news. We're at the top and it'll be all downhill to get to the restaurant."

I glare at him. "Don't you dare tell me I climbed that hill and almost died for nothing."

"Dramatic much?"

"Always."

He grins. "It wasn't for nothing." He sits up and points to the horizon. "Look."

I follow his finger and then gasp. I was so busy racing down the hill that I didn't stop to notice the view. It's perfection. A sea of trees sloping into turquoise water sparkling in the sun. All of that with a backdrop of Istanbul, a busy and crowded city. The

Asian side in front of me, and European in the distance to my left.

I should've brought my iPad so I can draw it. A photo can't do it justice. I'm not sure if I can even do it justice. The colors alone are inspiring, and I pop to my feet and head to the edge.

The mixture between the raw beauty of the mountains and hills in the background and the man-made beauty of the city is so interesting.

"Wow," I breathe.

He stands by my side. "This is my favorite place in the entire city."

He stares at the view like me, with longing.

"Why didn't you buy a house here?" I ask. "On the island? If you love it so much."

"I used to want that. To make enough money so I could afford a place here on the island."

"But?"

He lifts his shoulder, his expression almost lost. I've only seen him as confident and carefree. It feels like a glimpse into something deeper, something more than the jokes and the laughter.

"I'm not sure," he says. "Life got in the way, and I got too busy. I bought the house we're staying in as an investment. Easy to rent out, easy to sell. I thought I was fulfilling a dream by buying it, but now... I don't know."

"Dreams change. It's not too late to figure out what your dreams are now."

"Do you really believe that?" He faces me.

"Yeah, I do."

"What's your dream?"

I swallow. "I don't know. I thought I knew, but everything changed recently and I'm still trying to find my way."

We stare at each other for a long moment. There's a tug in my abdomen, as if a new connection is forming between us. One full of mutual lost dreams and the desire to rediscover them.

He breaks eye contact first and looks back out at the view. He's still frowning, and for some reason, I want to help him get out of it. So, I do what I do best and lighten the mood.

I grab my phone and throw my arm around his waist.

"Selfie?" I ask.

He groans, but I adjust our stance so the view is in the background and take a few photos before I put my phone away.

"You'll need to send me one of those," he says.

"Only if you feed me."

"Fine, but only if we take it easy going down."

I jut my bottom lip out, like a petulant child. "You're no fun."

He stares at my lip for far too long. "Don't tell me I'm about to lose another letter." And just like that, the Hayden I've come to know is back.

"You're about to," I tease.

"Well, then I'm going to dock your letters too. Just to make it even and all. Bree Adler. That's nine letters."

"Congratulations, you can count. But it's pointless because I'm perfect. So, there'll be no reason for you to remove any letters."

"You sure about that?"

"Obvi."

"Too bad, because you've just lost your first letter," he announces.

"For what?" I ask, outraged and a little scared to know why he'd remove a letter. What have I done to deserve it?

He draws out the moment, keeping me on my toes, before he finally says, "For having red hair."

I blink at him in shock. That's the last thing I expected him to say. "You—"

"Ah, ah, ah. I won't accept appeals. Come on." He laughs at whatever expression is on my face. "Let's discuss your faults over lunch."

"Hey now, those are fighting words."

He grins and hops on his bike. He takes off down the hill and calls back to me, "I'll fight with you anytime, baby."

THE RESTAURANT IS part of a white and blue Victorian-style house. There are a few seats outside on the sidewalk and they scattered the rest throughout the bottom floor of the house and its courtyard. The seats on the street are partially shaded from the building across from us, which is a relief. But even if it wasn't, I'd still want to sit out here. It feels wrong to be holed up inside on a beautiful day.

Hayden stands and hugs the old woman who comes out to serve us. They speak in Turkish for a few minutes before she gestures toward me a few times. Once they're finished, she goes back inside, and he returns to his seat.

"Friend of yours?" I ask.

"Yeah, used to come here all the time. She makes the best *mantı* on the island."

"And *mantı* is?"

He grins. "Meat stuffed pasta topped with yogurt and a spicy tomato paste."

"Yogurt and pasta? That's… different."

"Trust me, you'll love it."

"Well, you haven't steered me wrong yet."

"Yet? I take my job seriously as your tour guide."

Yeah, he does. The past couple of days have been amazing, and I'd never have experienced any of it without him.

"I'll be sure to leave a review of your capabilities once our trip ends."

"As you wish."

I'm about to make a quip about *The Princess Bride*, but I'm interrupted by a meow.

And not just any meow. The most pathetic meow I've ever heard. I search around, and Hayden does too, but we don't spot any cats.

Another meow. This time, from under the table. I peek under the tablecloth, but there's nothing by our feet.

Meow.

Hayden pulls the tablecloth up further and sitting in the table is a ginger and white cat. It's at shin level, on the support ring of the table legs.

The cat's face lifts towards Hayden, and it meows again. He reaches his hand out and pets the damn thing without a care in the world. Without questioning if it'll bite. What is he thinking?

"Aren't you a cutie," he coos.

Okay, so his cooing voice is adorable.

Screw you, traitorous hormones. We aren't supposed to consider a guy who has an expiration date.

"Did you ever have an animal when you were growing up?" he asks.

"No. The apartments we lived in didn't allow it. I guess I never got accustomed to having them around." Mom tried her hardest to make sure we always had food on the table and a roof over our heads. And it worked, but we never had the luxury of thinking about owning a pet.

I'm not sure when my disinterest toward animals started. Maybe it was when I begged Mom for three months for a cat, but we couldn't swing it without losing the apartment. Or maybe the time a friend's dog bit Jules and she needed to get stitches in her arm. Or the time when that same dog chased me five blocks one day while my "friend" laughed the entire time and didn't do a damn thing to stop it.

Or maybe it was this past January when my life flashed before my eyes as a dog attacked me.

"I also begged my parents for an animal," he says. "But we moved around so much it wasn't feasible. Not when the animal had to go to quarantine for months to be allowed into a new country. So, I went without."

"And now you're trying to save as many as you can."

"Yeah." He scratches the cat under its chin, and it arches into his touch. "It's a nice break from my daily work."

The same woman from before brings the food out, and the scent of meat and mint with something spicy underneath makes my mouth water. If it tastes as good as it smells and looks, this just might become my favorite food. She places a Turkish tea in front of each of us and says what I assume is a version of *enjoy your meal* before leaving.

The first bite confirms my assumption. That's it. I'd move here for the food alone. The yogurt pairs so well that I may never eat normal pasta again.

Damn him for being right yet again.

"You like?" he asks.

"I love."

His grin is full of arrogance at my response. "See, told you I'm the best tour guide."

"We'll see about that."

We eat in silence for a few minutes. Eventually, the cat ventures out of the table and stands up to place a paw on my knee. I freeze.

"Do you want me to move him?" Hayden asks.

"I…" Do I? The cat blinks at me slowly, as if daring me to touch him. "I don't want to get bitten."

"He won't bite. He smells the food and is curious. If you reach your fingers out, he'll sniff you and then he'll bump his head into your hand asking you to pet him."

Am I going to do it? Before I can process the question, I reach out to touch it. As if my hand has a mind of its own.

I slowly extend my fingers and the cat's pink nose twitches as he leans forward. I'm as still as I can be, waiting. Cats can't bite my hand off, it'll be fine. Even knowing this, I'm still a little afraid. I haven't petted an animal since January. Since the attack. And I guess I'm about to do it in the middle of the most beautiful place I've ever been, with the most beautiful man I've ever seen.

"You're doing great," Hayden says.

The cat sniffs my fingers for a few seconds before bumping his head into my hand. Just like Hayden said it'd do.

I snatch it back.

"He just wants some love."

"Where?" I glance at him.

"Under his chin would be perfect."

Taking a deep breath, I reach out again and the cat bumps my hand with his head.

"Demanding little fucker, isn't he?" I say.

"Definitely." Hayden laughs. "I'd name him Apollo if he were mine. The sun god because of his coloring, but since he's a god, he'd be a demanding prick."

I grin and my entire body relaxes as I scratch under the cat's chin. Oh, wow. I'm touching a cat. I can't believe it.

"Quick, take a photo," I say. "Jules will never believe this without proof."

Hayden whips his phone out and snaps a photo faster than I can say "please." It's as if he's had his phone in his hand and ready this entire time. He takes a photo from multiple angles and even gets down on his knee to get the perfect shot.

I laugh at his antics as the cat leans further into my hand and jumps onto my lap. I raise my hands, not sure what to do, and Hayden grins.

"I think Apollo likes you."

"If I get a disease from him, you're footing the bill."

"Only if you continue to eat."

I ignore the cat germs on my hands—which is way harder to do than I thought it'd be—and pick my fork back up.

"Do you like what you do?" he asks.

It's a purposeful distraction, but I'll take it. The longer Apollo is in my lap, kneading my thigh, the easier it is to remember that he will not hurt me.

"Yeah," I say, "it's a nice way to bring my love for helping people together with my love for art. But AI is taking over the industry and eventually I might end up without a job."

He nods once. "So that's why you're reevaluating your dreams."

"Yeah, I guess I need to figure out what I want out of life. I just feel lost."

"How so?"

Well, I walked myself into that question. Great, now I've got to say something.

"I… the attack happened six months ago, and I'm still processing everything. I'm not sure if Seattle is the right place for me, even though Mom and Jules are there. I've always wanted to leave Seattle, but now…" The guilt inside of me raises its head and gives me an accusing glare at the thought of leaving Mom and Jules. A year ago, I would've moved, and I was seriously considering it. But now? After almost losing Mom? I can't bear to leave her permanently. Even if I'm pushing her away and constantly traveling now, I'll always return to Seattle. To her.

"I feel that way about Portland sometimes. It's like…"

"… the pieces don't fit anymore?"

"Exactly," he says.

"Where would you live? If you didn't have any restrictions."

"I'm not sure. Growing up, I never stayed somewhere for longer than a few years. If I stayed somewhere for more than that, I'd get antsy and felt the need to get out."

I feel that statement in my soul. It's like he's describing me. I've never met someone else who desires change as much as me. Most people seem content living in the house they grew up in and raising a family there. But not me.

"I get that," I say.

"Yeah?"

"Yeah. It's like this pull inside here." I place my hand over my chest.

"Exactly." He points his fork at me.

We eat a few more bites in silence before he asks, "What's your logo making schedule like right now?"

"Why?"

"Because I want to hire you to make the logo for the work I'm doing here."

I can't tell if he's being serious or not. He must have a long list of graphic designers at his disposal. And yet… he wants to work with me?

I've never been one to say no to money, especially when I could use it to fund my travel habit.

"I'm finishing up a project at the moment, then I have a small gap," I say. "But if you're serious about this, I'll need more info about the company and what they're looking for."

"Of course, I'll get you anything you want."

Well, there goes my focus with that sentence. For a split second, I imagine him saying those words to me in another context related to us. That he'd get me anything, anytime, anywhere. Okay, so I expanded that a bit, but hey, it's a fantasy.

The cat chooses this moment to beg for more attention. And he couldn't have chosen a better time because I was in danger of reading too much into a throwaway statement.

Never thought I'd be grateful for a cat.

CHAPTER 16

$\mathcal{H}$AYDEN

BEFORE GETTING BACK on the ferry, Bree insisted on going inside every tourist shop on the way. She wanted to see all the offerings before settling on four magnets and two tea towels for her sister and her mom.

Every shop she went into, she drew the eye of everyone inside. All they saw was her appearance, and they have no idea how amazing her personality is.

On the ferry, the wind picks up and it rocks with the waves. But Bree just grins as if she were on an amusement ride. I like how she turns everything into a fun experience.

"Why don't you come to work with me tomorrow?" I ask. "Meet Deniz and ask her any questions you want."

"That's not necessary. I can do it all over email."

"I insist." If she meets Deniz and sees her passion for

what she does, then maybe she can understand what we're trying to accomplish.

"Is this a deal breaker for you?" she asks.

"No, but I can guarantee you there won't be any dogs where we're meeting. I'll warn her in advance. I would never put you in an uncomfortable situation if I can help it."

"Fine, as long as you promise I won't see one."

I catch her gaze. "I promise."

She nods once, short and jerky. "Then I'd like to stay in tonight. I'm tired."

"Sure," I say. "But can I ask you a question?"

She nods.

"Why did you come here for Bilet if you're scared of dogs?" It's the question that's plagued me since I've discovered her fear.

"I..." She focuses on the water. "I had this crazy idea."

"I like crazy ideas."

She glances at me. "I'm sure you do." She sighs. "But I never intended to book the ticket. I was drunk and annoyed and apparently Drunk Me shouldn't be around computers and a credit card."

"That's some excellent life advice right there."

"Right? I should put that on a coffee mug and sell it on Etsy."

I wait her out, but she doesn't continue, so I try a different angle.

"Why were you drunk and annoyed?" I ask. It seems like the easiest place to start in the story.

"I broke up with my boyfriend." She presses her lips together.

"Must've been some breakup for you to fly halfway across the world."

She gives me a strange look. "Not at all."

"Let me get this straight. You broke up with your boyfriend and you're not sad about it." I pause and she nods. "But then you accidentally book a flight to visit Bilet for some mysterious reason that you won't tell me about."

"That about sums it up."

I snort. "That doesn't make sense."

"Maybe you don't need to understand." She huffs.

"But what if I *want* to understand?"

"What's the point? In a little over a week, we'll never see each other again. That was part of our deal. Why would I open up to you?"

She's got a point, and I get where she's coming from. It's how I've lived my life for the past twenty-nine years. But I'm a firm believer that people come into other people's lives for a reason. At the exact moment we need to learn something from them.

And Bree bulldozed her way into my life. There has to be more to this than a ten-day trip of fun together. I'm tired of being nothing more than a temporary source of happiness for others. What I truly desire is to etch myself into her memory, even if our paths never cross again. To be more permanent to someone and not just a random fling while we're traveling.

Memories are forever. And sure, we're going to have a blast here, but I want more. If we can both somehow look back on this trip when we're older and pinpoint it as a defining moment in our lives, it'll be a success.

But how to make that happen?

I gaze at Bree and think about what I know about her. All the little tidbits she's given me. She loves competition and winning, being spontaneous and enjoying life to the max, and her family. But she's also dealing with trauma and has lost her way in life.

As the ferry jostles us, Bree slides closer to me on the bench.

The perfect idea pops into my head.

If we both worked through our shit together and figure out what we want in life, that'd be more than memorable. That'd be epic. Even though we'd never see each other again after this trip, we'd still be part of each other forever.

"What if," I say, "we make a game."

"I love games."

"I'm not sure you're going to love this one, but I'm hoping it can help us both."

"Are you sure you're experienced at selling things?" she asks. "That seems like the wrong thing to lead with."

I laugh. "Have I told you lately how much I enjoy you busting my balls all the time?"

"Not lately, but go on. I'm all for some flattery."

"You're the most interesting, unique, fun, hilarious, bewitching, and gorgeous woman I've ever met." Her face softens at my compliments, and she opens her mouth to say something, but I cut her off. "And I think if we play a continuous game of truth or truth, we could work through our life issues and figure it all out by the time we part."

"I'm not following how that'd help. Explain it to me like I'm five."

"We're a lot alike," I say. "We keep people at a distance and don't allow them to get close. Everyone except our family, but even then, we have our limits. What if we need to talk everything out, tell someone our deepest, darkest secrets and desires so we can discover what we really want?"

"That's called therapy."

I laugh. "And this is called *free* therapy."

She scrunches her nose, but I place a finger on her perfect lips and say, "It's the *best* idea, and you know it."

"You're only saying that because it came from you."

"Well, I am known for my amazing ideas."

"This is the craziest idea I've ever heard," she says. "And that's saying something coming from me."

I remain silent while she searches my face, for what I'm not sure, but I remain still and steady. It is a ridiculous idea, but it feels right.

"How would it work?" she asks. "How do I know you won't leak my secrets out into the world? Or vice versa." The seriousness of her tone causes me to pause. She's really worried about this.

"We could use an NDA." That would help me too. I don't need my personal information leaked to the media. Especially not when there's so much going on with NomNom. A scandal is the last thing I need. "But we have to be brutally honest. About everything. We're not allowed to shy away from a question or water down the answer."

"But what if a question is too hard to answer?"

"Then we take a shot of our favorite alcohol and still answer it."

She looks down at her fanny pack with a frown. "I'm going to need a bigger one to carry around a bottle of alcohol at all times."

"Don't worry, you don't have to give up your gorgeous fanny pack. I'll be in charge of the logistics of that."

"This is ridiculous," she says. "I hate truth or truth games."

"But this one will be fun, because by next week, we'll have our lives figured out. Gone will be all the uncertainty and doubts. Just imagine what that will feel like."

She takes a deep breath and stares at the water. After a few minutes, she turns to me. "You've got yourself a deal. But..." She looks me up and down. "We start tomorrow, so it'll give us time to get that NDA sorted. And I don't want to be bombarded by questions the second it's morning."

"Fair, and the same goes for you. I don't want you sneaking into my room at midnight to ask me what my favorite color is."

"That's actually the best idea ever." She laughs.

"See? I told you. I'm known for my amazing ideas."

She rolls her eyes. "We'll see about that."

"You keep saying that, but I haven't been proven wrong yet."

She winks. "And that's why you haven't lost another letter... yet."

* * *

WHEN WE ARRIVE BACK at the house, Bree's new clothes are hanging in garment bags in the kitchen.

153

"My clothes," she cries and rushes to them and snatches them up. "I'm going to try them on."

She runs up the stairs before I can respond. I smile at her antics and grab a beer from the fridge. I make my way to the desk in my room. A quick message to my assistant, and she sends an NDA over. Whether or not Bree was serious, it's a good idea to have one. Just in case.

I perfect the wording, making it straightforward and simple. I print off a copy and sign my name.

What's better than dinner with a side of NDA? I message my chef and request a variety of Turkish food to be delivered at eight. I don't want to have them cooking for hours in the kitchen, not when I want some peace and quiet.

I yawn and drink another sip of my beer, debating what to do next.

According to my email app, I have four hundred unread emails. My finger hovers over the icon, but I can't bring myself to click on it. It's too daunting. I'm already exhausted just seeing the number, let alone all the issues that await me inside. And it's my vacation. I don't want to work.

Chugging the rest of my beer, I set my alarm for an hour from now. A power nap will help me recharge. Then... I can deal with everything else. I settle into the bed and close my eyes.

The next thing I know, something drags me into consciousness. I check my phone, but only thirty minutes have passed.

What woke me?

I wait it out and there it is again.

A... moan?

I sit up. It has to be Bree. If she's hurt...

I'm across the hall and in front of her door before I can comprehend how I got there. I hesitate. If she was in pain, she'd be making more noise.

There's another drawn-out moan that doesn't sound like pain, that's... is she pleasuring herself?

I'm hard before I can complete the thought. The door is cracked a few inches, and I toe it open a few more. And there she is. Naked, on the bed. Her creamy skin flush with arousal. Her perfect nipples pebbled. Her hand working furiously just out of view.

She throws her head back and arches as another moan slips out of her.

I palm my erection through my pants. She's a fantasy in the flesh, and she's only a few feet from me. Almost on the brink, if her rapid breathing is any indication.

I need to turn around, to give her privacy. But if she wanted privacy, wouldn't she have closed the door fully? Why isn't she somewhere more private or trying to keep quiet?

Unless she's doing this on purpose, trying to get me to break our agreement. But if I stay here any longer, I'm going to do just that. She's sly, I'll give her that.

I stride back into my room and lean against my door. I can't have her... yet. But there's nothing stopping me from masturbating across the hallway to the delicious noises she's making.

I unzip my pants and take out my heavy length. I rub my thumb over my tip a few times before spitting into my hand. She moans again, and I stroke myself slowly.

The more she works herself into a frenzy, the louder she gets.

If she's this vocal by herself, I can't wait to hear how she'll sound when I'm balls-deep inside her. Tomorrow night can't come soon enough.

I increase my pace, trying to match her moans. Pleasure builds, and I explode into my hand at the same time as she crescendos into a climax.

Bree's pushing me to my breaking point. I've never reacted to a woman this way. Normally, they're fun and a decent lay, but disposable.

And I'm disposable to them.

But I'm not so sure how I'll feel once Bree and I part ways.

"SOMETHING SMELLS GOOD." Bree breezes into the kitchen in her new bathing suit and some sort of sheer turquoise coverup thing that's not covering her up one bit.

I ignore my instant hard-on and say, "I thought we could eat on the patio."

"Great idea."

We fill our plates full of meat kebabs, Turkish-style rice, green beans cooked with tomatoes and onions, hummus, and pita bread.

"What would you like to drink?" I ask.

"Do you have any beer?"

"Yeah, I'll bring it out."

She takes our plates and I grab the drinks and silverware. We settle into our chairs, and she lifts her beer in the air.

"To a gorgeous sunset," she says, "and an amazing day."

She's right. Istanbul is showcasing its beauty tonight. The sky is a beautiful blend of oranges, yellows, and reds as the sun sinks closer to the horizon.

"Cheers to more adventures," I say.

We clink our bottles together and take a sip. I can't keep my eyes off her as she takes her first bite. The V between her breasts is making me hungry for something besides food. What I wouldn't give to lick her there. To worship her.

"How do you like the new clothes?" I ask.

"They're perfect. Thanks again for getting them for me."

"We should go for a swim after dinner. Test it out."

She grins and takes a bite of green beans. "You going to pop these clothes' cherry?"

"Of course. My life goal is to pop every single one."

She shivers and I arch an eyebrow. "Cold?"

She glares, and I laugh.

"Swimming sounds perfect," she says. "But you're putting me at a disadvantage."

"Oh? How so?"

"The last time I used your pool, you saw me practically naked."

"Best day of my life," I say instantly.

"You must live a boring life." She arches an eyebrow. "But... it's got me thinking."

"Uh-oh."

She grins. "If I'm going to spill all my secrets to a

stranger, then you also need to have some skin in the game."

"You do realize I'm also going to divulge all my secrets to you too?"

"Potato, pah-tah-to."

I laugh. "If you want to see my dick that badly, all you have to do is ask."

"I want to see it for the sole purpose of creating endless jokes."

I lean closer toward her. "I can assure you the only jokes about what I'm packing is how it's going to fit inside you."

"Hmm." She licks her fork, all seductive like. "I somehow doubt that."

"I'll swim naked if it makes you feel better." I slide the NDA across the table. "But only if you sign this first."

She shoots me a look. "Had this just lying around, did you?"

"I'm a man of many talents."

She rolls her eyes and reads through everything before meeting my gaze. "Somehow, I'm surprised it's so straightforward."

"What? You thought I'd trick you?"

"You never know." Her tone is just a little too serious.

"Who hurt you?"

She startles and gives me a surprised look.

"No one," she says quickly. Too quickly.

"Our agreement means you can't lie. Not to me."

"And this whole thing isn't supposed to start until tomorrow," she snaps back.

I chug half my beer in one go, annoyed. "Fine."

"Fine," she says tersely and sets the pen down. "Maybe this is a mistake. We're already arguing, and we haven't even started this thing."

"We're arguing because we've already started. Because it's getting real."

"This sucks." She blows out a long breath.

"I know."

After a few minutes, she nods sharply and mouths something to herself.

"I better not regret this." She picks up the pen and signs her name in a flourish.

"How could you when you're about to see my dick?"

She huffs and chugs the rest of her beer.

"Another?" I ask.

She nods and I take the NDA inside for safekeeping before bringing the entire pack of beer outside.

"There's nothing like a cold beer after a hot day." She grabs one and settles back into her chair, the tension from before seemingly forgotten.

I tilt my bottle toward hers. "Amen."

The conversation for the rest of dinner revolves around rehashing the day, all the funny parts and nothing serious. When we finish, I bring the plates inside and use that moment to undress and head back outside. A deal is a deal.

"You ready for a swim?" I ask.

She turns her head and does a double take when she finds me naked.

CHAPTER 17

REE

HOLY SHIT.

Hayden wasn't lying about his size.

He's sporting a semi, and yeah… is it possible to trip and land on his dick? Because I need to take him for a ride.

I gulp and try to cover my reaction by nodding at his dick. "Aw, isn't he cute?"

"Cute?" He snorts. "That's not what I'd call him."

He walks into the water. Holy shit, his ass is perfect too? I don't think I've ever seen one so round. And he's got those little indentations on the side near his hips that only come from working out. Who knew I was an ass girl? I thought I was more of a six-pack and dick one, but Hayden's converted me. Maybe I should start a religion just for asses and he can be the star of the show.

"Oh?" I clear my throat. "And what would you call him?"

He turns to face me. "Magnificent, a gift to all womankind… something along those lines."

"You're very modest," I say sarcastically.

"This is me being modest."

Is this guy for real? Because I'm even more tempted to fuck him just to test it out. I can't stop my gaze from dipping down to his glorious dick.

"You're drooling," he says.

"Out of the two of us, I don't think I'm the one drooling."

"Oh, really?" He grins. "Why don't you come in and we can get a closer look? Settle this little debate."

This is a stupid idea, I know. But I can't help it if I love to play with fire. Besides, I've never been one to back down from a dare, even an implied one. Maybe I can get him to break, to make a move.

So, I do the only thing a sane and rational woman would do—I dive into the cool water. But if I get too close to him, I'm going to lose our challenge. Every time he takes a step closer to me, I move to the opposite side of the pool. This happens twice before he smirks and starts swimming some laps.

I stare at the stars and replay our conversation. When he asked who hurt me, it hit too close to home. The answer is everyone. Every single person, starting with my father. I don't like when anyone sees me as weak, and I especially don't like when Hayden sees it. And this stupid agreement will allow him to see me like that constantly.

I agreed because I'm just floating through life. Waiting

for something to happen. Something bad since those are normally the cards dealt to me. I try to enjoy life and not think about what will happen next. But the key word there is "try." I do think about the future. I just don't know what to do with that thinking. It never materializes into anything, and it never progresses into action. I'm always left annoyed and in need of a distraction.

When he asked me to imagine what it would feel like to have no uncertainty or doubts... it was like he was speaking directly to my soul. To the scared kid who's stuck in the past. And she listened to him and wanted to take a chance to feel better.

Opening up to him won't be that big of a risk. I won't see him again after this trip, and he can't use anything against me because of the NDA. I'll be protected on that front at least. Hell, I'll probably not like him that much after learning his secrets. I hope at least the sex will be good.

I have nothing to lose and only hope to gain.

I float starfish-style while he does his little workout. I'm still waiting on the floatie he promised to buy. But now I feel like a penis float would be a better idea than a unicorn. I make a mental note to research this online tonight while I talk to Jules.

After what feels like his hundredth lap, the next time he reaches my end of the pool, I call out to him, "Are you done yet?"

"Sorry." He stops and brushes the water off his face with his hand.

"Do you ever relax and enjoy the moment?" I swim to the edge of the pool, overlooking the Bosphorus.

"Depends on the moment." He settles next to me.

"And now?"

"I'm not sure if it's a good idea if I relax."

"Oh? Why not?" I ask.

His gaze dips to my breasts and back to my face slowly as if in a caress. I'm not the one naked here, but it sure feels like I am when he looks at me like that.

"I think you can figure it out," he says.

I glance away and swallow hard. I love that he can barely contain himself when he's around me.

"Let me take you out tomorrow night. Dinner, drinks, and fun," he says.

I glance at him out of the corner of my eye. "I could use some fun."

"Hey, I take offense to that."

"No, you don't." I laugh.

"Okay, I don't. Because I know I'm an amazing and fun person."

"Only people who aren't amazing and fun would say that."

"Touché." He grins. "But seriously. Let me take you out."

"Fine, but I demand the best food ever and even better drinks if we're going to do this truth thing."

He raises an eyebrow. "Wow, never knew telling the truth would be such a hardship."

"Oh, it is."

"Because?"

"Because it is."

"Good argument there," he says.

I bump my shoulder into his. "I thought so."

"I wonder if it's midnight yet."

"Thankfully, that's an impossibility because the sun just set like an hour ago."

He laughs. "Well, it *is* midnight somewhere."

"You did not just say that."

"It was the best one-liner ever and you know it."

"If you say so." I roll my eyes. "I need to call my sister."

He nods and swims to the steps. Once he steps out, I'm reminded yet again of how hot he is as the water runs down his body. Water I wouldn't mind licking off him.

Tomorrow. I just have to wait until then, until our agreement from the plane ends, and then I can have my fill.

He hands me a towel and we head up the stairs together. Silent, but surprisingly comfortable.

When we're at my door, I say, "Goodnight."

"Goodnight," he says before smiling. "And if in the middle of the night you need some relief, you can always find me."

"Relief?"

He gives me a look, one that takes me a moment to decipher. And then it hits.

He heard me masturbating.

I mean, it wasn't like I was trying to be sneaky about it. When I checked on him, he was asleep, so I thought it was safe to get some relief from the constant arousal I feel in his presence.

But I refuse to be embarrassed by that, because it's not like it's something he hasn't done or seen.

"Did you enjoy the show?" I ask.

"It'd only be considered a show if I had a front-row seat."

"Okay then. I'll keep that in mind."

"You do that." He leans close to my ear and whispers, "Next time, you can watch me too."

Heat washes over me, and my pussy flutters at the thought of watching him.

"That might be considered cheating in regard to our challenge," I say, trying to act unaffected.

"Would it though? It'd be like watching porn."

"Stretching that definition as far as it can go, I see."

He laughs and places an arm above me on the door-jamb, all casual like. "What can I say? I like to break the rules."

"And that applies to the dictionary?"

"Apparently."

I grin and push against his muscular chest. "Goodnight."

"Night beautiful." He steps back and enters his room.

I shut the door behind me and lean against it. Glad it's dark in the room, so no one can see me smile.

Damn Hayden for making me like him. Too bad tomorrow's going to change everything between us.

CHAPTER 18

$\mathcal{H}$AYDEN

Anders: What's with the radio silence, Hayden?

Me: I'm jet lagged.

Theo: That's never stopped you from texting us at all hours before.

Me: And I'm on vacation.

Anders: Seriously? You're finally listening?

Theo: Who has your phone? Blink once if you're in trouble.

Me: I can't blink through text, idiot.

Theo: I demand proof of life from whoever I'm talking with.

Anders: We don't accept ransoms, you can have him.

I SEND a picture of me flipping them off.

Me: Good to know where I stand with you, assholes. There'll be no Turkish delight for you lot when I fly back.

Theo: Hey now, you don't have to do anything as drastic as that.

Anders: Don't worry, I can buy us all some when we visit him next week.

Theo: But Hayden is the only one who knows the best place. The one he refuses to tell us about.

Anders: Shit, you're right. We're sorry.

Me: I bet it hurt to say those words, huh?

Anders: Not really, not when Zoey makes it feel all better.

Me: Ew, TMI, bro. TMI.

Theo: Get it, bro.

Me: Theo, do you really want to be reminded of Christmas and what went on in the bedroom we'll never enter again?

Theo: Good point. I bet Zoey wouldn't appreciate you talking about your sex life with us.

Anders: Get your head out of your ass. I was talking about her helping me admit when I'm wrong.

Me: Oh.

Anders: If you text her, Theo, I'm going to enlist Hayden to help me prank you.

Theo: Fine, you're no fun.

Anders: I've never been fun. Hayden, let us know how it works out with Deniz.

Me: Will do. I'm meeting with her this morning. I've enlisted some help to get the marketing materials going.

Theo: Help from whom?

Me: No one you know.

Anders: Is it the woman you met?

Me: Going through a tunnel, can't talk.

Theo: Hayden is in looooveeeeee.

Me: Fuck off.

I TOSS my phone on the bed and grin. Today, I'll not only get answers from Bree, but we can finally have sex. I hurry through my morning routine and practically run down the stairs to the kitchen.

Bree's already there, in her new T-shirt dress thing. She's so stunning it takes my breath away.

"Good morning."

"Dark fern," she blurts out.

"That's the most interesting response I've ever gotten to a good morning."

She laughs. "I like to mix it up."

"I like it." I grab a coffee mug and nod to her half full coffee cup. "You want a refill?"

"Actually, do you know how to make Turkish tea?"

"Of course." I open the cabinet and get out the tea. "So let me guess, dark fern means you slept well?"

"No." She snorts. "It's my favorite color."

"I don't think I've ever met someone who has dark fern as their favorite color."

"I aim to please."

"So does this mean you're ready to get started on our little agreement?"

"Not really…"

"You don't have to sound so scared." I laugh to lighten the mood. She's totally scared and I get it. Being brutally honest is tough. Approaching this topic slowly and easing into is the best course of action. I don't want her to be uncomfortable.

"I'm not scared." She straightens her shoulders and tries to act unaffected.

I ignore her reaction and change the subject. "My favorite color is yellow."

"What shade?"

"Lemon yellow."

"Huh, our favorite colors complement each other," she

says offhandedly.

"It's meant to be then."

She looks at me and smiles. "Something like that."

We finish up our teas and breakfast before being driven to Deniz's office. The entire time, Bree twists her hands together.

"It'll be fine." I place a hand on hers.

She shoots me a grateful look before returning her gaze to the window. I keep my hand on hers, unable to help myself.

Deniz's place is a two-story, small building on the Asian side. The white paint needs a refresh, power lines crisscross above us, and the apartment buildings on either side have laundry hanging on the balconies.

But there's a yard in the back for the dogs to run around in.

My driver pulls up to the side of the street and we exit together. My hand finds its way to Bree's lower back, and I guide her through the door.

The scent of dog fills the air, not in a bad way, but in a way that makes it clear many animals live here. The ground floor of the building has the receptionist, two treatment rooms, and the kennels where the dogs are housed. Upstairs is the offices, supply room, and a small bedroom and bathroom for the person on the night shift.

I greet the receptionist and she leads us up the stairs to Deniz's office, bypassing all the animals.

Bree's entire body is stiff as we walk. When we get to Deniz's office, she stands from behind her desk and greets us. Her brown hair is thrown back in a messy ponytail, and her navy scrubs match the color scheme of the room.

One of the walls has five photos hanging on it. Each photo is of a person hugging a dog they've adopted from here. My goal is for this entire wall to be covered in photos. Deniz has a small organization right now, so she needs my help to grow.

"Welcome," Deniz says, "Please have a seat."

We sit in the two chairs before her desk. Someone comes inside and places teas in front of us.

"I'm so glad you're willing to help us out with some marketing material," Deniz says.

"No problem," Bree says. "Happy to help."

"What if Bree asks her questions first and then we can discuss some of the next steps?" I propose.

"Sounds good. Ask whatever you need."

Bree takes out her computer and iPad and transforms before my eyes. She glows as she asks about Deniz, her company, and her goals for it. Bree types so fast, she could be typing word for word what Deniz says. She's personable and engaged 1,000 percent in what Deniz is saying.

Bree asks about the target audience, what logo they have now, for Deniz to narrow down some words to describe the company, and so on. She's thorough and it's impressive. Bree's got a knack for making someone feel at ease, for showing a genuine interest in another person's passion. Deniz talks more than I thought was possible for the woman who prefers the company of animals to humans.

Watching Bree work is quickly becoming my new hobby.

When they finish, Bree doodles ideas on her iPad while Deniz and I talk about concrete next steps and how she'll use the funds to grow. She shows me her business plan and the new location she wants to move to since this one is at its limit size wise.

After an hour, Deniz excuses herself to help one of her employees.

I glance at Bree and she's staring at me with an intensity I can't place.

"What?" I ask.

"Nothing, I just haven't seen that side of you."

"Which side?"

"The confident businessman who knows the exact right question to ask. Who has an apparent gut feeling of how to direct the business."

"It's all about experience. Somehow, I have a knack for it." It shocked the hell out of my brothers when we started our business, especially when I failed every subject in school.

"It's impressive."

"Funny, because I find what you're doing more impressive."

She blushes. "Drawing some pictures isn't the same thing as what you're doing."

"Don't you dare discount what you do."

"I'm not discounting it. But I am realistic."

"Come here." I stand and grab her hand to join me.

I lead her to the photos and point to them. "These dogs were lucky to find a home. Deniz has been getting by with word-of-mouth, but the dogs downstairs? They won't find homes if we don't market this. They'll be left here to die. Is it better than the streets? For sure. But they won't know the love they could know if we don't reach more people. And the people who need a dog, or want a dog, won't get to experience the love only an animal can offer. That's where you come in."

She studies the photos, running her finger over the ones with smiling kids.

"I've got an idea," she says before returning to her iPad.

As I sit down next to her, she sketches something. A line-style drawing of a dog that looks like Bilet takes shape. One ear is sticking up, and the other is floppy. He's wearing a pair of heart-shaped sunglasses. Engrossed in her task, she writes the name of the company and tries fitting it in the sunglasses, or around the dog. She settles on making it look like a tattoo on the inside of the upright ear.

It's cool and cute even with it being a rough sketch. It's exactly the image Deniz needs to portray to get new customers since we're aiming for a variety of age ranges. We want it to be cool to adopt a dog.

"That's the one," I say.

"You can't decide for Deniz. Let me come up with a few more designs for her to choose from."

"I'm telling you, that's the one."

"You can't know that."

"I can. I've always gone with my gut in business, and it's never steered me wrong," I say. "Let's show her when she returns. You'll see."

"But I… that's not how this works."

"Who cares? Why not try something different?"

"Fine, but if she hates it, you better explain that I'll give her more options."

I laugh. "Don't worry. You'll see."

When Deniz returns a few minutes later, I show her the sketch, and she immediately approves it. I shoot Bree an "I told you so" look and she rolls her eyes in response.

We finish the meeting shortly after that, and before we leave, Deniz asks to speak to Bree in private.

Bree agrees, and I wait outside the door to find out what in the world Deniz wants to say.

CHAPTER 19

REE

"You hate it, don't you?" I ask the second the door closes. "The logo, I mean."

"Not at all," she smiles kindly. "It is the perfect design. But I wanted to ask you a personal question if that's okay?"

I nod, wondering where this is heading.

"Hayden mentioned you aren't a fan of dogs?" She asks it like a question to be polite, which I appreciate. But I refuse to lie to her.

"Yes, but that won't influence my ability to work on this project." It's true. Although I may not be passionate about the dog rescue mission she's got going on, I'm a professional and give my best effort to each project I take on.

"I know. You're clearly passionate about what you do. But do you mind sharing why you don't like dogs?"

"One attacked me earlier this year."

Her face softens. "I thought it might be the case. I'm sorry that happened to you."

"It's not your fault."

"Did you know most dogs mirror the emotional state of their owners?"

"Really?" I ask.

"Yes, dogs aren't inherently bad. It's mostly about how they're raised and their owners that influence their actions."

I blink at her a few times, trying to process this information. I never thought about it like that. I always thought that dogs are aggressive because it's their nature. Not because of the influence their owners have on them. It makes sense, and it's shifting my entire perspective.

"But what about the street dogs?" I ask. "They don't have an owner and yet they can be aggressive."

"Well, it depends on the dog. Most haven't been trained or socialized properly and that can lead to some poor habits. But once they're in a loving environment, they can be rehabilitated easily."

"I'll have to take your word for it."

"Have you worked on overcoming your fear?" she asks.

"Not really. But I'm trying."

"I can send you a list of tips and tricks to help if you want?"

"Sure. Thank you," I say, giving her my number. I rejected therapy because I don't want to rehash what happened, but I'm not opposed to some hints or tricks to help make walking down the street easier.

"Let's get you back to Hayden before he comes looking for you."

I laugh. "I doubt he'll come looking for me."

"Hmm," is all she says and gives me a knowing smile.

I'm not sure what that means, but when she opens the door, Hayden's leaning against the opposite wall.

Deniz grins and says her goodbyes before we leave.

Once we settle back into Hayden's car, he asks, "How are you feeling?"

"Good. Great, even. That was easier than I thought it was. Deniz is an amazing person."

"She is. But not as amazing as you."

I roll my eyes. He's smooth, I'll give him that. He opens his mouth to say something, but my phone pings with a message.

I open it to find a text from Deniz with techniques to get over my fear.

"Who's that?" Hayden asks.

"Deniz." I hand him the phone so he can see for himself.

"Do you want to grab some food and find Bilet again?"

"Yes to the food, but I'm nervous about the Bilet option."

"I'll make sure nothing happens to you," he promises.

His promise endears me toward him. Well, more than I already am.

"Okay."

* * *

ACCORDING TO HIS INSTAGRAM, Bilet's on a ferry today. The one that goes between the Asian and European sides. We hop on at the Asian side and find a group of men and women in workout gear, from all different ages, chatting in the row behind Bilet.

Hayden guides me to sit in the row across from them. He positions himself between me and Bilet by taking the aisle. My heart stumbles at the protective stance. No one outside of Mom and Jules has protected me before. Hayden protecting me with such a simple gesture means more than I care to admit.

Bilet's relaxing his head on his paws as the ferry chugs through the water. He looks the same as last time. I'm not sure what I was expecting, perhaps more of a sign that he's living on the street.

The people provide constant chatter for the entire twenty-minute ride to cross the Bosphorus. When the ferry docks, everyone gets off except us and the group. Hayden tells me to remain seated while he gets up to talk to one of the workers.

When he comes back, he sits next to me again.

"Do we need to get off?" I ask.

"No, we can stay. I explained to the operator that we were following Bilet."

"What about them?" I ask, nodding to the group in workout gear.

"They're here for Bilet too. I assume they do this regularly because he didn't ask them to get off."

"Interesting."

"Pardon," Hayden says, getting the attention of the people near us. He follows up with something in Turkish.

"I do," one of the women says in English. She looks like she's in her twenties with golden streaks in her brown hair.

"I asked if anyone speaks English," Hayden tells me, "and said you'd like to ask them about Bilet."

I glare at Hayden, but he just smiles in response.

I turn my attention to the woman who spoke and ask, "I'm curious about Bilet and was wondering if you follow him regularly."

"Every Wednesday we meet and track him down. Ayla started the meetup about a year ago." She gestures to another woman close to her age.

"What made her start following him?"

The two women talk in Turkish for a moment before the one who speaks English says, "Bilet is very intelligent to navigate the public transport so smoothly and with no help. He knows exactly what line to take and has preferences. I doubt any other city can say they have a dog like ours. Ayla wanted to celebrate him and bring like-minded people together."

Huh, I guess he is intelligent to do all that. I never thought of it that way. Without Hayden guiding me, I'd have a hard time figuring out all the transportation options here.

"Makes sense," I say. "How long do you normally follow him?"

"About an hour. We use the time to catch up on each other's lives and anything interesting Bilet did during the past week. This is one of his favorite lines, by the way. We all think he likes the rocking of the ferry. But it's fun. You should join us next week."

"Thank you for the offer," I say. "I'm supposed to fly back home then, but I'll see if I can squeeze it in."

"We'll be here," she says simply.

She already knows what she's going to do every Wednesday for the foreseeable future. I'd find that confining, but apparently, they all love it.

But what's most surprising is that Ayla has built a community here. All because of a dog. I don't even have that in Seattle. Making friends as an adult is way more difficult than people acknowledge. Especially when I don't have kids or any real hobby.

I purposely severed ties with everyone I grew up with. There's no need to keep toxic people around. But that only leaves me with Mom and Jules, and the random men I sometimes date. Maybe I should try a hobby and make a friend or two when I get back. Maybe I'll feel more settled that way.

"You doing okay?" Hayden asks.

"Yeah, just trying to wrap my mind around the fact that so many people love Bilet just because he's a dog who rides public transport."

"Loving an animal differs from loving a person."

"How so?" I ask.

"They're innocent creatures who don't have underhanded motivations in their actions," he says. "They're driven by love, loyalty, and instinct."

I chew over his statement. Everyone's convinced dogs are these amazing creatures, but if that's the case, how is it possible for me to have misjudged them so much?

I never looked at them as anything more than an

annoyance, even before the attack. Just needy little creatures that demand too much love and attention. They always appeared like more trouble than anything else.

They got more love than me.

Years ago, I forced Jules to drive us by our dad's house after finding him on social media. When she finally gave in, we found him in his front yard with his new family. A little boy and girl ran around in the sprinklers. The house was big, so much bigger than the apartment we could barely afford. Dad knelt in the grass and a Labrador bounded toward him, wet and slobbery. He scooped the dog up and kissed it as if it meant more to him than anything else in the world. Like a dog meant more than we did.

Maybe to him, it did.

I swallow back tears. I haven't thought about that day in forever.

"Hey, what's wrong?" Hayden asks.

"Nothing."

"You're not supposed to lie."

"I just thought about my dad for the first time in a long," I say, staring at the water.

"Will you tell me about it?"

"Only with tons of alcohol."

He snorts. "I'll write our driver and make sure he has some in the car."

"The perks of being rich."

We're silent for a few beats before Hayden murmurs, "Fuck it."

He puts his strong arm over my shoulders and pulls

me into his side. I tense for a moment, surprised. But after a second, I melt into him.

And most surprising of all is that I like it.

CHAPTER 20

*H*AYDEN

W**HEN** **WE** **GOT** **BACK** to the house, Bree insisted on working for a few hours on the logo for Deniz before sending it off. She was motivated, so I left her to it.

Anders also texted to inform me that Zoey accepted his proposal. As if she would ever say no. I'm so happy for them, and it's time to have fun and celebrate.

Bree wanted to experience the heart and soul of Istanbul, and tonight I'm delivering.

We end up between two multi-story buildings on a side street near Taksim. Around sundown, the restaurants on either side of the alleyway put out small stools and tables. They're more suitable for children in size, but it somehow adds to the atmosphere. Everything wobbles on the cobblestones, but it doesn't deter people from coming.

There's not a single empty table on this street or any of the surrounding ones.

I order us this restaurant's special—fried mussels—with beer. It's perfect for a summer night. I could've brought her to a swanky rooftop restaurant, but I have a feeling I'd lose another letter if I did that.

"I know why I lost my letter," I say.

"Let's hear it."

"It's because of that one time I filled every cabinet in our kitchen with plastic balls."

"Don't tell me your mom opened it," she says.

"Well, I was trying to prank my dad. But he was onto me when I kept asking for things from the kitchen, trying to get him to open one. But my mom walked into the room, overheard my request, and said she'd make me a snack."

"Oh, no." Bree's eyes are wide as she leans into the table. "What happened?"

"Let's just say my fingers are still pruned from all the dish duty she put me on."

"Your mom sounds cool, because you totally deserved that."

"Yeah, I did." I laugh. "But it was pretty epic."

"And let me guess? Did I lose another letter?"

"Of course," I say lightly. "You're too brave, facing your fear of dogs."

She gives me a soft smile. "I didn't think I could do it, to go to Deniz or Bilet again."

"But you did."

"Yeah, thanks to you."

"I was just the arm candy. You did all the hard work."

"I should put that on a shirt and sell it," she says.

"I'd buy it, but only if you're walking next to me while I wear it."

"Deal," she says.

The server brings us our beers and sets them on the table.

"I wish they had a place like this back home," Bree says, looking around in awe.

"I agree. It's pretty amazing. We're lucky the rules have changed recently. For a time, this was outlawed." Because of the views of the government regarding alcohol. But to me, this makes Istanbul, Istanbul. It's an atmosphere that can't be replicated, no matter how many places I visit.

"Lucky indeed." She clinks her beer against mine. "To a fun night."

"And to a fun afterparty." I give her a hooded glance, one full of promises.

"Only if you can last a few more hours without breaking."

"You mean only if you can be honest in our truth or truth games, or no sex for you."

She inclines her head and we both take a healthy sip of our drinks. The food comes out fast. The plate is piled high with skewers, each skewer filled with multiple fried mussels. There's also walnut and yogurt tartar sauce. I put five sticks on Bree's plate and a healthy serving of the sauce on the side. She waits until I serve myself before eating.

"Tell me more about this," she says, referencing the plate I gave her. "You mentioned your dad does it for your mom."

This is the first real question she's asked me all day. I was waiting for something, anything, from her, but she didn't ask me a single thing, and then I didn't want to push for my own answers. Even if she agreed to this in principle, coming at her with nonstop questions wouldn't help my cause.

But now, she's cracked. And I'm delighted.

"He's done that for as long as I can remember," I say. "The rule in the house is that none of us are allowed to make our plates until Mom gets hers. I remember my dad setting us straight real fast when we complained."

"That's cute. He sounds like a good dad." She takes a bite of the mussel with the sauce. "This is so good."

I grin at her enjoyment. "He is a good dad. What about yours? You don't talk much about him."

"Because he left us when I was a baby."

"I'm sorry."

She lifts her shoulder. "That's life for you."

The words are practiced, as if she's said them a thousand times to discourage any follow-up questions. But I won't be deterred. Not when it's time to dig deeper.

"Has he contacted you since he left?" I ask.

She shakes her head.

"What an asshole," I say.

She avoids my gaze and stares at the table next to us and the friends laughing together.

"Hey," I say, reaching for her hand. "I know it's hard, but I'd really like to find out more about you."

"Because of our deal?"

"I wouldn't have made that deal if I wasn't interested in you."

She blows out a breath and chugs the rest of her beer.

When she finishes, I pass her mine. "Just in case we don't get new ones in time."

She huffs out a laugh and then turns serious.

"He ruined our lives when he left," she says. "Mom's dream was to be a stay-at-home-mom, and he supported that with his job as a dentist. Their arrangement worked great until Mom had problems getting pregnant after having Jules. Her dream of having tons of kids close in age stayed just that... a dream. After I was born, years too late, he cheated on Mom and left us with nothing. Mom had no relevant work experience and could only find minimum wage jobs, so she worked three jobs just to make rent and keep food on the table."

"But what about child support?"

"He had better lawyers and was able to walk away with paying a low amount. That money kept us from being homeless."

"Did you ever reach out to him?"

"Once." Her expression sours.

"And?"

"I saw him from afar. With his new family, house, and dog. I knew then it wasn't worth it to connect with him again."

"I'm sorry," I say again. Those words are so inadequate, but it's all I've got.

"At least I have Jules and... Mom."

"Why the hesitation?"

"No reason."

"Bree..."

"Ugh, fine," she says. "My relationship with my mom has been strained since the beginning of the year."

"Since the attack?"

She gives me a jerky nod.

I don't know what that means, or why she seems upset. Was her mom not there for her or something? I still don't understand what happened to her. It was obviously traumatic, but that's all I've deduced from it.

"I know what you're about to ask," she says. "But I can't go into the details when we're around so many people. If you insist, I'll tell you later about it."

"Fair enough," I say, noting the slight shake in her hand as she picks up her fork. There's no need to push for more when we're in public.

"How about you?" she asks. "Tell me more about moving around. Was it hard?"

"It used to be when I was young. I hated the moving and blamed my dad and his job for uprooting us so often. But as I got older, it just became the norm. I knew what to expect regarding friendships and how we'd never keep in touch once I moved again."

"Why wouldn't you keep in touch with a friend after you moved?" she asks.

"That's not the lifestyle." And it killed me every time a friend didn't keep their promise to call regularly. I'd call them, and they wouldn't answer. Or if they did, it was only for the first couple of weeks. Then it trailed off to once a month... and then nothing. Our friendship meant nothing to them, and I became disposable.

"That's sad."

"I guess," I say, not wanting to delve deeper into those wounds.

"Do you have many friends now? In Portland."

I pause.

Do I?

I hang out with my brothers, or friends of my brothers. But the longer I think about it, the more I realize I don't have any of my own.

What the hell does that mean?

I grab my beer as the waiter finishes refilling and chug it. "I thought I did, but I guess I don't have any that weren't friends with my brothers first."

She looks at me with something akin to pity in her expression.

"Don't you dare pity me," I say.

"I don't pity you, you idiot. I understand where you're coming from."

"Yeah?"

"Yeah." She nods. "I don't have any friends either, besides Jules. And I tolerate her friends at best."

"Huh. Who knew we'd have this in common? You up for a rapid fire round of truths?"

"Sure. How about three truths?"

"Five?" I counter.

"Let's do four then."

"Deal." I grin. "I'll even go first. I hate heights. My second favorite country after Turkey is Vietnam. I love the beach, and I almost failed out of high school and college."

"But you're so smart. How did you almost fail?" she asks.

"I didn't like school. I didn't see the point when we moved so often. It wasn't until we made NomNom, our reservation platform, that I applied myself. There was finally something bigger than me to dedicate myself to."

"Huh, I never would've guessed that about you."

"Alright, your turn," I say.

"I hate heights as well." She smirks. "My favorite country just might be Turkey. I also love the bea—"

"I see what you're doing here," I interrupt, equal parts amused and annoyed at her humor.

"Sorry, I couldn't help it." She laughs. "But just so you know, they were all true. Okay, let's see... I started drawing when I realized my friends all had dad's and I didn't."

"How old were you?"

"Five? I always liked art, but it was Jules's idea to get me more involved in it."

"And did it help?"

"Yeah, I finally had an outlet for all these feelings I couldn't even begin to explain."

"Do you still like it?"

"I do." She lifts her glass in the air. "Whew, that rapid fire round was intense. Let's celebrate by taking a break from the whole truth thing?"

We clink our glasses together and spend the rest of dinner talking about anything and everything. Nothing too serious, but we stay at the table for hours, eating and drinking. We switch to drinking raki halfway through to enjoy the slow pace.

After we finish eating, we're both unstable on our feet as I guide her to one of my favorite spots. Locals and tourists alike fill the streets, and it's so busy, it's hard to walk to our destination.

I guide her down another alley and to my favorite bar. It only serves shots and doesn't open until around midnight. All the shot glasses have something along the rim. Everything from sugar, to salt, to crushed up nuts or candies depending on what's ordered.

Music from a DJ fills the alley and there's a crowd of people milling about. Most people are standing, but some lucky ones are sitting on the ledges that are placed sporadically on the walls. A few bars line the alley, but the bar I want consists of just a window to order from.

I order two variety boards for us. Each one has five of their signature shots and it's a good introduction to the place. We find a small ledge halfway down the alley to place the wooden shot holders on.

"This is the coolest bar I've ever been to," she says, looking around with wide eyes.

"It's my favorite bar in the city." I grab us each a pale yellow shot with sugar around the rim. It has an apple slice inside and a dash of cinnamon on top.

"I despise mangos," I say, and drink the shot.

She grins. "Well, I hate all forms of melon. Watermelon, cantaloupe, honeydew. It's all disgusting."

Her shoulder brushes against mine as she sets the empty glass back in the holder. And it's like giving a teaspoon of food to a starved man. It ignites my appetite for her, and that small touch is not enough. Not when I need more of her. Not when it's been four days, and our deadline is officially up.

She sways to the music, and I turn to her. The blue and

green strobe lights fall across her face, highlighting her features. Her gorgeous eyes meet mine. I could stare at her for a million lifetimes and it still wouldn't be long enough. I've never felt like this with another person.

The longer we stare at one another, the stronger this connection between us grows. Time stumbles forward, as if it feels our moment and is having as hard a time regaining its balance as I am.

Someone bumps into her, breaking our eye contact. She falls into me, but I catch her with my hands around her waist. Her arms somehow end up around my neck, and maybe it was an instinctual move on her part, but I don't care. Not when she's touching me, and I've finally got her curves under my hands.

"Why hello there," she says, laughing.

"Hi." I smile. "You good?"

"I'm perfect."

She just might be.

"Shot time," she says, pulling away. I feel her absence like a physical ache.

She chooses one that's red with crushed chocolate candy on the rim and lifts it in the air.

"Tell me a secret," I say. "Something important that no one knows."

She thinks on it for a moment before saying, "I don't like Seattle."

"Ah, ah, ah," I say, putting my hand on her arm and stopping her from downing the shot. "You already told me that."

"I know." She lowers the shot and glares at it, as if it's

the one responsible for getting caught trying to take the easy way out.

"Come on, you can do better than that," I taunt. "I can't believe you tried to cheat your way out of that one."

"It was worth a try." She grins. "But just so you know, I'm giving you more than I give most people."

"I don't want to be most people to you." And isn't that the truth? I desperately want to leave a lasting impression on her. For once, I don't want to be forgotten when I leave.

"It's difficult to just open up when I've spent my entire life holding everything in." She slams her lips shut after saying that, and I tuck away that information for later.

"Come on, what about our agreement?"

She stares at me for a beat before bringing the shot glass to her lips. "Fine," she snaps. "I'm so angry with my mom, and I don't know if I can ever forgive her." She slams her shot back as if it personally offended her, and I'm left gaping at what she said.

She wipes her mouth with the back of her hand. "Your turn."

"I'm scared to tell my brothers that I don't enjoy work anymore. That I want to quit. When we sold our company, it was part of the agreement that I'd stay on and work for the new owners. But I'm... tired."

I down the shot and place it back in the holder without looking at her. The urge to brush off the words, to make a joke and lighten them, runs through me. It's what I'd normally do after getting a bit too close to telling the truth. But I refrain, and it's uncomfortable as fuck.

"Shall we have another to ease the burn of that last one?" she asks.

It did burn, in more ways than one. We need to lighten the mood before we have sex, so I latch onto her idea and grin.

"Now that sounds like a good idea."

We pick up a lime green one with a cucumber on the edge and salt lining the rim. No clue what this one is, but I don't care. It goes down a lot smoother than I thought it would.

"I think I figured it out," I say.

"Enlighten me."

"I know why I lost my letter."

"Oh? Do tell."

"It's because of that one time I tried to prank my brother Theo by using cling film to block the doorway and trying to get him to run into it. But he noticed, so he pushed our dad into it instead to get me in trouble."

"No." She gasps. "Please tell me that didn't happen."

"It did. Anders, my other brother, filmed the entire thing."

"I'm going to need to see that one day." She laughs with her whole body, as if every cell inside her finds it funny. We both must be feeling the shots because her laugh makes me laugh.

"I think I can dig it up for you."

"How did your dad respond?"

"Oh, he got me back with a pie in the face a couple of days later."

"Your family sounds like fun," she says.

"They are. And you'll get to meet Anders and his new

fiancé at the end of our trip. But fair warning, he's a grumpy asshole."

"I'm sure I can handle him." She rolls her eyes, as if she thinks I'm joking. "But honestly, I'm surprised you didn't use our new agreement to demand to know why you lost your letters."

"I think it's more fun to guess. For now, at least." I'm hoping she'll eventually tell me herself. So far, I've had to drag each truth out of her, and I'd like her to tell me this one thing on her own. "But I've got news for you."

"What is it?"

"You've lost another letter," I say.

"Let me guess. It's because I'm difficult."

"No, it's worse," I say. "It's because you're too fun to be around."

"Rude," she says, outraged, before breaking into a smile.

I turn to the shots and grab an orange with a cut strawberry on the edge. "Truth time."

"Ugh, not this again. I thought we were having a break." She takes her shot from me.

"Let me rephrase. My turn for a truth. It's after midnight."

"Meaning?" she asks.

"It's been four days. And I want you."

CHAPTER 21

REE

Oh okay, wow. I thought by now he'd have lost more letters, or wouldn't want me after hearing more of my truths. Logically, I should be running away, desperate to leave him.

But I'm not. I'm ready. The buildup from the past days has been so intense and I'm dying for release. For him.

"Let's get out of here," I suggest.

"Lead the way."

He whips out his phone and types something before guiding me down the alley, our shots forgotten. He walks so fast, as if he were being chased by a paternity test. All I notice are twisting side streets, the scent of cooked meat, and the pressure of his hand on my back.

Before I know it, we're in the car.

As soon as we set off, he places his hand on my thigh.

After a few minutes, he slowly, oh so slowly, raises my dress until it's as short as it can go without showing my goods.

He stares at me the entire time and I do nothing to stop him. Instead, I spread my legs, making room for him.

"How drunk are you?" he asks.

"Not that drunk. I'm able to give my consent and don't you dare question that. I love sex. Drunk sex, sober sex. With someone I know or a stranger... it doesn't matter."

"Are you sure?"

"Yup." I roll my eyes. "We've only got a week left. There's no need to waste any more time. I'm clean and have the implant."

"I'm clean too."

"Good. So... get on with it."

"Get on with it?" He chuckles and leans close to me. "Oh, baby, just you wait. When I'm finished, you'll be ruined and no one else will be able to do it for you like I can."

I shiver at the words and turn my face so that we're eye-to-eye.

"It's only a week," I say.

He grins. "Hmm, I'll be reminding you of those words."

Normally I find cocky guys a turn off. But with him? It's hot. I close the gap between our lips and kiss him.

It was supposed to be a quick kiss, but he grabs the back of my head and pulls me closer.

I melt into him and his lips. He kisses like a Casanova who wrote a bestselling book about kissing.

And hey, I'm not about to complain. Not when I get to reap the benefits.

His hand works its way further up my leg and skims my inner thigh. I'm about to combust, and we're barely getting started.

He drags his tongue across mine as his hand drifts further up. His fingers brush across my core. My bare core.

He pulls back and raises an eyebrow. "No underwear?"

"I didn't pack too much."

"Thank you for that miracle."

I laugh, but it turns into a moan when he rubs my clit.

"Ah, ah, ah," he says. "You need to stay quiet." He flicks his gaze to the driver. The man who can look at the mirror and see us at any time.

Hayden places my hands on the headrest behind me. "Keep them here."

I nod and bite the inside of my cheek as he teases me. He sucks on my neck and runs a finger through my folds, using my wetness to coat his fingers. He swirls his finger around my clit but doesn't touch it. I jerk my hips up into his hand, needing more.

He sucks harder on my neck. He adds another finger into the mix, but all he does is play and tease. I squeeze the leather of the headrest, desperate for more. After days of sexual frustration, I need release from more than myself.

His fingers are the only thing I can focus on. It doesn't matter that there's a driver in the car with us. Or that he can most likely hear me.

Nothing matters.

Hayden asks the driver something in Turkish and he turns up the music louder. It sounds similar to the tradi-

tional restaurant he took us to, the meyhane. All instru-
mentals and vocalization.

He trails kisses along my neck and shoulders as his
fingers move in time with the vocals. Every time it goes
high, he moves toward my clit. Every time the voice goes
low, he moves to my opening. And when they do some
sort of yodeling type thing… oh my fuckity fuck.

It's maddening.

I tug on his hair to get his attention.

"If you need tips on how to please a woman," I say
breathlessly, "I'm happy to show you what to do."

The lights from the city flash across his face and illuminate his smirk. He gives a pointed look to my hands,
and I put them back on the headrest.

"I'd be more than happy to watch you finger your
pussy, but I know exactly…" He dips a finger inside me.
It's shallow, but I clench around him, as if my body is
refusing to let go. My hand grips the headrest behind me
in a death grip.

"… what…" He lazily pumps into me a few times.

"… I'm…" He flicks my clit and I'm close to seeing
stars.

"… doing." His fingers dive inside me.

I crash my lips against his in a bruising kiss as my hips
lift off the seat. He fingers me so fast I can hear the wet
suctioning sound.

I moan into his mouth, and he swallows it down.

"But by all means," he says, pulling away from the kiss,
"show me how to do it better." He removes his fingers and
sucks on them one by one, without breaking eye contact.

My pussy clenches at the sight.

"You taste like rainbows." His lids become hooded as his tongue swirls over his wet digits, clearly enjoying my taste.

"Fuck off. No one knows what rainbows taste like," I pant, ashamed at how husky my voice sounds.

He leans close to my neck and inhales deeply before sinking his fingers back inside me. He pumps them a few times. My pussy pulses around him, ready for release. But he doesn't give in, no he removes them and holds them an inch from my mouth.

"Taste for yourself how much you want me," he demands.

The next thing I know, my lips are sucking his fingers clean, following his command before my brain can process it.

"Oh, baby," he rasps. "We're going to have so much fun if you're this responsive."

I can't help but moan at his words. "I wish I was tasting you instead."

"Soon." He licks my neck.

"I need you." My voice is so pathetic and needy, even to my own ears.

"Don't worry. When I'm done with you, you'll be so exhausted from the number of orgasms I give you, you'll be begging me to stop."

"How much longer until we're home?"

He looks out the window before saying, "Only a few minutes."

It's surely possible to wait for a few minutes for an orgasm. But it feels impossible.

Like if I don't come right this instant, I'll die. Never

thought I was this dramatic, but Hayden is surely bringing out that personality trait.

My body is so tense as he continues to play with me. And play is all he does. It's like he has a sixth sense about when I'm close because then he pulls back each time.

A few minutes have never felt like years before. Time must be taking lessons in torturing me, playing its little tricks just to mess with my sanity.

By the time we exit the car, I'm a mess. I can barely walk, can barely think of anything but Hayden.

The second the front door shuts behind us, he stalks toward me. My brain's too scrambled to think about moving, to do anything more than just keeping me upright.

I'm wound too tight. I'm about to combust. I need... everything.

He doesn't talk as he lowers the zipper on my dress and unclasps my bra all in one go. He stands in front of my naked body and places my hands on the buttons of his shirt. I undo them one by one. His hands remain on mine down the entire length of the shirt. It's only when I'm finished that he shucks his shirt off.

He grabs my hands again and runs them over his pecs and down his six-pack. Damn, he's so hard everywhere. Our descent down his body ends when we reach his belt. He raises an eyebrow at me, as if I don't know where this is going.

I unbuckle the belt without looking away from him, then I unbutton his slacks and shove them down his legs.

His dick springs free. Holy shit. Can a dick be perfect? Because it's even better than I remember. It's so thick and long, it'll be a tight fit. Wait, is his dick the superpower he hinted at before? To dick-mesmerize unsuspecting women? Dickerize? The dictionary needs to add that word to it and have a picture of Hayden next to it.

"Not a fan of underwear?" I ask.

"Nope. Looks like we have that in common." He steps out of his pants and tweaks my nipple. "Follow me."

He doesn't let go of my pebbled bud as he leads me through the house and into the kitchen. I just follow, too dickerized to put up a fight. To do anything but put one foot in front of the other, willingly letting him lead me to my destruction, my salvation.

Every step is a form of glorious torture, tugging and twisting in the best of ways. He lifts me onto the granite island and, before I can say anything, he feasts on my left breast as if starved. His other hand snakes up and rolls my other nipple between his knuckles.

I arch into him, and he grins. "Needy are we?"

"I've surpassed needy," I pant. "Please…"

"Please, what?"

"Please fuck me with that glorious dick of yours."

"Glorious, huh?"

"You know it. Now show me what it can do," I demand.

"But I haven't tasted you, not fully."

"If you don't fuck me in the next second, I'm going to scream."

"We wouldn't want that to happen." He seats himself fully in one thrust and I cry out at how full I am. "That's right, baby." He circles his hips. "I only want to hear you shout in ecstasy."

"Shut up and move," I say. "Or else I'm going to finish myself off with my dildo."

"That's not a threat." He thrusts into me so hard my ass scoots back on the granite. "I'd love to use it on you."

He pounds into me, and I lean back and take it. He's fucking me exactly how I like. Fast and hard. He slaps my breasts a few times and lifts my leg, changing the angle.

My eyes roll back into my head. "Don't stop, I'm so close."

He actually listens, not like all the other guys who decide to change it up at the worst moment. As if I don't know what I want or need.

Seconds later, bliss becomes my frequent flier, jet-setting away from me as my body remains grounded in the land of the living. I've heard about people experiencing out of this world orgasms, and I always thought it was a lie.

How wrong have I been?

I must have hit the reset button on my perception because suddenly everything's in HD. And holy shit, what a world it is.

Hayden grunts with his own release, and I'm still in a pool of ecstasy. He pulls out and sinks to his knees.

"What?" I can barely form words, my brain still lost.

"You think I'm done with you?" He nuzzles my pussy. "Not in the slightest. Do you think I can wring ten orgasms out of your body before you pass out?"

"T-ten?"

"More?" He arches an eyebrow.

"I've never had over three in a night." Is it possible to

die from multiple orgasms? If so, it'd be a hell of a way to go. And I'm down to try it.

"Good." He licks me from slit to clit before lazily lapping at me. "Because when I'm done with you, and when you're ready to pass out… be ready. I'm keeping my dick inside you while we sleep."

"Wh-what?"

"Cockwarming. It's my thing."

My pussy clenches at the thought, but my brain comes back online as a million questions filter through my post-orgasm haze.

"You sure you're big enough to stay inside me the whole night?" I tease.

"It doesn't matter if I slip out. Whenever I wake up, I'll put it back inside."

"But don't you risk breaking your glorious dick? Are you a statue when you sleep? What if I move? Or turn while I'm asleep?" I need answers to these like I need my next orgasm.

"I'll be fine." He smirks. "But good to know you care about my dick this much."

"If you end up breaking your dick because of this, I'm going to kill you in retaliation."

"Agreed." He laughs.

"Alright, I'm down. Let's try it."

"Good. Because I'm about to fuck you until you see shooting stars."

CHAPTER 22

$\mathcal{H}$AYDEN

I COULD GET USED to having Bree in my arms when I wake up. I slip back inside her with ease and pull her closer to my chest.

Last night she made it to ten orgasms, barely. She's so amazing. It's like she was made just for me.

I circle my hips and my cock is ready for round... who the hell knows?

Bree opens one eye. "I'm not going to be able to walk after this."

"Then I'll carry you."

"I'm going to hold you to that."

I pull out a few inches before lazily pushing back into her. The frantic need from last night has abated, and there's nothing like starting the day with some slow morning sex. I pull her into my body, my hands on her tits.

I tug and tweak her gorgeous nipples as she arches into me. She tries to move her hips, to speed up the pace, but I don't allow it.

"You're driving me crazy," she says.

"Good."

"No, not good. I need more. Harder. Faster."

"Don't you know by now that I'll give you what you need? Or do we need a repeat of last night to remind you?"

Her pussy clenches around my dick at my words, and I chuckle.

"Aren't you a greedy little thing?" I ask. "Does your body remember what I did to it? How I controlled how many times you came? How we soaked the bed with our come?"

She makes an unintelligible sound and I pick up my pace.

"Say that again," I demand. "I couldn't hear you."

"Yes, I love it all."

"Good girl." My fingers drift down to her clit, playing with her as I slow down my pace again.

The sounds she makes, her building pleasure, almost cause me to lose control. To fuck her so hard, she won't be able to walk the rest of the day.

It's tempting, more than tempting.

But then she clenches around me, and I jerk into her. She laughs and says, "Two can play this game."

She clenches again, and I'm done for. My plans fly out the window between one instant and the next. I push her onto her stomach and pound into her, seeking the oblivion that awaits us both. She pushes up and into me with every thrust, making it that much more forceful.

"I'm close," I pant.

"Me too," she moans.

A quick adjustment of her hips and she's coming in no time. I follow her into ecstasy.

When I can see clearly again, I collapse onto the bed next to her.

"So... what's the plan for today?" she asks nonchalantly, as if she didn't just rock my entire world.

"Even though it's touristy, I have a feeling you'll like this underground cistern. There's a statue of Medusa heads. Or we could do a cooking class."

"Can we do both?"

"Greedy, huh?" I laugh. "I like it."

She grins. "I'm all about living life to the max."

"Then get your fine ass ready, and we'll start with the cistern. Then we can learn how to cook something Turkish before a surprise for dinner."

"Race you. First one to get ready gets bragging rights and drinks the first tea of the day." She hops out of bed and sprints out of the room.

This woman is something else.

BREE's silent as we step inside the Basilica Cistern. After descending the stairs into the concealed sanctuary, darkness envelops us, wrapping around us in a familiar embrace. The chamber is full of graceful arches, sturdy vaults, and elegant marble columns. It must be the size of a couple of football fields.

Gentle illumination highlights the columns and arches, creating a mesmerizing sight. Water flows through the area, forming a tranquil presence, and a pathway amidst the pillars ensures we remain dry.

A musty scent tinged with dampness greets our noses, the telltale signature of an underground haven.

I've always felt that here, in this hidden realm, it's almost possible to feel a connection to the ancient past. Where secrets are whispered between shadows and history, echoing through every stone. It's as though time itself has sought refuge in this subterranean place, offering a haven from the relentless march of the world above.

"Wow," she says. "What was this place originally?"

"It was a basilica that was used as a water filtration system for the palace in the fifteenth century."

We work our way toward the true spectacle: twin colossal Medusa heads, nestled at the base of two grand pillars.

One of them reclines, as if caught in a dream, while the other is turned upside down. The water veils half the tresses of the inverted medusa and playfully obscures a fraction of the watchful eye belonging to her companion.

Bree's enthralled with the sight. Just like I knew she would be. I've always thought they exuded an air of enigmatic allure, as if holding the secrets of an ancient world within their stony gazes. There's an undeniable pull, a magnetic force that draws people closer, urging them to ponder the stories and myths hidden behind their ageless expressions.

"Why are they turned?" she asks.

"There's a lot of speculation about that. Some say it was just rubble used when they were building. Others say it was done on purpose to belittle the religion. But I prefer to think it's because they wanted to minimize her gaze and save anyone passing by from turning into stone."

"It's eerie. There's a contrast somehow between strength and vulnerability, with one being upside down and the other sideways. It's like a balance between power and fragility."

"That's the perfect way to describe it," I say. "There is something captivating about it for sure."

She stays standing in front of the statues for longer than anyone else. Others leave within a few minutes, but she remains. I'm curious to know what she's thinking about, why she's so interested in them. But I don't ask since she appears lost in her own world. Instead, I watch her observe them. She walks back and forth and pauses at different spots. Her fingers twitch, as if with the urge to draw. I'm going to have to carry her iPad around, or at the minimum, paper and a pencil for her.

She tilts her head to the side before her lips curl into a subtle smile, like she's sharing a secret between herself and the Medusa heads. When she's done, almost an hour later, she turns to me and says, "I'm ready now."

We walk out silently, and the sun blinds us when we reemerge above ground. We eat a simple meal of Lahmacun at a restaurant nearby.

"Now this needs to be brought over to America," Bree

says after the first bite. "Who knew a cheeseless pizza with minced meat, herbs, and spices would be so amazing?"

"I agree."

"Why don't you do it? Your brothers have a coffee shop and a bar. Why not make a restaurant with your favorite dishes from all over the world?"

"That's a good idea."

"Don't sound so shocked," she says.

"I just never thought of myself as a restaurant owner." I never had the desire to open a place like Theo and Anders did. I've also been too busy to even consider it. Now I'm busier than ever and I've lost the ability to even think about an after. I just need to survive the next couple of months. Maybe after, I'll have time to consider what to do with the rest of my life.

"Why not?"

"I don't know... I've always stuck more on the business side of things."

"You can still do all those things. It's not like you have to be the one cooking the food. You said you're tired of what you're doing now. So..." She shrugs and tucks a piece of hair behind her ear. "It was just an idea."

"Thank you. I'll think about it." I say it to be kind and to end the conversation.

We finish the rest of our food in comfortable silence. Once she's ready, we head to the address Ela sent me for baklava making. It'll take us a few hours, but I think she's going to love it.

We end up in a kitchen attached to a high-end bakery,

and a middle-aged woman wearing a chef's apron greets us.

"Welcome," she says. "My name is Elif and today I'll teach you how to make our amazing pistachio baklava."

"I'm so excited." Bree beams at her. "I've never had baklava before coming to Turkey."

"To me, Turkey has the best baklava in the world," she says. "I'll show you the basics and then you both can work together to recreate everything."

She guides us through every step, and Bree listens with rapt attention. When Elif finishes showing us everything, we get to work.

"First, we need to roll the phyllo out to be super thin and about the length of the table," Bree says and passes me the thin rolling stick. "You're the muscle, so you get to do it."

"Is that the only reason you're keeping me around?"

"Duh." She grins and I laugh.

Once the dough is rolled out, Bree nudges me aside.

"My turn," she says.

She sprinkles crushed pistachio across the entire thing. Then, she takes the stick and rolls the dough around it. We're supposed to keep it tightly coiled as we roll, but it doesn't quite work out that way.

Bree laughs when she eyes her lopsided log. "I think I've found my calling in life."

"That you have." I laugh.

"Keep working at it," Elif says. "It takes practice and repetition. I'll leave you to it and come back to check on you. Fill the three pans on the table and then come find me. I'll be through those doors if you need me." She points to the swinging doors on the wall, then waves and walks out.

"Well, that was unexpected," Bree says.

"This is the strangest cooking class I've ever been to since our instructor just left after a few minutes."

Bree lifts her shoulder. "It's fine. I actually prefer it this way. It's not like I'm a decent cook, so if she stayed, it could get embarrassing."

"You? Not a decent cook? I would've never expected that."

"Hey now." She smacks my shoulder. "Just because I like eating food doesn't mean I know how to make it."

"Good thing you have me around."

"Yes, good thing." Bree grins. "Because I'll have fun watching you work."

She hands me the stick and points to the dough that needs rolling.

"I'm always down for hard work." I make sure to flex while I press into the dough.

When I grab the next piece, I finger it in the same way I fingered her last night. I also slap it, like how I slapped her ass.

"You did not..." She bursts out laughing and points to the dough. "Just..." She mimes smacking it and fingering it. She laughs so hard she's crying. Leaning against the counter, she can't talk, can barely breathe.

"It wasn't that funny," I say, put out. I saw a guy do it once on TikTok. Apparently, it's harder than it looks to pull it off.

She sucks in a breath, trying to keep a straight face. But when she looks at the dough again, she loses it.

"Sorry," she gasps out. "That might've been the funniest thing I've ever witnessed."

"Well, it seemed like a good idea in my head."

Another laugh bursts out of her. "Uh-huh."

"Hey, I could totally make a killing doing that. I just need… practice."

"Practice. Right. Well, my job here is done." She dusts her hands together. "We found your calling in life— making suggestive baking videos. I guess this truth or truth thing really works."

"Speaking of truth or truth…"

"I totally walked into that one." She groans.

She did, but I will not pass up the opportunity here. "Have you ever met the family of someone you're dating?"

"Never," she says.

"Well," I draw out. "I invited my brother and his new fiancé to visit us in a few days."

"Wait, I thought you were joking when you mentioned it earlier. Why would I meet them?"

"I was telling the truth. As for why… why not?"

"That's…" She spreads the crushed pistachio across the dough.

"A great idea." I finish with a winning smile.

"I was going to go with weird, but sure, let's pretend it was a great idea."

"I haven't seen my family much since Christmas. It's been nonstop work and travel and I've barely had time to breathe. Anders and Zoey are in Finland right now and have just gotten engaged. The invitation just happened."

"It's okay. I get it," she says. "I can find somewhere else to stay."

"Wait, no. You don't get to get out of this."

"Yes, I do," she says.

"Give me one good reason why not."

"It's just not my thing," she says.

"That's not a good reason." I give her a look and she rolls her eyes.

"Ugh, fine. It's because all my previous boyfriends never made it that far. I don't fuck people I actually like."

I turn to her slowly. "Are you telling me you don't like me?"

"No, you're an exception. But it feels too relationship-y to meet your brother."

"I mean... a fling is like dating someone. We spend every minute together." And a fling while on vacation is even more intense and faster paced than would happen in the real world.

"Is a fling with an expiration date really considered dating? We only have one week left and poof, we're done."

"But isn't that what you normally do if you date people you don't like?" And not to mention that letter removal thing she's got going on.

"It's not the same thing." She glares at me. "And I find that offensive."

"I find it offensive that you don't want to meet my brother."

She drops another piece of dough against the counter, next to where we're working. It lands with a loud smack. She presses the rolling pin into it aggressively.

"Listen," I say, gently placing my hand on her arm.

She stops what she's doing but doesn't look at me.

"I only have a limited amount of time off until my life

becomes a whirlwind of travel and nonstop work," I say. "I don't want to choose between spending time with you and spending time with my brother. Not when I can have you both."

"But you're not considering how I feel," she says.

"Because you're not telling me *how* you feel."

"Because I don't know how I'm feeling," she shouts and then takes a deep breath. And another. "I don't know why the thought of meeting someone's family makes me feel like my chest is being crushed in a vice. It's like I can't breathe."

Her voice cracks on the last words, and I pull her into a hug. She buries her head in my shoulder, and I'm not sure how to respond, so I just provide her with my presence. A safe space to feel whatever she's feeling.

"Isn't it enough," she says, sniffling through her tears, "that I'm being honest with you? Why do I have to go a step further and meet your family?"

I tilt her chin up, so she's forced to look at me. "Because if something is this scary, there's something deeper behind it. Avoiding it won't do you any good. It's like what you're doing with Bilet. You're putting yourself out there and meeting him, even if it's scary."

"But avoiding it is so much easier."

"I know. But I really think you'll like Zoey and Anders. They're fun. Well, Zoey's fun. Anders is... Anders."

She grins and says, "Fine. But if it's awkward or boring, I reserve the right to leave."

"Of course. All I ask is you try it."

"Okay," she says.

We work in silence for a couple of minutes. But I miss her, even though she's standing next to me.

"Do you want to roll this together?" I point to the almost complete roll we abandoned during our spat.

She nods and I pull her between my arms, her back to my front. I lean forward and inhale her vanilla scent. I can't get enough of it.

She places her hands on the rolling pin, and I place mine on top of hers. We work slowly, oh so slowly, while we try to get the baklava just right.

When we finish, it looks like the one Elif did.

"We did it," Bree says, turning her face slightly so she can see me.

"We make a great team."

"We do," she whispers.

I tilt her chin up, and my lips brush against hers in a soft caress. She kisses me back for a few seconds before pulling away.

She smiles softly. "You know you're not going to mesmerize me into having sex with you here, right?"

"I bet I can change your mind."

"I'm sure you could, but as much as I don't like cooking, I really want to finish this."

"You're no fun." I pout.

"My middle names are Fun Killer. Are you really that surprised?"

"Baby, with a middle name like that, you've got to pick a struggle."

"See." She grins. "Now you know the root cause of all my issues."

I laugh. "It all makes sense now."

"Come, let's finish these."

"Fine," I say, "but we're staying like this and working together on every single one."

"Deal."

We do everything slowly, savoring every moment. There's an effortless rhythm to our collaboration, an unspoken understanding that transcends words. Laughter. Meaningful glances. Entwined hands. Her scent lures me in every time she shifts.

It's a dance where we connect on a level that surpasses the physical. It's a fusion of minds, hearts, and spirits. Each gesture, each touch, carries the weight of a million unsaid feelings and desires, drawing us closer together with an irresistible force.

When Elif comes back, we break apart, and the loss is stark. The connection dissolves like the sugar syrup we pour on the baklava.

CHAPTER 23

REE

WHEN WE REEMERGE into the late afternoon sun, with four boxes of baklava in our hands, my phone rings.

I glance at the screen and it's Jules wanting to make a video call.

I stop walking and say, "It's my sister. I should take this."

"Of course." Hayden guides us to a bench to sit on, and I answer.

"Good to see you're alive and well," Jules deadpans. Her fake stern face is in place. It's fake because when she's really mad, her eyes blaze like they'll burn me on the spot.

"Sorry for the radio silence. I've been busy."

"Oh, I see. I'm about as relevant as an expired coupon in your life." Jules places a hand dramatically on her forehead.

"At least I'd keep you."

"More like stuff me in the drawer along with all the other junk you keep."

I grin and she laughs.

"How are you?" she asks.

"Fantastic." I hold up the box of baklava. "We just made baklava and I wish you could try it."

"We?"

"Um… Hayden and me?" I turn the phone and show Hayden.

"Hi," he says, waving. "Nice to meet you."

"You too," Jules says before I turn the phone back to me. "Wait," she says. "Hold out the phone so you're both on the screen."

"Why?"

"I deserve something nice to look at after you ignored me for a day."

"Rude." I laugh but do as she asks.

"For as much research as I did on you," Jules says to Hayden, "your photos don't do you justice."

"Right?" I say, laughing. "I told him he should get a better photo."

"I'll add that to the top of my to-do when I get home," he says. "Or maybe I'm just not photogenic."

"If you're fishing for more compliments, you're looking in the wrong place," Jules says.

I snicker, and Hayden grins.

"I see where Bree gets some of her humor from," Hayden says.

"And now you're buttering up?" Jules says. "What are your intentions with my baby sister?"

I groan, embarrassed Jules just went for *that* question like an overprotective mother.

"It's just for the trip," Hayden says.

"Only the trip?" Jules asks, glaring at him, as if she's offended on my behalf by that information.

"Only the trip," I say firmly.

"You better give Bree the best trip of her life," she demands. "Or else…"

"Be nice," I say, rolling my eyes at her implied threat. "He's too good in bed to scare off just yet."

"If I'm that good," he says, "add back my missing letter."

"Wait, he knows?" Jules squints at the phone. "What voodoo have you worked on my sister?"

No one has ever known about the letters. They've never picked up on it, or if they did, they never cared enough to ask. Only Jules knew. Mom wouldn't have approved, so we never included her in the fun.

"Eh, I'm trying out something new," I say.

"That sounds ominous," says Jules.

"It is," I say. "I'm test-driving honesty."

"We both are," Hayden says.

Jules looks between us a few times before laughing.

"What's so funny?" I ask. "I thought you'd be over the moon about this experiment."

"Oh, I am." Jules singsongs the last word and has this annoying secretive smile on her face, as if she knows more about Hayden and me than we do. "But if you're testing out honesty, why don't you work through why you won't call Mom even though you promised to last time we spoke."

"I texted her—"

"Oops, sorry," she says. "Going through a tunnel. Love you."

Jules disconnects, and I stare at the black screen for a beat before turning to Hayden. "She totally hung up on me."

"She did." He chuckles. "She's funny."

"Uh-huh. Sooo funny," I say sarcastically.

"She also loves you dearly."

"What can I say? I'm very lovable."

He grins. "Come, let's go eat. I have the perfect place in mind."

"So, you're not going to ask? About my mom?"

"I most definitely will. But I was thinking you could tell me over food?"

"Ugh, fine."

Hayden guides us down enchanting tree-lined avenues, branches arching gracefully overhead. The cityscape reveals a myriad of stories etched in the facades of buildings that reach skyward, around six stories high. The buildings themselves are a canvas of colors, each telling a tale of its own. Some buildings are a calming beige. Others shimmer in the purity of white. In contrast, a few are drenched in coral, painting the town with the hues of fiery love and unbridled emotions.

There are charming little shops and cozy cafes, their inviting atmospheres spilling onto the sidewalks with chairs and tables ready to greet anyone passing by.

I never thought it was possible to fall in love with a city, but Istanbul has cast its spell on me. I'm helplessly, hopelessly in love with it.

And I have a feeling this is only the beginning.

* * *

HAYDEN BRINGS us to a spot near the Galata bridge, on the shores of the Golden Horn. Colorful boats are docked in a row. Each with ornate carvings, everything from swirls to flowers to sea life. But what makes them even more impressive are the vibrant colors in yellows, blues, greens, and reds that accent the carvings.

"What is this place?" I ask.

"These are *balık ekmek*—fish and bread—boats."

Each boat, around twenty feet long, has a huge grill near the middle. The scent of cooked fish fills the air along with the smokey smell that only comes with grilling.

"This is so cool," I say.

"I knew you'd like it."

He orders us two sandwiches and I give all but one box of baklava away to the people working on the boat we ordered from.

They're so surprised, they give us our food for free. I insist Hayden pays, and he agrees. After he does, he shakes the hand of the man who took our order.

Hayden grins and says something in Turkish before coming back to me with the sandwiches and some lemon wedges.

There's no place to sit. Standing or walking are our only options, so we stroll along the riverside. I take a huge bite and it's amazing. There's a slight smokey and charred taste to the well-seasoned fish. The bread is the perfect balance to it. It's light but filling, flavorful but not over-bearing.

"This is delicious," I say.

"It's a favorite of mine. Simple but amazing."

"Sometimes the simplest things are the hardest to get right."

Hayden glances at me. "True."

When we finish, I sigh. It's time to tell him. I can't delay it any longer.

Somehow sensing this, he asks, "Are you ready to tell me about your mom and the attack?"

"I don't think I'll ever be ready..."

"I know, but we promised to be honest."

I say nothing, trying to build up the courage, and Hayden waits patiently, not at all in a rush.

"My mom and I used to meet up a few times a week to jog," I say. "Well, we called it jogging, but it was more slow walking, full of gossip and catching up on life."

I swallow hard and wring my hands. Taking a deep breath, I try to center myself.

"We were in a park when the dog attacked. It was off leash and there was no warning. Between one step and the next, I was pulled to the ground. It got ahold of my jacket."

I close my eyes, able to see its sharp fangs in perfect clarity. The pure malice on its face. The growls. The jerking of its head from side to side as it ripped through my coat.

"I tried to kick it away, but it wouldn't let go of me." My entire body shakes and sweat pools on my lower back. I don't think I can continue.

"It's okay, you're safe," Hayden says.

"When it let go to re-grip, my mom threw her arm between us and the dog latched onto her instead—"

I gag, all the delicious food I ate threatening to come back up.

"Shh, it's okay." He places a hand on my lower back. "You don't have to continue if you don't want to. I'm so sorry, I didn't know it'd be something like this."

"There was so much blood," I whisper, not able to register his words. I'm completely caught up in the memories overwhelming me, playing on an unending loop. "So much damage."

I shudder.

My vision tunnels. Sweat lines my forehead. It's like I can see Mom and all her injuries all over again. Right in front of me. I can see the stick in my hand...

"She's still not able to use her left arm or hand well. She's got a ton of scars on her face. It's... I... it should've been me."

How many times have they told me it wasn't my fault? How many times have I pretended to believe them when I don't? The guilt and pain have been gnawing at my soul, a festering wound I couldn't bear to expose. Someone I cherish, and a person I would do anything to protect, suffers because of me.

The mere thought is a blade through my heart, shattering any semblance of strength within me. How can I live with myself, knowing that my existence inflicts such torment on those I love? The anguish is unbearable, and I fear it might break me completely.

Strong arms pull me into a hug, into safety. Hayden

guides us to the side of the street and shields my body with his.

"Shh, I've got you." He rubs my back.

I duck my face into his shoulder and cry. Cry at the burden of my deepest truth—of how I stopped the dog. It's a truth that's suffocating, but I can't bear to acknowledge it. It's something I've never talked about.

Once I calm down, I wipe at my face, hoping it won't be too obvious to the people passing by that I was crying.

Hayden keeps his arms around me, refusing to let go.

"I imagine it's completely normal to feel that kind of guilt," he says, meeting my gaze. "Thank you for sharing that with me."

I nod once and let out a shaky breath. "I'm the worst daughter in the world."

"No, you aren't. You're processing a traumatic event. Have you considered therapy?"

"No. My mom and sister have gone, but I can't bring myself to go."

"Why not?" he asks.

"Because it feels too scary. I don't want to relive it all over again each time."

"How often do you relive it all now?"

"Anytime I'm not distracting myself," I whisper. It's easier not to obsess over everything when I'm not physically in Seattle.

"You deserve to heal. I'm pretty sure rehashing it with a therapist won't be any more difficult than rehashing it alone within your own mind. At least the therapist will have the experience and tools to help you."

"I… I'll have to think about it," I say.

Fear grips me like a vise at the thought of talking through the memories in detail and not the glossed over version I just gave Hayden. It's a terror far more haunting than overcoming my phobia of dogs. To confront the truth that "it should've been me" is to stare into the abyss of my survivor's guilt, a labyrinth of emotions I've long avoided. I'm not sure how I'll find the courage to go through with it.

But most of all, I'm tired.

Tired of dealing with everything alone.

CHAPTER 24

ℋAYDEN

My heart breaks for Bree. For what she's endured. For what her mom endured.

She shuts down after her confession. I can't help but feel a little guilty for wanting to know what happened, for inadvertently causing her pain.

I guide her along the Bosphorus until we reach the store I'm looking for. I have her wait outside while I go in and buy some colored pencils and a blank notebook. It's not of high quality, but I hope she'll like it.

I select a bench for us to sit on and pass her the plastic bag.

Bree stares at the bag for so long, as if it has all the answers to life, but she's not able to understand its language.

"I'm sorry," I say.

She startles and glances at me. "For what?"

"For asking you to tell me your story. For making you relive it. I didn't... I shouldn't have... I didn't know it'd be something so horrific."

"Thank you for your apology." She lets out a long breath. "But I agreed to this whole thing, and I made the conscious decision to tell you. It's not your fault I'm messed up."

"Don't you dare talk about yourself like that. You're not messed up, you're perfect." I nod to the bag. "Open it."

She does and takes out the notebook and pencils.

"You got me drawing stuff?" she asks, as if it's not obvious.

Shit. She hates it.

"Yeah? If you don't like it, you don't have to use it. I don't even know if colored pencils are your thing. I just wanted..."

Who knew gifting her something so basic would cause an internal freak out? The clothes I bought her were nothing compared to this. It was just money for those things, and she got to pick them out, so I knew she'd like it. But this? This is a personal gift and I'm feeling exposed for even trying. I'm also kicking myself for not paying more attention to how Theo chooses gifts. He's the most thoughtful one out of all of us, and now karma is biting me in the ass for not learning from him.

Bree touches my arm. "It's perfect, thank you."

She smiles, and all of my worries float away.

"Do you mind if I draw something now?" she asks.

"Please."

Opening the notebook, she takes out the black pencil.

She puts the notebook on her knees and sketches. It takes me a moment to realize she's drawing one of the Medusa heads from the cistern.

But she makes the upside down one have tears in her eyes, while her snakes strangle her. The one laying on its side looks on with only one eye open and a sneer on her face, her snakes laughing at the other Medusa. Bree draws a wave behind both of them. They can't see it, but it's about to destroy them.

She's drawing their final moments.

It's dark and haunting and I get goosebumps the longer I look at it.

"Can I have that one?" I ask.

She glances at me. "It's not that good."

"It's gorgeous. I'd really like it."

"Sure, let me color it in and I can give it to you when it's done?"

"Promise?" Somehow, I have a feeling she'll never give it to me.

"Ugh, fine. I promise."

I grin. "Now I know why you were staring at the heads for an hour."

"Oh, shut up. You loved it."

She doesn't wait for my reaction before she dives back into her drawing. As she works, I stay silent and stare at the water, relaxing into the moment. At the slight breeze brushing against my face, at the warmth of the fading sun on my skin.

Being around Bree somehow helps me live in the moment and stop worrying about work.

"How would you feel about leaving for the beach tomorrow?" I ask.

She glances at me. "Don't tempt me with a beach and it be a joke."

"Noted. Never joke about the beach with you." I grin. "But seriously, we can leave for Bodrum tomorrow and have a long weekend there."

"Let's do it."

I love she doesn't have to think about it. That she's so spontaneous. I have great memories of Bodrum. I used to go there all the time with my ex, Mutlu, but it was always fun. We'd rent a house, or stay with her parents, and invite our friends from school to join.

"We can come back a day before the flight if you want," I say.

"Yeah, I want to see Bilet before I head back to Seattle. But I think a long weekend of fun and relaxation will be a nice reprieve from focusing on my dog trauma."

"Fair enough. There are strays in Bodrum, but not as many as here."

"Cool." She goes back to her drawing, seemingly pleased by that.

I message Ela so she can organize everything. Then I shoot a text to Anders telling him to come to Bodrum instead of Istanbul.

Anders: What are you planning? What's in Bodrum?

Me: Why? Afraid?

Anders: When it comes to your plans…
always.

I LAUGH, and Bree looks at me.

"What's so funny?" she asks.

"Anders thinks Bodrum is a prank. I can't wait to see his reaction when you whip out a bottle of alcohol from your fanny pack and randomly drink from it while telling a truth."

"What a great impression that'll give… so naturally, I'm down."

I grin. "I think I've met my match with you, Bree Adler."

"Good." She catches my gaze and smiles. "Because I think I've met my partner in crime with you, Hayden Watson."

My heart stumbles over itself at those words. Funny how a simple throwaway comment can mean so much to me when it's said at the right time. Bree is implying that she likes me because of me. Not because of my job, or my connections, or my money. But because of my personality, my brand of humor. Even if that brand of humor has gotten me into trouble on more than one occasion. It's the most refreshing thing anyone has ever said to me.

It always felt like my flings were putting up with me, rather than enjoying me. They were in it for the sex or the gifts or the possible social elevation. And that was all fine and mutually beneficial.

But to be desired for more?

Is this how people feel when they're with the right person? Because I may not show my real emotions most of the time, but that doesn't mean I don't feel them. Or that I don't need validation too.

I lean into her shoulder and we sit there, soaking up the sounds. The birds in the air. The boat horns in the distance. The snippets of conversation from people passing us by.

It's in this moment, amongst the stars, when the universe seems to align that I realize something.

I'm falling for Bree.

And for the first time, I'm certain. It's more than sex. More than attraction.

It's her.

WHEN WE ENTER THE HOUSE, I lead her straight to the kitchen. I need something, anything, to tame the desire running through me. I feel out of control, like my realization that I'm falling for her is calling on my instincts to go full caveman on her. To fuck her so hard she'll never forget me.

It's messing with my head.

"Drink?" I ask.

"Sure. Whatever you're having." She sits on the counter, and I wash the outside of the bottle of beer in the sink. She watches with curiosity, but I don't explain. I can't, not yet.

She looks so hot sitting on my counter. I nudge her legs apart and stand between them. She reaches out for the bottle, but I pull it away. Instead, I run the cold bottle across the back of her neck, her collarbones, her chest, over her nipples.

Everywhere.

Her eyes become hooded as she watches me. I lift her dress slowly and run the bottle up her calf, her thighs, teasing her. She shivers when the bottle touches the inside of her thighs, barely brushing her pussy.

She's so responsive and taunting her is too fun. But I need to see all of her. If she had packed more clothes, I'd rip this dress right off her.

"Off," I demand, tugging on the material.

She maneuvers the dress off, and I unclip her bra so she's bare. Her body is perfect and pleading for the pleasure it knows I'm about to give. Every part of her is like a siren, singing her deadly song and luring me in. Pebbled nipples begging for attention, glossy and plump lips begging to be kissed, her creamy skin begging to be licked.

She makes no move to undress me and instead widens her legs once again for me to return to my place. I'm so hard, the zipper on my pants is in danger of breaking. But I love foreplay. I love restraining myself for as long as possible. It makes it more amazing when I finally sink into her heat.

I pop the top off the beer and drink most of it in one go. I bring the bottle to her mouth and tilt it up so she can drink.

She swallows and keeps her gaze on me the entire time. I lick the top of the bottle, as if searching for any last drop of her on it. Exactly like I'm going to do to her pussy soon.

She squirms and makes a needy sound.

"Not yet," I say.

I run the bottle across every part of her body. From her ribs, trailing down to her belly button and to her hips. Over her arms and shoulders. To her cheekbones and lips. She arches her back and shifts to the side, trying to get me to touch her breasts with it.

"Have I told you lately how amazing these are?" I ask.

"Hmm, they're begging for your attention. Why not get a closer look?"

"You mean like this?" I place the cold bottle against her nipple.

"It's a start."

"How about now?" I bend down and flick her other nipple with my tongue.

"Closer," she moans.

I suck and nip at her.

"Yes, like that."

"I love how needy you are."

Her hand presses against the back of my head and pulls me back into her breast.

"Enough talking," she says. "More action."

I continue running the bottle over her body with one hand while playing with her full breasts with my mouth. Attention to the right, then to the left. Her eyes close and she tips her head back.

"How many orgasms do you think you can handle tonight?" I ask.

"Enough to kill me."

"How about one before that?"

"I don't care, because what a way to die."

I place the tip of the bottle against her pussy opening, and her gaze snaps to mine. "Okay?" I ask, teasing her entrance with the bottle.

She nods and licks her lips.

"No. I need you to say it with words."

"I want you to fuck me with the bottle," she says.

I lean back to watch as the bottle's neck disappears into her glorious pussy. I push it in and out slowly, loving the sight. With my free hand, I pull my dick out of my pants and stroke myself. She moans, her gaze flicking between the bottle and my dick.

I take the bottle out of her and lick the rim before chasing the last drops of beer inside the bottle.

"I can't get enough of your rainbow taste."

I tilt the bottle toward her lips, and she drinks the very last drop. She pushes my hand back toward her pussy and I take the hint.

"You like when I fuck you with this? Your greedy pussy needs to be full, huh?"

"Yes." She moans when I insert the bottle back inside her.

I pump it in and out, faster this time. I want her to orgasm around the bottle to complete this experience. I need it more than anything. My pleasure can wait. This is too amazing to focus on anything else.

I flick her clit with my other hand and play with her as she builds and builds. When she can't keep her eyes open anymore, I know she's close. Her hips rock in time with the pace I set. I rub her clit in the perfect place, playing her body like I'm an expert musician.

Her entire body tightens, and she explodes. I help her ride out her orgasm, and it's the most glorious sight I've ever seen. Her chest and cheeks flush with pleasure. Her eyes glassy. Her wet pussy ready for another round.

I'm so close. Just the sight of her is enough for me to come.

I place the bottle to the side and stare at her pussy while I grip my dick. Taking in every part of her, I stroke myself. She watches with hooded eyes and in record time, I'm ready. I bring my dick close to her pussy and come all over her.

I reach out and rub my cum into her skin, cementing the fact she's mine.

Marking her as mine.

She leans forward and captures my mouth with her own. She kisses me with so much passion, my knees go weak and I grip the edge of the counter to keep my balance. This kiss is like being hit with a sledgehammer, more powerful than the orgasm I just had.

I'm not sure what it means, but I sink into the feeling. The feeling of rightness. She kisses my lips once, twice, and three times before pulling back and grinning at me.

"Well, that was a new experience," she says, panting as if that kiss affected her as much as me.

"I'm keeping this bottle for the rest of my life."

She swipes it from the counter and stares down at the mess I made of her pussy before scooping up some of my cum and placing it on the lip of the bottle. She licks it and sucks it off.

"You taste so good." She moans. "Next time, I get your dick in my mouth."

I blink, at a loss for words. Why was that the hottest thing I've ever seen in my life?

"If you insist," I say hoarsely.

She grins as if she knows what she's doing to me. Then she hops off the counter and wraps her hand around my semi-hard dick. She tugs and walks across the kitchen. I'm literally being led around by my dick, and it's glorious.

"What's your plan?" I ask when we reach the steps.

"To go to bed. The counter was hurting my ass."

"We can't have the counter hurting your ass." I slap said ass. "Only me."

She looks over her shoulder. "Is that so?"

"It is." I continue to stare at her perfect ass.

She leads us to her bed.

I open the drawer of the side table, the one that was open when I saw her masturbate. I pick up her pink dildo and examine it. Perfect. It's also a vibrator.

"Are you ready to black out from pleasure?" I ask.

She crawls onto the bed.

"Do your worst."

CHAPTER 25

REE

HAYDEN'S FINGERS trail lazily up and down my ribs, as if he doesn't even realize he's doing it.

He delivered on his promise to have me blackout from pleasure.

I don't know how sex with him can be so amazing, but it is.

I open my eyes and Hayden's facing me. His arms are around me and his dick is still inside me.

"How are you feeling?" he asks.

"Amazing." I clench my pussy on purpose.

"Don't tempt me." He slaps my ass. "You need a break."

"Do I?"

"Behave."

"I've never had a dick in me most of the night," I say. "Until you."

"And?"

"I might not be able to sleep any other way again."

"Good." His hips buck.

"You're not doing so well at this whole 'giving me a break' thing."

"You're just too tempting." He slowly pulls out and slides back in. "Are you sore?"

"Nope," I lie. I only have a few days left with this man, and I refuse to lose out on a single moment. I'm sure I can convince Hayden to carry me around if needed.

"Stop lying." He gives me a stern look.

"How did you know?"

"I'm good at reading people."

"Fine, I'm sore," I say. "But I refuse to spend the limited time we have left not fucking. So go buy some painkillers for me and get on with it."

"Are you sure?"

"Walking is for losers," I say.

I push him onto his back and follow, keeping him inside me. I squeeze my tits and slowly ride him. He grips my hips and lets me pick the pace. Lets me do all the work. He's the type of man who likes to be in control in the bedroom, and it's sexy. But when he relinquishes control? That's even sexier.

I grind into him and place his hands on my breasts. He rolls my nipples and plays with me while I set a nice and slow rhythm.

It's torturous. It's perfection.

He remains still as I come all over his dick. Once the last spasm finishes, he sets a punishing rhythm. He fucks me so hard I have to grip the headboard to avoid falling over.

He shouts his release and I fall to the side, spent.

"Wow, baby. How is every time with you mind-blowing?" he asks.

"I'm just magical."

"No." He kisses my shoulder. "We're magical together."

After he kisses me senseless, I slip into the bathroom to clean up. When I return to the bed, his phone pings nonstop, but he ignores it.

"Maybe it's important?" I say.

"It's just my brothers. They're not important."

"Now I'm even more curious what they could be texting you about in the middle of the night their time."

"Come here." He pats beside him. "I'll show you."

I jump onto the spot and cuddle into his side. He opens his phone and hands it to me.

Theo: Assholes, why are you both asleep at the worst time?

Anders: What do you want?

Theo: It's an emergency.

Anders: The last time you said it was an emergency, you couldn't decide if you should add cinnamon to one of your cocktails.

Theo: This one is a real emergency. I can't decide what to eat for dinner.

"This is an emergency?" I grin.

"No, he's just nosy and wants to know what we're up to."

I grab his phone and type out a response.

> Hayden: Try some raw horse meat. It's delicious.

> Theo: I'm trying not to gag right now.

> Anders: Same.

> Hayden: It's a delicacy in some parts of the world. Don't knock it until you try it.

> Theo: I think I'll skip dinner now.

> Anders: I think I'll never eat again.

> Hayden: My job here is complete.

I pass the phone back to Hayden and he reads the messages before laughing.

"You're a genius," he says.

"Of course, I am. I'm me."

He smirks and throws his phone onto the side table. "I've been thinking."

"That sounds serious."

He grins. "I know why I lost my letters."

"Hit me with it."

"It's because of that one time my friend dared me to enter his house unannounced with only his older brother

241

home. His brother had never met me, so he had no idea I wasn't some random person. I walked in, said nothing, grabbed the milk from the fridge and left."

"You didn't." I choke on my laugh.

"I did. The look on his face was priceless. I wish we had a hidden camera set up to capture it."

I giggle and his gaze softens at the sound.

"That just means you'll have to reenact it," I say. "Oh, or better yet, I can do it to one of your brothers."

"That'd be hilarious. But not Anders. He's far too protective to take a joke, especially if Zoey's around."

"That's cute." I snuggle further into his side and yawn. "Did I lose another one?"

"Yeah, for being too amazing in bed."

I laugh and yawn again.

"Sleep, baby," he says, putting his dick back inside me and maneuvering us so that we're comfortable. "We can leave for Bodrum whenever we want."

"M'kay," I say and drift off into a dreamless sleep.

WE ARRIVE at the Bodrum house after taking a private plane and car. I guess being a millionaire has its perks.

"Is this place yours?" I ask in awe.

The modern four bedroom, four bath monstrosity screams money. It's decorated in beige, white, marble, and wood. The entire house is angled to show off the view of the Mediterranean. Every room showcases it. The back is full of decking, an infinity pool, and entertainment areas.

"No, just renting it. There are some steps to the side

that lead down to a private beach. It's shared with some other homes, but it's all inclusive. Food, drinks, lounge chairs, everything."

"Sounds amazing."

He pulls me into his body. "Not as amazing as you."

"You're too much." I push away from him and laugh.

"Choose the best room and we'll stay there."

"What makes you think you're staying in the same room as me?" I arch my eyebrow.

"What makes you think you have a choice?"

"You're demanding."

"You love it."

"You're lucky I do," I say, "or I'd have to remove more letters."

"Hmm. You better be careful. I've just docked another letter from your name because you're stunning when you smile."

"You're ridiculous."

"But you love it." He swats me on the ass. "Go pick a bedroom and let's go check out this beach."

I choose the largest room and Hayden stashes his suitcase and my backpack in the closet. We quickly change into our bathing suits and head down a path of stone steps, through a gate, and then our feet land on the sand.

A man greets us and leads us to a private cabana. It's a huge mattress with gauzy drapes, giving it tons of privacy. The server hands us each a menu and promises to return with some cold water.

Hayden spreads the towels on the mattress for us and helps me up. He totally cops a feel of my ass and I love how he can't seem to stop touching me. It's the biggest confidence boost.

We scan the menu and order some cocktails and pasta to eat. We fall into an easy conversation, talking about nothing important as we wait for the drinks to be delivered.

In record time, the server returns and hands us the drinks. He promises the food will be out soon and leaves us alone.

I take a sip and sigh in contentment. "I love frozen drinks on a hot day."

"Nothing can beat beer for me," he says, his gaze zeroing in on my pussy.

I lean closer to him. "Are you thinking about the last time we had a beer together?"

"I think about it all the time."

"Good." I grin. "I like being on your mind."

"You never have to worry about that."

We stare at each other, lost in each other's gazes, before the server interrupts and delivers us our food.

Hayden takes my plate in his lap and twirls my fork in the carbonara pasta and holds it out for me.

"I can feed myself," I say. "Don't let your food get cold."

"I enjoy taking care of you," he says. "I don't care about my food. You're the priority."

My chest feels full, bubbly. Like champagne. All it took was words. Words that no man has ever told me. I've never been a priority to someone outside of Mom and Jules, and it's addictive.

I close my mouth around the pasta and it's delicious.

He prepares another mouthful for me and I take a bite again.

"I could get used to this," I say.

"Which part?"

"All of it," I say honestly.

And that's scary. I like being around him. I like that he's so fun but also caring and supportive. I like that I can be myself and talk about anything and everything and that he doesn't judge me for it.

I just like him.

Which is what I wanted to avoid when we met, but now that I'm here, it's not as scary as I thought it'd be. Not when I'm pretty sure he likes me too. Not when we've built a connection between us that started out with our silly challenges but grew into something more secure. Something I could be okay with perusing after our trip ends.

"I'd take a million flights again if it meant we'd end up right here, together." He smiles, and it's blinding.

I place my hand over his mouth and look around. "You've got to be careful with that smile. You may cause some random women to stumble if they see it. Or fall in love with you."

He grabs my hand and kisses my palm. "Another superpower unlocked."

I laugh and he prepares me another bite.

"Thank you," I say.

"For what?"

"For taking care of me."

"Anytime."

CHAPTER 26

HAYDEN

I'M in heaven with Bree's legs around my waist, my arms around her. We're enjoying the water of the Mediterranean together.

We ended up in this position because I promised to share my body heat with her when she yelped at the coldness of the water. But really, it was an excuse to get her into my arms.

The sand cushions my feet as the water laps at my chest. The sun beats down on us and it's perfection. I should've listened to my brothers and taken a vacation earlier. This is the most relaxed I've felt in far too long.

"Why do you hate your job?" she asks.

I frown and she laughs.

"You get to ask me all the difficult questions," she says. "It's only fair you have to respond too."

"I guess I'm bored and tired. Maybe I'm just burnt out."

"Well, when did it change?"

"In December."

"Did anything happen in December?"

"Yeah, I guess it did. Anders brought Zoey to Christmas dinner. When you meet Anders, you'll understand why it's so shocking he found someone to like his grumpy ass."

"And what? You were jealous?"

"Not at all. And it wasn't about him finding love or me desiring it. It was more the fact that I missed his birthday party because of work. Because I was in Singapore and couldn't get back. That party was the moment Anders and Zoey took their relationship to the next level."

"It sounds like you miss your family."

"Yeah, I guess I do."

"Then I should make Zoey and Anders a congratulations banner. Remind me to work on that before we go to dinner."

"Okay." I grin, loving that she wants to do something special for them.

We sway with the water for a bit before she asks, "Do you like what you do?"

"I..." I pause. Do I? "Not anymore. I'm good at it, but I don't love it. It's become routine and more of a hindrance than anything else."

"Well, I've noticed you light up when you talk about Deniz and her program. Or you get excited when you share your favorite foods with me."

"I do?" I ask.

"Yup. To me, it's clear where your passion lies. It's in supporting others or sharing new things with them."

Huh, I never thought of myself like that. For most of my life, I was the jokester. And when we made NomNom it was because we experienced this issue while we were living in Asia. It's not like I went into it with anything but the potential success on my mind. The money is what I was after at first. And the money is the reason I've stayed on as long as I have. Well, that and my pride at seeing it through to the end.

But money makes me useful to my family. What enabled them to live their dreams. What Bree's saying differs from what I've identified myself as. I'm not even sure who I am anymore, so how can she be so certain?

"What about you?" I ask, needing the focus off me. "Tell me more about your plans for your business."

"Lately, it's getting slow since there are free websites that can generate a logo in seconds. And they're decent. It's not something I need to find a solution for tomorrow, but I need to be prepared. I'm just not sure what to do."

"Well, what did you want to be when you were a kid?"

"A dentist."

"Like your dad?"

She nods. "But then I realized I didn't want to be anything like him, so I nixed that idea real fast, and was left with nothing. One day, I created some marketing material for Jules's practice as a joke since they hired someone to help them rebrand, and it was shit. But they liked what I did, and that's when I just kind of fell into logo making."

"I feel you could easily combine your artistic ability with another industry. Like your love for food."

She laughs. "I don't see how."

"I could think of a few things off the top of my head. Packaging design, menu and food concepts, interior design. Hell, you could even make murals inside restaurants."

"Wow." She blinks at me. "I didn't expect you to actually answer."

"I have a lot of experience in the food industry."

"Hmm, I guess you do. I'd have to find something in Seattle though. I can't leave Mom. Not now... not after..."

"Seattle has a fantastic food scene. I'm sure you'd be able to find something."

"All this talk of food is making me hungry again," she says.

"We can't have that happen." I laugh.

We swim back to the beach and order more drinks. The conversation flows effortlessly between us, and we both find ways to touch one another. A hand, an arm, a thigh. We can't go for a few minutes being separated. It's no surprise when I get hard, because how can I not when she's next to me?

"Seems like you've got a problem there." She licks her lips as she stares at my swim trunks.

"Let's head back to the house."

She shakes her head. "What if we take care of it now?"

I glance around. "Here?"

"Why not? It's private-ish." She closes the gauzy material. "Please, I can't wait."

I nod and her hands immediately go to my swim trunks.

She pulls my dick out and licks the tip like it's her favorite ice cream flavor. A few pumps of her hand and then she sucks as much of me as she can take. She gags but sucks me deeper and deeper each time.

I hold on to her hair, keeping it to the side so I don't miss a single second. Her eyes water and a tear drips down her cheek. It's so hot watching her struggle to take my length.

There's no way I'll last with her mouth on me. There's no way I'll have the time to give her orgasm after orgasm like I want to. Instead, I need her fast and hard. I tug on her hair, and she comes off my dick with a pop.

"I need to be inside you right now," I say.

In one smooth motion, she pushes me flat on my back. She climbs on top of me and moves her bathing suit to the side before impaling herself on my dick.

"Fuck, baby," I say, closing my eyes, relishing the feel of her tight and warm pussy.

"I know," she pants.

I can't have her set the pace, not like this morning. Not when I'm so needy. I grip her hips and hold her still as I piston in and out of her.

"Yes, just like that," she moans. "You fuck me so good."

She snakes a hand down to her clit. A few circles of her finger and she's falling apart along with me.

She collapses onto the mattress next to me, and I lean over to adjust her swimsuit so she's fully covered once again. I tuck myself back into my shorts before I climb on top of her. I frame her face with my hands and kiss her for all I'm worth.

Our chemistry is like being hit with a supernova every time we come together.

* * *

BREE SPENT a couple of hours making the celebratory banner, and now we're in one of my favorite restaurants here. It's full of marble floors, outside seating, pergolas covered in bright pink flowers, and views of the Mediterranean and Bodrum.

It's on the fancier side, but I love this place. I used to come here every time I was in town with my friends. They have the best octopus and I want Bree to try it.

The server guides us to our table, right next to the glass barrier that protects guests from falling down the cliff they built the restaurant into. The tables aren't designed for much privacy, but I don't mind. Not when Bree's face lights up as she takes in the surrounding details.

"This is gorgeous," she says.

I take out a folded piece of paper and her colored pencils from the inside of my blazer and pass them to her.

"In case you need it," I say.

"You're ridiculous." She laughs. "But thanks for bringing them. And for being my purse since you refused to let me bring my fanny pack."

"I think it might've clashed with the atmosphere."

"I don't care about stuff like that," she says. "Because if

I did, I'd be self-conscious that I'm underdressed for such a fancy place."

She's wearing her emerald dress again, my favorite of hers. Even though she has new clothes, she only uses them occasionally and I find that so interesting.

"You're not underdressed," I say. "You look gorgeous."

"Oh, I most definitely am not hitting the style of this place. But I don't mind. I'm never going to see these people again. They can judge me all they want."

I frown, scanning the people around us. The women are wearing dresses like Bree's, but they're all wearing heels. Does that really make or break an outfit?

"Don't think too hard about it." She unfolds the paper and squints at me. "Stay still. I'm going to draw you."

"Am I Rose in this situation? Do I need to be naked?"

"That'd be hilarious if you started striping right here." Bree laughs. "But fair warning, if I'm Jack, you better make room for me on that door."

"I doubt we'll die of hypothermia in the water here."

"I don't know… it's freezing to me."

"You're dramatic." I grin.

"I'm a water temperature snob, sorry not sorry."

I laugh and she smiles.

When the server comes over, I order the octopus, various seafood, and a wine they recommend pairing with the food.

Once the server leaves, she sketches. I can't help but watch her the entire time. It's easy to connect with someone strongly when traveling, but it's always felt fake before. A way to temporarily rely on someone, or make a fast friend, to ease loneliness while on a trip.

Not with Bree though. It feels real, too real. I'm kicking myself for including the end term in our agreement. Because the more I learn about her, the less I want to let her go. Even if she can't leave Seattle because of her mom, I'd still be willing to try.

After our wine arrives, she glances at me and says, "You're staring."

"I like the view."

She gives me a soft smile and draws for a few more minutes until she says, "Done."

When she passes me the paper, I snort. It's a drawing of a cat with its ears and tail made of flames. It has the words "Purr-sonality for days" written above it. She laughs at whatever expression is on my face.

"Just to be clear," I say, slowly, "*this* is supposed to be me?"

"Yup. Can't you tell? It has your eyes and your face shape."

I turn the paper to the right and left and squint hard. "I can see it."

She laughs and attempts to take the picture back, but I hold it out of reach.

"This is mine now," I say, placing the drawing to the side of the table.

"I'm going to have to start charging you for my drawings if you like them so much."

"Oh, I can pay you alright… in orgasms."

She licks her lips and—

"Hayden?" a woman asks. "Is that you?"

I glance at the intruder and am shocked at who I see.

It's like my past is coming back to bite me in the ass at the worst time.

"Hello, Mutlu," I say, standing and kissing both of her cheeks in greeting as per the custom here. "It's been a long time."

Understatement of the year. We were friends through high school, but we dated for the last few months of my time in Istanbul. When I left, we tried a long-distance relationship, and it lasted one month before she cheated on me. My entire life friends, relationships, anything really, never worked out once I moved. No one followed me. And she was the last person I let ghost me. Since then, I've refused to be in a serious relationship, and I definitely never expected to see her again.

"It has," she says, still wearing the same floral scent she used to when we were teens. But her dark hair is now long and straight, nothing like the curls she used to wear. "I'm with a friend, celebrating their birthday, and I thought I spotted you. I can't believe you're here, in my favorite restaurant."

"Small world," I say.

"Remember when we used to come here all the time?"

I make some sort of noise, but I don't know what to say. I forgot she was the one who introduced me to this place.

"You look good," she says. "Really good."

"Thank you. Now, if you'll excuse me, I need to get back to my date." I gesture to Bree, and Mutlu frowns at her.

"I see. Well, if you're in town for longer, or get bored,

call me." Mutlu grabs a colored pencil from the table and scrawls her number on the paper next to my place.

On the drawing from Bree.

Shit.

She hands it to me and sashays away before I can tell her it'd be a cold day in Hell before I'd ever call her.

"So that was Mutlu," Bree states. There's no emotion in her voice, nothing to indicate how she's feeling.

With the paper clutched tightly in my hand, I take a moment before I speak because I'm raging inside that Mutlu ruined Bree's drawing. "Yeah…" A wave of pain crashes inside me. Mutlu is a stark reminder that long-distance relationships are doomed from the start. And even if Bree and I lived in the same city, it'd still be long distance with all the traveling I do for work.

Mutlu is a burst of reality into this fantasy bubble Bree and I've got going on.

It makes me question if Bree and I could ever really work together after we return to our normal lives.

And it fucking hurts to think that I might have to give her up.

CHAPTER 27

REE

AFTER HAYDEN'S gorgeous ex dropped in on us, we cut the suddenly awkward dinner short. He's been in a funk since she left, insisting he's fine. But he's clearly not. I didn't pull the truth card to get him to open up. Not when I'm scared to hear what he has to say.

Does he still love her? Is he just working through the shock of seeing her? Does he want to see her again?

I don't have a clue, and it's driving me crazy. The thought of him calling her makes me want to burn my drawing when we get home.

Instead, I use the drive back to his place to devise a plan to pull him out of this sadness that's enveloping him. He needs a distraction and I'm hoping we can get back to how we were before that she-devil interrupted us.

Once we're back in the house, I start opening and closing all the cabinets in this massive place.

"What are you searching for?" he asks.

"For fun."

He gives me a curious look but follows me around anyway.

"Aha," I say, "I found it." I hold up a game of Monopoly with a winning smile.

"You want to play a board game?" he asks in confusion.

"Not just any board game. Strip Monopoly."

"I have no idea what that means, but you had me at strip," he says.

I grin, glad he's in the mood to play with me.

"We have one minute to prepare," I shriek before running to our room, him hot on my heels. I rip my dress off and then open his suitcase, proceeding to pull on his T-shirts, one after another. I also add some socks, my headphones, and my yoga pants.

"What are you doing?" he asks.

"Hurry, you only have twenty seconds left."

"To?"

"Prepare for strip Monopoly. Pile on as many clothes as you can to make the game last longer."

He laughs and looks down at his light blue collared shirt that's unbuttoned at the top and black slacks. "I'm going to keep this outfit."

"Suit yourself. You're going to be naked in no time."

"I like to live dangerously."

"Then I'll allow you to start, since you're at a clear disadvantage." I laugh and he grins.

I open the game on the floor and pass out the money to each of us.

"Let's lay down some rules," I say. "First up, we have to remove an article of clothing if we land on someone else's property."

"Sounds good. And we have to ask the other person a question with each roll of the dice."

"Agreed," I say. "Anything else?"

"Nope. But let me get some drinks to make this more interesting."

"This is shaping up to be one hell of a game." I laugh. "A drinking game combined with truth and truth and a strip version of Monopoly."

"I aim to please," he says, hustling to the kitchen and returning with two bottles of wine.

He opens one and pours us each a glass.

"So…" Hayden rolls the dice on the board. "When did you start traveling?"

"Hmm." I shift uncomfortably on the plush carpet. Out of all the questions he could've asked, why does it have to be this one? "I guess it started when I was sixteen and dealing with my first breakup." I stop there, not wanting to remember all the horribleness of it.

When I say nothing more, he picks my glass up and hands it to me. "Is this enough or do you need a bottle of something?"

"It's not a fun story, and I wanted us to have fun. Can you ask something else?"

"No. I don't care about fun. I want to know more about you. Please tell me?"

Ugh, it's the *please* that does it for me. I chug the rest of my wine, trying to ease the phantom pain.

"We were only together for a couple of weeks," I say, "but he cheated on me with my friend. I actually liked him, and was devastated, but it was even worse because of school. My friends took his side, and they started spreading rumors about me. Nasty things that made him look good and me bad. Between one day and the next, I was friendless and boyfriendless. It was fucking miserable."

"That's a dick move from your friends."

"I guess they were never really my friends..." I try to push down the emotions I thought I had buried ages ago. Or at least gotten over. They're part of the reason I don't trust people enough to become friends with them now. My entire experience is why I don't date people I actually like.

"Sorry," I say, waving to my face and the tears that are building. "I don't know why I'm crying."

Hayden scoots next to me and frames my face with his hands. "There's nothing to apologize for." He wipes my tears away with his thumbs and brushes his lips over mine.

"Thank you," I whisper, kissing him again. "Jules must've seen how hard of a time I was having, and she took me on a weekend getaway to Vancouver. It was so freeing to be somewhere where no one knew me, or what happened. It was like a light bulb went off. One that said I don't have to stay anywhere if I don't want to and can restart at any time."

"I get that. It's freeing to restart your life whenever you feel like it. Have you been traveling ever since then?"

"Yeah, I guess so, but it increased more after the attack." As a way to not face all the hurt I caused. Even if I leave Mom for short periods of times now, I'll never be able to leave her permanently after what she did to save me.

"How many trips have you taken since January?" he asks.

"Umm, I think about twelve? I guess I'm averaging twice a month."

"Aren't you getting tired of it?"

"Not really," I say. "I only travel internationally once a month."

"Only." He grins. "That's a flex if I ever heard one."

"I guess so." I laugh. "What about you?"

"I travel to Singapore about twice a month now."

"When will you go back?"

"I'm sure my boss will demand I go ASAP. But I don't want to. I'm tired of his demands."

"Why don't you quit?"

"Because I can't," he says. "I'm locked into the contract I signed when we sold our company to Adrien, my boss."

"There has to be an out..."

He sighs. "I mean, I guess I could quit and then take the hit to my salary."

"So? Why not do that? You have tons of money."

"Because it's important that I see it through," he says. "That I finish what I started."

"Is your family the supportive type?"

"Yeah, why?"

"Because I'm sure they'd understand if you talked to them."

"Maybe." He looks away and picks up the dice. "Your turn to roll."

I roll and move my piece six places, buying the property.

"Do you still have feelings for Mutlu?" I ask in a rush. This was supposed to be a light and fun game, but it got deep real fast. Might as well ask him what's on my mind. It also helps that I've chugged some wine and have a little buzz to ease my nerves.

"Not at all. But seeing her was a shock, and it brought up a lot of pain from the past."

Whew, so he's not still in love with her.

"I'm pissed she ruined my drawing by writing her number on it," I say.

"Me too."

"I'll make you another one later." I pass him the dice. At least I could squeeze in making a banner for Zoey before his ex ruined our dinner.

He picks up the dice, but doesn't roll, "Have you thought any more on what you're interested in work wise?"

"I'm thinking I should find a sugar daddy. Work just isn't for me." He scowls at me, and I laugh. "Kidding. Maybe. But I kind of liked your idea of combining my love for food with art."

I never considered finding another way to use my talents, but I've been thinking about his proposal more and more.

"I could connect you with some people if you want?" he asks.

"We'd have to stay in touch after the end of the fling," I say, my eyebrows raised. This is the first time he's ever hinted at an after, and I'm curious where he stands concerning this. Especially when I'm stupidly hopeful we won't just end abruptly.

"I mean… we could, especially if it's to help you."

Ripples of excitement pulse through me. He wants to keep in touch. He. Wants. To. Keep. In. Touch.

It's like winning the lottery. I'm so happy.

"That's sweet of you to offer," I say, desperate to not shut down the idea of communicating with him after the trip ends.

But I wouldn't feel comfortable using his connections or his help. I've had to work hard to get where I am, and it feels like I'm cheating the process if I skip all the beginning parts.

"But here's a better idea," I say. "Let's both quit and open something together."

I say it like a joke, but he nods. "That might just be the best idea you've had yet."

"I'm not sure if I should be offended or proud."

"Proud. Definitely proud."

He finally rolls, and he lands on the property I just bought.

"Oh, strip, baby, strip," I yell and whistle. "Should I grab some money and make it rain?"

"You want a show?" He stands and walks to the other end of the room. "I'll give you a show, baby."

He undoes one button on his shirt before ripping the

entire thing right down the middle. He shakes his junk as if he's fucking someone hard. I fan myself with my hands because that move was hot.

This game was my best idea ever.

Skidding on his knees, he slides right to me, stopping just before my legs.

Holy shit.

Stick a flag in me because I'm fucking conquered with that move.

He grabs each of my hands and kisses my palms before placing them on his abs. Using our hands, still joined, he runs them all over his chest and abs.

"Maybe you should quit your job," I say, "and join one of the Magic Mike shows."

He laughs. "I'll apply as soon as I'm back. But only if you attend my opening night."

"I'll pencil you in."

"You do that." He grins and pulls away. "Come on, we need to finish the game before we fuck."

"Wait," I say, "doesn't Monopoly last hours or days even?"

"Uh-huh. That means no dick for you until we finish."

"Hold on, that wasn't the goal here. We're supposed to fuck once we're naked."

"New rule," he says with a shrug.

"What about some finger action in the meantime?"

"Nope."

"Or mouth?" I ask.

"Nothing," he says, grinning.

"You're a cruel, cruel man."

"Rules are rules, baby."

"You know what they say about rules?" I ask.

"What's that?"

"That they're just suggestions for amateurs."

"I'll have to remember that." He laughs. "You should also put that on a T-shirt and sell it."

"Let me grab my iPad. Might as well work on that now, especially since I won't be getting dicked anytime soon."

"Smartass," he says.

I wink. "Always."

* * *

A COUPLE OF HOURS PASS, and we've spent most of the time talking, revealing more secrets. Only occasionally do we pretend to roll the dice and play the game.

He knows all about that time when I was seventeen and a teacher told me my art was shit and I should focus on something else if I wanted to be successful in life. How I cried myself to sleep that night.

And that I never went to college since we couldn't afford it.

And how my mom cried in her room more nights than not when she thought no one could hear her. I've never even talked to Jules about that, but she must've heard since we were sharing a room.

I learned about the time he was sixteen and his brothers were off to college and how he felt so alone without them. How he always hated he was the youngest and how school never came easy to him. That he went to college just because he felt like he had to since his brothers went.

And I know about the time when he was eight and there was a huge earthquake in the middle of the night. He was living on the thirty-second floor of a building and he thought it would never stop swaying and shaking. It terrified him, and he thought he was going to die. It's why he hates heights.

The wine has been flowing all night, and I've drunk my fair share. Surprisingly, not to help me reveal truths, but to stop myself from jumping Hayden.

When I insisted he visit my favorite restaurant in Mexico that serves the best mole in the country, he said we should go together. After that, he's dropped small hints here and there that he wants to see me again after this trip.

He's too amazing for his own good. It's as if he's a living embodiment of all the qualities I never realized my heart craved. I always thought I needed someone stable and boring to help ground me. Turns out I was dead wrong. Hayden is the opposite of all of that, and I've never felt closer to another person before now.

Not even Jules.

The more I tell him, the more he wants to know, as if my existence is a never-ending love story, and he's determined to be its most devoted reader.

"What's the scariest thing that's happened to you while traveling?" he asks during his turn, moving his piece five spaces.

I glance at him, and there're two Haydens swimming in front of my drunken eyes. Ha, that'd be fun if there were two of him. But that also means I'm close to black out drunk.

"Bree?"

"Hmm? Oh, yeah, you asked me a question." I laugh, trying to determine which of the two Haydens is the real one. "It was probably when I was in Switzerland and had to take a four- a.m. train from the city center to the airport. There was almost no one around, and on the platform was this guy who wouldn't stop bothering me. I didn't know what to do. It was one of my first times abroad and I wasn't prepared for something like that."

"What happened?"

"There was another woman on the platform. She was older than me, came to my side, and protected me. She told the guy off like a badass. When he eventually left, she asked if I was okay and stayed with me the entire time."

"Come here," he says, all growly.

I crawl across the carpet to him, hoping I chose the right Hayden. But I don't need to worry because when I'm within his reach, he scoops me up in his arms. He places me on his lap, my knees falling on either side of his legs.

"Better?" I ask, his hands cupping my bare ass under the last T-shirt I'm wearing.

"Yes. Even though this happened years ago, and you're clearly okay. I just… I wanted to feel that you're alright with my own two hands."

"Aw, aren't you just as sweet as pie?" I pinch his cheeks and steal a kiss.

"And I think we need to cut you off from alcohol for the rest of the night." He grins. "Come, let's get you some water and put you to bed."

"I'm too full to drink anything more right now." I rest my head on his shoulder. "Can we stay like this a little longer?"

"We can stay like this forever."

"Don't promise me something you can't give." I yawn, suddenly tired.

"Who says I can't?"

"Hmm." I'm scared to hope for more from him, from us. Even if I want it with every fiber of my being.

He rubs my back and holds me.

"You didn't answer my question," I say.

"You didn't ask a question."

"No?" I laugh. "I did in my head. It was the same question you asked me."

"I haven't had many scary encounters. More close calls, like being followed by some guys at night or needing to have an armed guard escort me around in another country for protection. But I was fine."

I lift my head off his shoulder and run my hands over his arms and into his hair. I now understand his need to touch me and make sure I'm okay.

"Come, let's pause the game and get you to bed," he says.

"I'm not tired," I say and then my body betrays me by yawning again.

"Uh-huh." He laughs and lifts me onto the bed. "Be back in a moment."

I blink and he's back with some painkillers and a bottle of water.

"Here." He hands me both things.

I take them and then reach for the hem of my shirt. He covers my hands with his, stopping my movements.

"What's wrong? Don't you want me?" I ask.

"I always want you, but you're close to passing out."

"That not your thing?" I joke.

"No, because I want you to feel and remember every orgasm I wring from your body."

My pussy clenches.

"Why do you get to be naked and not me?" I ask. He lost all his clothes a while ago.

"Because I'm allergic to underwear."

"Hmm, that's a tough problem to have. My breasts just so happen to be allergic to shirts."

He laughs. "Lie down, you."

He positions me so my head is on his chest and my leg is over his hip.

"Just so you know," I say, "you don't have to worry about consent. You breathe in my direction, and I want you. Being drunk doesn't change that."

"Good to know, but we always have tomorrow."

"No, we don't. Your brother is coming and—"

"And nothing. We'll definitely still be fucking. Why do you think they're going to be in the room furthest from us in the house?"

I laugh and close my eyes, snuggling into him and trying to sleep. But it doesn't come. Something's missing.

After a few minutes, I say, "I can't sleep."

"Any reason?"

"Uh-huh. You've ruined me. I need your dick inside me to fall asleep."

"Bree…"

"I'm not saying we'll have sex, but you've converted me. I'm now the number one fan of cockwarming." And it's true. That's what's missing. I thought I'd get an infection or some shit with it, but so far, so good. And I love having him inside me.

"You're testing my patience. I'm trying to do right by you," he says.

"Is that a no?" I pull his already hard cock toward me. "I promise to stay still."

"Screw it. Fine, but no sex and no orgasms." He maneuvers me around to be the little spoon.

"You're no fun."

"I'm so much fun." He thrusts into me, and his chuckles turn into a moan.

I bite my lip to keep my own moan at bay. I promised him I'd stay still, but I never promised not to play with him. I tighten my pussy around him multiple times. Thank you, Kegels, for finally paying off.

"I know what you're trying to do, you naughty, naughty woman." He slaps my ass cheek.

"Who me? I'm soooo innocent."

"Innocent, you say? Then what do you call that?"

"Oh, this?" I clench around him again. "I'm just doing my daily Kegels. I forgot to do them today."

"Is that right?" he chuckles.

He slowly pulls out, and I try to keep him inside with the force of my pussy alone. But it doesn't work. When just his tip is inside me, he thrusts back inside so fast, so unexpectedly, that I see honest to fuck stars.

"Oops," he says, "I forgot to work on my hip flexors."

"Oh fuck, please work away." I moan. "Hip flexors are very important."

He stills. "Good night."

"Wait, no, that's not supposed to happen," I whine.

He laughs. "Just imagine how it'll feel when I finally fuck you in the morning."

"I'll be hungover and will totally throw up all over you with all the jostling."

"You paint a nice visual there."

"Please," I say. "I don't want to miss out on a single moment with you. If I only have a few days left, I need to bottle up all this pleasure to hold me over."

"Hold you over until when?" he asks, all growly, maybe thinking I mean until I meet someone new. But that's not it at all.

"Until I die. I'm confident no one will ever give me what you've given me."

And I mean that in more ways than one. Not just the pleasure, but the friendship, the fun, the fact I can be me, messy bits and all. He hasn't run away after learning about all the scarred parts inside. Instead, he leans into them, as if all those parts make him like me more.

I open my mouth to tell him all of that, to explain. But even in my drunken state, I know I should wait until I'm sober. He might brush it all off as drunken ramblings and I don't think I'll be brave enough to tell him how much I like him a second time.

All of my feelings for him swell, and tears drip onto my pillow. Tears of happiness that I might've found someone, but they're also tears of loneliness, of past hurts.

Ugh, Drunk Bree is an emotional mess.

I sniffle and try to hide it with an exaggerated yawn. But he must've seen through my attempt to cover my reaction because he maneuvers me, so I'm on my back and he's on top of me. His weight is the most delicious feeling in the world.

He kisses away my tears and brushes his lips across my cheek and to my ear.

"I understand exactly what you mean," he whispers, before moving his hips.

He doesn't fuck me.

He doesn't have sex with me.

No, he makes love to me.

I never understood that term until now. Until this moment. It's like our souls entwine and the act of joining our bodies together brings us closer than any words could ever achieve.

It's the most heartbreakingly beautiful moment of my life.

CHAPTER 28

$\mathcal{H}$AYDEN

PLAYING strip Monopoly will go down as one of the best nights of my life.

Though Bree was worried she'd have a hangover this morning, she doesn't. Thank fuck, because we just finished a marathon sex session and Anders and Zoey will arrive any minute now.

Bree shooed me out of the shower so she could get cleaned up before they come. Just in time, because as soon as I get dressed, the doorbell rings.

"Oh, thank the stars," Zoey says when I open the door. "You're alive." She turns to Anders. "See, told you he would be."

"And why wouldn't I be?" I ask, confused.

"I've been calling you since we landed," Anders says, "and you didn't answer."

"Oh... I've been busy." Busy being buried balls-deep in Bree. "Sorry about that. Come in."

Anders claps me on the back. "Good to see you."

"You too," I say, meaning it. "Congrats, you two. Show me the ring. Tell me everything."

"It was life changing," Anders says. "We kayaked to an island, and I proposed."

Zoey holds up the emerald cut, canary diamond I helped Anders pick out, but I act like I haven't seen it before.

"It was perfect," Zoey says, staring at Anders with a dreamy expression. "The best vacation I've ever had."

"I'm so happy for you guys. Bree will be right out. She's just getting ready," I say.

"And Bree is the mysterious woman you're with?" Zoey asks.

"Yeah," I say, leading them to the kitchen and the banner Bree made before dinner.

Bree did all the work. All I had to do was tape each piece of paper together. On each paper is a letter that Bree stylized and colored using the pencils I bought her.

It spells out "Congratulations On Your Engagement" in bubble letters. But she made each letter unique. The C has ferns drawn around it, as if growing from the letter itself. She left the C white but colored everything else around it. For the O, she drew bees and flowers inside the letter.

"Hayden, did you do this?" Zoey asks, her blue-gray eyes widening. "I didn't know you could draw. Anders, why didn't you tell me? This is amazing."

"He can't draw," Anders says, frowning in confusion.

"Yeah, I don't have an artistic bone in my body," I say.

"Then how?" Zoey asks.

"It was me," Bree says, breezing into the kitchen with her fanny pack over the T-shirt dress I had made for her. "Sorry I'm late."

"Anders, Zoey, this is Bree," I say, standing next to her. "Bree, meet my brother and his fiancée, Zoey."

Bree waves to them.

"It's so lovely to meet you," Zoey says. "Thank you so much for making this. I'm going to get it framed and hang it in my house."

"Yes, it's beautiful," Anders says. "Thank you for making this for us."

"I'm glad you like it," Bree says simply, as if she didn't spend hours on it.

"You guys want some food? A drink?" I ask.

"That'd be great," Zoey says.

"I'll cook," Anders says, guiding Zoey to a bar stool at the kitchen island and kissing her on the cheek. "Any allergies?" Anders asks Bree.

"Nope."

"But she hates potatoes," I say.

"I don't hate *all* potatoes," Bree insists.

"What kind do you like?" Anders asks, opening the fridge and looking through it.

"Vodka," Bree says.

"I think we're going to get along fabulously." Zoey laughs. "Come, sit next to me."

Bree pulls out the stool next to Zoey and sits.

"Your ring is gorgeous," Bree says, reaching for her hand.

As Zoey and Bree discuss the ins and outs of engagement rings, I make my way over to Anders.

"Congrats, bro," I say, glancing over at the women.

"Thanks. How are you doing? You look good." Anders starts chopping mushrooms and tomatoes, but I don't offer to help. We both know he's a way better cook than me.

"Well, I finally followed your advice and took a vacation."

"Did you really take my advice," Anders says, looking over at Bree, "or was there finally someone more important than work?"

"Aren't you clever?"

He grins. "How has Adrien handled your time off?"

"Good, he's supportive," I lie. Admitting the truth would be like admitting I'm a failure. That I'm sliding back into how I was as a teenager, joking around all the time and not taking anything seriously. That I can't hack a few years of dedicating myself to one thing.

"I've been wondering why you aren't extending your contract? Since you like it so much."

"I don't know." I rub the back of my neck, uncomfortable. "I was looking forward to some time off. It's been nonstop, you know?"

"That's because you don't have a healthy work-life balance."

"Hmm." I mean, he's right, but it's also not possible to have a work-life balance with Adrien as the owner of the company. "Can we not talk about work right now? It's our vacation."

Anders opens his mouth to say something, but Zoey interrupts us.

"Hayden," Zoey says. "Bree says you took a long-ass flight and were prepared to just sit there with nothing to entertain you."

I grin. "Sounds about right."

"That's…" Anders says.

"Brilliant," I finish. "It was strategic, and it worked out for me."

I wink at Bree, and she rolls her eyes.

Anders plates up omelets in no time and pours some spiced coffee concoction he pulled out of his ass. But for Zoey, he makes hot chocolate.

Zoey gives him moon eyes when he passes her the drink with a kiss.

Bree takes a sip of the coffee, and her eyes widen. "Holy explosion of flavor."

"I know. I don't know how he does it," I say. "But they don't own the two best coffee shops in the Pacific Northwest for nothing."

"You should come to our newest shop in Portland sometime," Zoey offers. "It's called A Cup of Zodiac."

"I'd love to," Bree says. "I live in Seattle, so it's not too far away."

"What brought you to Turkey?" Zoey asks.

"That's a long story," Bree says. "But the short version is I came to stalk a dog."

"You… what?" Anders asks.

I laugh and pull up Bilet's feed on Instagram. When I pass my phone to Zoey, she coos over the photos.

"He's so cute," she says. "Are you really into animals?"

"Not at all," Bree says airily.

Zoey and Anders look at me as if she's speaking another language and they need a translator.

"I'm confused," Zoey says. "Why would you travel halfway around the world for a dog if you don't like animals?"

"Now that's an even longer story," I say. "One that doesn't need repeating."

Zoey frowns and Anders shrugs, but Bree? Bree's looking at me like Zoey was looking at Anders a moment ago.

Like diverting the attention away from her was akin to making her homemade hot chocolate. I mentally take note and add it to the "things that make Bree feel good" file I'm keeping in my brain.

For some reason, I want to make sure she's happy all the time.

* * *

THE DIMMED LIGHTS of the dance floor cast a sensual glow upon the crowded club. Bodies move in harmony to the music, as if there's a collective heartbeat of the night.

We left Zoey and Anders at the table an hour ago, and Bree and I have been dancing ever since. It's been a game of restraint, with both of us refusing to touch the other for longer than a few seconds.

I'm not sure when the game started, but we somehow both knew the rules. Even without either of us explicitly stating them.

When our gazes lock, they're full of unspoken

promises. She entwines our fingers together. The miniscule contact between us ignites a spark that seems to electrify the air around us. With a gentle tug, I pull her closer. I'm so close to surrendering to the intoxicating game we've been playing.

The music's tempo shifts, becoming a slow, sultry melody that matches the cadence of our breaths. We sway, bodies brushing against each other, yearning for more.

I rest my hand against the small of her back, drawing her impossibly closer. My heart races faster as we tease each other. At the palpable energy between us, enough for me to get drunk on. Fuck, let's be honest. I've been drunk on it, on her, for days now.

Our gazes lock again. Bree's desire mirrors my own, and she presses herself into my body. When she grinds against me, it's game over. My need for her is so intense, I can't resist anymore.

As the music swells, I trace a path up her arm, over her neck, and fist her hair. I capture her fuckable lips with my own and deepen the kiss.

She responds in full.

It's raw, animalistic, and wild.

With each beat of the music, I pull her impossibly closer, until she's practically fucking herself on my leg.

"Home." She pulls back and demands. "Now."

"Needy, are we?" I ask.

She nods.

"Let's get Anders and Zoey."

I lead us back to the table. Anders and Zoey are as lost in their own world as we are.

"Ready to leave?" I ask them.

"Yes," Anders says, not looking away from Zoey.

When the van pulls up, I rush to claim the backseat with Bree. Anders gives me a weird look, but I just shrug in response. Anders and Zoey settle into the row in front of us, and I ask the driver to turn up the music.

I nuzzle Bree's neck and place my hand on her leg. Bree grabs my hand and sticks it under her dress, guiding it until I'm touching her pussy.

I pull back and raise an eyebrow. "What are you doing?"

"If I'm a good girl and stay quiet, can I get a reward?" she whispers into my ear.

She glances at Anders and Zoey. They're chatting away, snuggled up to one another. Bree licks her lips and opens her legs further.

Even if it's not an appropriate time or place, I'm helpless to resist her. The fact we could get caught at any moment adds to the anticipation that hangs heavy in the air.

"Please?" she whispers, begging.

It's the look in her eye that causes me to break. The one that promises adventure and fun. The same one that caught my attention back on the flight.

I run a finger through her wetness before sucking it off my finger.

"No playing," she whispers. "I can't wait."

Same. I'm one move away from coming in my pants, but I need to wait until we get home before sinking into her.

I play with her clit and fall into a languid rhythm that has her lifting her hips off the seat. When I insert two fingers, she bites her lip to hold in her moan. She's panting as if she's running somewhere. I love how I can do that to her.

I grip the back of her neck and pull her mouth into mine. She bites my bottom lip before licking it. My cock pulses in time with the throbbing of my lip.

"You're so fucking perfect," I whisper, sliding two fingers in and out of her.

She covers her mouth with her hand to quiet the moans that slip out.

"Are you going to come for me?" I ask, whispering. "Come all over my fingers like they're your favorite toy?"

Her pussy spasms at my words and I grin.

"What are we doing tomorrow?" Anders asks, turning his face to the side, but luckily, not turning around fully.

Bree freezes, but I don't break my pace as I say, "It's a surprise, but we're waking up at the crack of dawn."

Bree's body shakes before going tense and she comes. Neck straining, head thrown back, hips lifted, lips parted in a silent moan. Beautiful.

"Why do we have to wake up early on vacation?" Anders grumbles while Zoey laughs.

"Good girl," I whisper to Bree while she comes down from her high.

She really is perfect for me.

"Holy shit," she whispers back. "I can't believe we just did that."

"That was just the beginning." I lick her neck and suck. "But don't worry, Anders owes Theo and me. After forcing us to listen to him bang Zoey all night long over Christmas. He should get a taste of his own medicine."

"You're fucked up," Bree says.

"But you love it."

"Fuck you." She rolls her eyes.

"Don't worry, you will in a few minutes."

CHAPTER 29

REE

THE BOAT gently cuts through the turquoise waters, enveloping me in a sense of boundless freedom and peace. Anders and Zoey are half asleep on the cushions across from Hayden and me.

Hayden woke everyone up with the sun to go on this boat trip. We've all barely slept longer than an hour or two, but I don't care. Our days here in Turkey are winding down and I want to enjoy them to the max. Especially since tomorrow we'll all fly back to Istanbul. Zoey and Anders will catch their flight back to Portland a few hours after we arrive.

Meeting them wasn't as intimidating as I had feared. It felt oddly natural, like catching up with old friends I'd forgotten I had. It's a relief to know that I can handle meeting someone's family like a pro. It also helps that they're the cutest couple. Zoey is so petite and classy, whereas Anders is gruff, tall, muscular, and tattooed. They're perfect together.

I pull my hair up into a ponytail and notice Hayden staring at me.

"What?" I ask.

"Nothing, you're mesmerizing."

My heart hiccups every time he says shit like that. Ugh, why is he so amazing?

"It's so different from what I expected," I say, gazing out at the scenery.

"What is?"

"The view. The mixture of hills with greenery interspersed with sand and dirt. It has a desert feel to it, but we're in the middle of the Mediterranean."

"I love how you describe things. I could listen to you talk all day." He gives me a soft smile. "Today will be all about the beauty of Bodrum."

"Where are we going first?" I ask.

"Cleopatra's cave and hot springs. Legend has it she was so beautiful because of it."

"That must be some cave."

"It is, and also the reason we're awake so early," he says. "I wanted us to go before all the tourists."

"Are you breaking my no touristy places rule?"

"Well, you loved the Medusa heads, and that was touristy."

"Semantics." I wave a hand in the air, as if dismissing it.

"So…" Zoey's gaze bounces between us. "How long have you been together?"

"We're…" I glance at Hayden and indicate he should finish the sentence. What are we? Still a fling? More?

"Together for the vacation," Hayden says. "I'm also her tour guide."

My heart sinks at his statement. At the time limit he put on it.

"What he means is he likes to *pretend* he's a tour guide," I say, covering my reaction with a joke.

"Pretend?" Anders opens his eyes and raises an eyebrow at that.

"What *she* means is that I'm the best fucking tour guide in the country," Hayden says.

"Well, I challenged him to show me only places off the beaten path," I say.

"And how has it been?" Zoey asks.

"He's not the worst," I joke.

"Deny it all you want," Hayden says. "But you know I'm amazing."

"Maybe," I say with a grin, knocking shoulders with him.

Zoey and Anders watch us raptly, and I'm not sure why. Hayden jokes around all the time. What's so different about this?

The rest of the trip is filled with silence as we all take in the sea's peacefulness. When we arrive at our docking place, there's a platform for us to stand on. There's a ladder we can use to get into the water and the sectioned off area for the cave. The cave entrance is all jagged, pale rocks that dip into the water. Above the entrance, the rock continues upward until some trees peek over the very top of the cliff.

I can't get over the scenery here. There's so much contrast that makes it raw, rugged, and beautiful.

Hayden passes us shore shoes and they're too big, but he promises we'll appreciate them inside the cave.

We descend the wooden ladder into the hot spring. Sulfur fills the air, but I quickly get used to it. The warm water welcomes us, and Hayden leads us to the cave entrance.

"Careful going in and watch your head," Hayden says. "Anders, go in first with the light."

"Why do I have to be the first one?" Anders teases.

"If you're too scared to do it, I'll go," Hayden says.

Anders flips him off. While they're busy focused on each other, I grab the light from Anders.

"I'll go first," I say, half swimming, half walking to the entrance.

Hayden sputters, but I'm too fast for him to stop me. The entrance is so small, two people can barely fit side by side. But that doesn't deter Hayden. He squeezes in right next to me before taking the light from my hands and surging forward.

"Hey," I say, trying to catch up to him without banging my head on the rock formations that dip into the water. I have to maneuver around it all to get to the light thief.

Once the space opens up, Hayden spins around so suddenly, I run into him.

He grabs my waist and plants a kiss on my lips.

Grinning, he says, "Finders, keepers."

"Losers, weepers." I laugh and splash him with water. I swipe the light from him and try to swim-walk away again. But I'm too slow and he drags me into his body.

"You're not going to get away from me that easily," he says, lifting me higher.

My legs automatically go around his waist. The light in my hand is the only illumination, and it feels like we're in our own world here. I kiss him, unable to resist, and he squeezes my ass. I'm not sure if we should kiss in Cleopatra's cave, but I'm so caught up that I can't stop. I take far too long to realize that he stole the light back from me.

"You play dirty," I say, trying to catch my breath.

"Obviously. That's the only way to play."

My nipples pebble and Hayden's gaze heats. He tightens his grip on my ass.

"You guys need some privacy?" Anders asks.

Shit, I forgot about them. All it took was a kiss and some words, and I lost my mind. Just like last night on the taxi ride home.

I laugh and push away from Hayden. "It's not my fault he can't keep his hands to himself."

"Right?" Zoey grins.

"I'm not mad about it," Hayden says, bringing the light to a ledge above the water. "That's the mud." He points to a sloped bit of land off to the side, big enough for two people to stand on. "People normally cover themselves with it from head to toe."

Hayden scoops up a handful of mud before passing it to Zoey and me. Zoey rubs it onto her arms and Anders takes some in his hands to help her cover her back. Hayden makes a small pile of mud at the edge of the water for us to easily reach.

He hops back in the water and dips a finger in the mud, then swipes it across my cheek.

"You've got something right here." He adds another stripe to my other cheek.

I grab a handful and rub it all over his torso, totally copping a feel as I go. "Oops. Looks like you've made a mess of yourself," I say.

He grins and we go back and forth, helping each other cover ourselves in mud.

Once we're covered, Anders splashes Hayden with water.

"Oops," Anders says.

I laugh when Hayden sputters before retaliating tenfold. Zoey and I move to the mouth of the cave.

"How long do you think it would take before they notice we're not here?" she asks, nodding to the outside.

"Anders will probably notice within a minute or two, max."

"And Hayden?"

"Maybe it'll take him all day," I joke.

She laughs and we wade our way out and into the blinding sun. I blink a few times, trying to adjust to the sudden brightness. She scrubs the mud clean of her skin and within one minute, Anders and Hayden come barreling out of the cave.

Zoey grins when she sees them.

"You were right," she says to me.

"Anders, of course, would notice," I say. "He seems to have a sixth sense when it comes to you."

"Actually," Anders says, "Hayden noticed first that you both weren't in the cave."

I shoot Hayden a look and he shrugs like it's not a big

deal. Zoey's grin widens at the admission, but she doesn't say anything else.

It doesn't mean anything that Hayden noticed it first. It's just a joke, but damn if it doesn't stop my heart from batting its metaphorical eyelashes at Hayden as if he were our hero.

Our captain calls from the boat to Hayden, and he translates for us. "We should get going. Our time here is up."

We all hurry to rinse the rest of the mud from our bodies and board the boat. Underneath the canopy in the back of the boat, there's a full Turkish breakfast laid out on the table. All the bread is piled to one side and there is a gap before the rest of the food. There's everything from scrambled eggs mixed with tomato and peppers to sliced tomatoes and cucumbers to cheeses and olives. It all looks so amazing.

But the best part is the Turkish tea. I could get used to having it every day.

"That's gluten-free bread." Hayden points to a plate on the other end of the table, far away from the other bread. "Everything else is safe for you."

Zoey gives him a soft smile. "Thank you."

"Anyone want some Turkish tea?" I ask.

The men agree, but Zoey says she prefers water. We all eat in contented silence as the boat starts back up.

"Does the cave get your seal of approval, or was it too touristy?" Hayden asks.

"Well, that depends."

"On?"

"If that mud works its magic and gives me beauty that rivals Cleopatra."

"You are already the most beautiful woman in the world, even before the mud."

Zoey lets out an "Aw" and warmth spreads through my body at hearing words that no one has never told me. Sure, I've been called pretty before, but it's never meant much because strangers or people I didn't care about said it. Their opinion meant nothing. There's always a roboticness to random compliments. It always feels like people dish them out left and right so often, it loses its impact.

And yet, with Hayden, it means something. Something more. Maybe because he knows me more than most people. Or maybe because it's just him.

But I like it.

Too much.

* * *

THE DAY SPEEDS BY, as if time pressed the fast-forward button on a remote. It's moments like this where I wish it were the opposite. Where I'd prefer the day to pass by at a snail's pace so I can savor every moment. Where I have endless time to engrave each memory into my mind to keep forever.

Today is easily in the top three best days I've ever had. It's full of laughter, fun, relaxation and sun. Zoey and Anders are easy people to travel with. They've perfected the balance of spending time with everyone while also going off on their own.

We all have champagne glasses in hand while the

waves gently rock our boat. We've literally been on here all day, but I could stay here forever. The sun is one pinky finger away from the horizon. According to our captain, that means it's about ten to fifteen minutes from setting.

I stare at the sparkling water, sad that the day is ending.

"You look contemplative," Hayden says, standing next to me, staring at the view.

I can't help but snuggle into his body, his warmth and the contentment I feel around him.

"I've realized that water is my happy place," I say. "And yet I do nothing to enjoy it back home. Even though Seattle isn't landlocked."

"I get that. Even after all the countries I've been to, my favorite are the ones that are warm and on the water."

"Hmm…"

"Hey, are you okay?" he asks.

"Just sad it's about to end."

He turns to face me fully.

"Me too."

"Yeah?" I ask.

"Yeah, I could stay here forever."

"Let's forget life and buy this yacht and stay on the Med." I say it like a joke, even if I'm somewhat serious.

"You'd be a lady of luxury, and I'd be your arm candy."

"Then we must go to Monaco and show you off."

He laughs. "Way to make me feel like a kept man right off the bat."

"You've got to know your place." I grin.

"Oh, I know my place."

"And where's that?"

"Anywhere you are."

I suck in a breath at his statement. I can't tell if he's joking or not. I wait for a few beats, but he doesn't crack a smile. He said it like he meant it.

But I do what I always do when I'm nervous. I make a joke.

"What if I was climbing the top of a bridge for funsies?" I ask.

"I'd be there, peeing my pants in fear and all."

"And what if I was imprisoned behind enemy lines?"

"I'd launch a rescue attempt and never stop until my dying breath."

"Fuck." I let out a long breath. "That's the most perfect answer ever."

"Well, I'm stealing it from a book, but it's true."

"What if I'm permanently disfigured from an accident?" Oh fuck, I didn't mean to say that out loud. I wish I could reel those words back in. I could've been injured like my mom, riddled with scars. And I didn't know it was a fear I had until now. "Hypothetically, of course."

"You're hot and all," he says. "But it's not your best quality."

"I can't tell if I should feel offended or not."

He gives me a soft smile. "It's your personality. Your fearlessness. Your desire to explore and your curiosity that makes you attractive."

"If that's the case, if I were a horse who could talk—"

"You just gave me a weird visual there," he says, shuddering.

I laugh.

"Shut up and accept that I like you," he says.

"I like you too," I say before he kisses me senseless.

"If you can stop sucking each other's faces for a minute, sunset's happening now," Anders calls from the other side of the boat.

I pull away and laugh.

"Fuck off," Hayden calls back. "As if you're not doing the same thing with Zoey."

I giggle and snuggle into Hayden's side as we watch the sun slip behind the horizon, closing out the best day ever.

CHAPTER 30

$\mathcal{H}$AYDEN

Even though we're all exhausted after an epic day on the water, we agreed to have a power nap and to get ready for another night on the town.

Bree slots into my family perfectly.

And it's equal parts exciting and terrifying. I still don't know how we'd really make it work. At least for the next two months, I'll be in Singapore. But afterward, maybe I can split my time between Seattle and Portland. Try to make long-distance work, even if it's never worked in the past.

I pour myself a whiskey in the kitchen, trying to stave off my building headache just thinking about it all.

"Hey," Anders says. "Pour one for me?"

I nod and bring the glasses over to him.

He leans against an edge of the kitchen counter and takes a sip.

"So… you and Bree, huh?" he asks.

"Me and Bree what?"

"Don't be dense. You like her."

"What makes you say that?"

"You look at her like she's your sun."

"That was poetic," I say, trying to deflect his nosiness.

"Fuck you. I'm serious."

"Fine, I like her, but we originally agreed that this'll end when we return to the US."

"Why?" he asks.

"It felt safer when we didn't know each other. But now… I'm not sure how to work it out. Not when Adrien and his demands will consume me for the next months."

Oh shit, I didn't mean to say that.

"What kind of demands does he have?" Anders asks.

"Nothing important." I try to brush it off, but Anders gives me a look that says he can see through my bullshit.

My phone rings and I glance at it. "It's Adrien."

"You going to answer?" Anders asks.

I don't want to, but I feel like I have to since Anders is watching. If I don't, Adrien will call me back until I answer. It's better if I get it over with and pretend everything is fine between us.

"Adrien," I answer.

"I know I promised not to call, but your vacation is almost finished."

"The key word in that sentence is almost," I say, turning my back on Anders and walking a few steps away.

"You're right. But I'm calling for two reasons. The first is I want you to fly directly from Istanbul to Singapore."

"No," I say, immediately. I'm supposed to fly back with Bree, and I refuse to not be on the same flight as her. Not when I've been looking forward to it all week.

"Well, I wouldn't be so hasty in saying that. Not when I tell you the second part. The board is prepared to give you an amazing offer if you extend your contract by one year."

My eyebrows shoot up. That's news to me. Adrien has been insistent that once my contract's up, it's over. That he'll take on the role of owner and CEO. I've also been adamant that I'm not interested in continuing to work with him.

"I'm not interested," I say.

"You might want to reconsider when I tell you how much we're offering."

I remain silent.

"Five million, plus bonus, for one year," he says.

That's a shit ton of money. Especially with the bonus. But it'll all come at a price. The question is, can I tough it out for another year or not?

"Let me think about it," I say and hang up.

"What was that all about?" Anders asks.

"Adrien offered me a contract extension." This is the worst thing that could happen. The one outcome I wanted to avoid—my family finding out I'm unhappy—is going to happen no matter what I do. Because now I have to decide and explain it to them.

Shit.

"We should celebrate the great news," Anders says.

"What good news?" Bree asks, coming into the kitchen

with Zoey.

"His boss just called," Anders says. "He wants to extend Hayden's contract for another year."

"And you're considering it?" Bree's lips thin.

"I don't know," I say. "I told him I'd think about it."

"What's there to consider?" Anders asks. "You love your job."

Bree glares at me, like she's mad at me for keeping up the lie. For not coming clean to him about how I feel. But she doesn't get it. It's not that simple.

"But does he really?" Bree asks it in a way that makes Anders frown.

He shoots me a look.

"Of course, I love my job," I glare at Bree. She has no right to bring this up. She has no right to out me like this, even if she said nothing specific. Her question could be interpreted a thousand different ways, but Anders looks between Bree and me a few times.

"What's going on?" he asks.

"Nothing. Let's go, the car's waiting for us," I say, shutting down the conversation.

Zoey picks up on that right away and drags Anders out of the kitchen.

"Why are you still lying to him?"

"Because I'm not ready to tell him the truth, and you had no right to tell him that. I told you how I felt in confidence."

"You're right. I'm sorry." Bree blows out a long breath. "I just... it kills me to see you unhappy. You deserve more."

"But it's *my* decision to make. Not yours."

"Yeah, but you haven't done it yet and you're scared. I get it—"

"No, you don't get it," I say. "This isn't the same as overcoming a fear. It's my life, my future, my job."

"I was just trying to help," she whispers.

"Well, you didn't," I say. "You made it worse."

"I don't think that I did."

"Why? Because you've known Anders for a couple of days and can read him perfectly? Get real. I've known him for almost thirty years. I know what I'm doing."

"Then do something," she yells. "Anything would be better than remaining quiet."

"I am doing the best I can. Sorry if it's not good enough for you."

I storm past her, too angry to continue the conversation. She's disappointed in me? Well, I'm disappointed in her and how she just unpinned a grenade and threw it in the kitchen minutes ago. I could've gotten around Adrien's offer with Anders. But what Bree did? I won't be able to get around that. I'll be forced to talk to him. It was supposed to remain a secret. I'd tough it out for another two months and then I'd be done with it all.

But this right here is a casualty of opening up to someone. Someone else has the power over my secrets. They can let them slip at any moment. Sure, we signed an NDA, but that doesn't stop her from accidentally, or accidentally-on-purpose, telling my family.

I need alcohol, ASAP. I wanted tonight to be fun, but that's not looking so promising now. Not when maybe it wasn't worth getting close to Bree, not when this is what happened.

CHAPTER 31

REE

OKAY, so I fucked up. I didn't mean to say it like that. I was furious Hayden would even consider extending his contract. He can't, not when he hates it. Not when it sucks all his energy from him. And I was even angrier that Anders had no inkling how much Hayden's been suffering. How he's not supporting Hayden.

But now? Hayden's pissed at me. He didn't even hold my hand in the car. I've gotten so used to him touching me all the time that the lack of it is shocking. I miss it. I miss him.

His aloofness is killing me.

My sorry doesn't seem to help, and I don't know what else to do because that's the only thing I've got.

Anders and Hayden lead us through the crowded, outdoor bar that pulses with music. Green and blue lights occasionally flicker, highlighting the view. We're surrounded by yachts and the Bodrum castle. It's gorgeous, but I'm too torn up inside to enjoy it.

Hayden finds us a high, white table to stand around while Anders hunts down drinks. I ask him to order a few rounds of shots for the table and he agrees.

"You okay?" Zoey asks quietly.

I shrug. I don't want to say anything in front of Hayden, and she seems to get that. She touches my arm and squeezes it lightly. I give her a strained smile in return.

Anders returns with a shit ton of alcohol. Each of us grabs a cocktail and three shots.

We all lift a shot, clink them together, and down them.

"I hate hearing people eat bananas," I say the second I finish swallowing.

Hopefully that's a random enough truth to distract Anders. I don't want to put Hayden in an uncomfortable position with him about what I let slip. I give Hayden a look, one that begs him to play with me.

"That's..." Anders shoots Zoey a look that screams *help me*.

Hayden remains silent and my heart sinks. I really messed up if he won't even play. And now I'm going to have to explain what the hell I just said and why and—

"I still have the teddy bear I used as a kid," Hayden says at last, but it's lacking the usual playfulness he has.

"I'm so confused," Zoey says.

"We like to say a truth when we take a shot," Hayden says.

"Of course, you do," Anders says.

Zoey grins and picks up another shot. "I hate coffee."

"It's supposed to be something we all don't know already." Hayden's lips twitch.

"Well"—she laughs—"I just wanted to make sure Bree knows that."

"But you own a coffee shop, right?" I ask.

"Yup," Zoey says almost proudly.

"Don't get her started," Anders says. "It's all my fault for getting her into it."

"Oh, wait. I've got another truth. A better one." Zoey pauses dramatically. "I love reality TV shows."

We're all silent for a few seconds before Hayden says, "You suck at this game."

I snort and Anders grins.

"Okay, fine. So truth telling games aren't my strong point," Zoey says, pointing a finger at Hayden. "But at least I can beat you all at flip cup."

"I'll make sure to be on your team for Christmas," Hayden says.

"Wait. You play drinking games at Christmas?" I ask.

"It's tradition," Anders says simply.

Huh, that's different... but amazing. I wish I did that with Mom and Jules. Maybe we can add some extra pizzazz to this year's festivities.

"I know it sounds weird, but it's fun," Zoey says to me. "Maybe you can come this Christmas."

Hayden tenses and shoots Zoey a wide-eyed look. All the levity at the table vanishes with his reaction. Zoey swallows hard and stares at everyone, seeming to realize her mistake five seconds too late.

"Oh, I mean... if you're still... together..." Zoey blushes

and tries to backtrack, but she's doing a shit job of it. "I'm going to go dig a hole and jump inside it. Be back... never."

Zoey tugs on Anders's arm and leads him away.

"She's funny," I say, trying to break the tension still lingering in Hayden.

"Hilarious," Hayden deadpans.

He doesn't say anything else. I get that he's angry with me, but is the thought of me coming to Christmas so dreadful that he cringed?

"Just so we're clear"—I nudge his shoulder with my own—"I'm expecting a Christmas invite, a wedding in Italy, and for us to move in together by the time our trip ends."

Hayden's lips twitch, but he still doesn't crack.

"Oh, and most importantly—there will be a surprise pregnancy."

"It's not much of a surprise if you tell me about it beforehand." He glances at me. "But I'll trade you a pregnancy for something else."

"You're right." I force a laugh. "I don't want kids."

"Ever?"

"Ever. Why? Do you?" I hold my breath, waiting for his response.

"I don't know," he says. "I never thought about it much."

"Hmm, so what will you trade me for it?"

He thinks on it for a few beats before proposing, "What about a hot-air balloon ride over Cappadocia?"

"Nice," I say, pleased he's finally playing along. "But I need something bigger, grander."

His gaze sparks at the challenge. "What about an announcement of our engagement slash wedding in the news? We'll ham it up in the media, make the nation fall in love with us, have our own hashtag and everything. Oh, and let's not forget the best part..." He pauses dramatically. "There will be merch."

"Okay, you win." I laugh. "I'll take that over a surprise pregnancy any day."

He grins and pulls me to his side. Finally, he's touching me again.

I take a sip of my drink. "Okay, truth or truth time."

"Hit me with it."

"Do you forgive me for the kitchen?"

"Yeah, but I'm still hurt."

"I understand, and I promise I won't do it again. But can I ask about your reaction earlier? When Zoey mentioned Christmas?"

"It was nothing."

"You're not allowed to lie," I remind him.

"I—"

"Is it safe to approach?" Zoey asks, returning with Anders.

I want to scream that she can't return. Not yet. Not until I find out why Hayden had that kind of reaction about Christmas. Because, right now, I'm thinking he's horrified for me to meet the rest of his family. And it hurts.

"Oh, good," Zoey says, looking us over. "You've made up."

"Yeah," Anders says, "because I was planning to rub it

into Theo's face that I got to meet your girlfriend and he didn't."

"Great idea." Hayden grins, his gaze lingering on me for a long moment before he focuses back on Anders. "It's about time I'm not the one missing out on something."

Hayden doesn't shy away from the girlfriend title, and a wave of hope washes over me. Hayden's falling for me like I'm falling for him. A future together seems increasingly promising.

Anders takes his phone out and snaps a picture of Hayden and me. "I'll just text him the news now."

Hayden takes out his phone also and I lean over his shoulder, watching the screen. The anticipation of what Anders is writing is so dramatic.

Anders: I've got news.

Theo: Oh? Did Zoey finally dig the stick out of your ass?

Anders: Nope, it's permanently wedged there. It's about Hayden.

Theo: I'm on the edge of my seat...

Anders: He has a girlfriend.

Anders: (sends a picture of Hayden and me)

THEO DOESN'T RESPOND and we all stare at the screen, waiting.

. . .

> Theo: Ha ha, very funny. Hayden doesn't date. But good job picking a hot woman to fake date him.

> Hayden: Bree is the one you were asking about earlier.

> Theo: Wait, wait, wait. Bree is the mystery woman? Is my baby brother finally ready to settle down?

> Hayden: Whoa, let's not get ahead of ourselves here. No one said anything about settling down.

> Theo: Fine, then you're finally in a relationship.

> Hayden: I'm not sure.

NOT SURE? *Not sure.* What the hell?

I glance at Hayden, but he's too busy texting Theo to notice. I shift my gaze to Anders and he's giving me a look full of pity.

Oh no.

I really believed Hayden was falling for me. He was mad at me, but we made up. Couples fight all the time.

Right? *Right?*

The last few times we've had sex, I felt something more. Something deeper between us. But I was completely off base.

Oh no.

Zoey's gaze swings to mine. "Bathroom time. Bree, come with me?"

I follow her to the bathroom robotically. I can't believe I was stupid enough to think he wanted more. Alcohol and me can't be trusted. It makes me project and feel hopeful and… wanted.

I inhale sharply through my nose, trying to contain the building tears. But it's not working and a few escape down my cheek. I hastily wipe them away before Zoey sees them.

Once we enter the white bathroom, Zoey turns to me.

"You okay?" she asks.

"Of course." I dab at the inside of my eye, pretending I have something besides a tear stuck there. "It's not like we're serious or anything."

"Could've fooled me."

"I knew from the beginning that we'd end when we leave," I say, trying to act unaffected. "It's for the best."

Zoey scrutinizes my expression. "It's okay if that's changed. If you want more."

"I thought…" I shake my head. "It doesn't matter what I thought."

"This is what Ruby must've felt like," Zoey announces, as if I know who the hell Ruby is.

"Care to explain?"

"You're falling for him and want more, but you're scared. Don't worry, I was in your shoes not so long ago. But a word of advice? These Watson men have a way of sneaking up on you."

"You've got it wrong. Hayden doesn't want me. I think he's made that abundantly clear with that text message."

Hope is a tricky bitch, and I may have fallen into her clutches the past few days, but I need to remember that Hayden hasn't made me any real promises. He definitely loses three letters—one for storming out of the kitchen, one for giving me the silent treatment, and the last for that text he sent Theo. He's down to just a *W* for his last name.

If he loses the last one by the time we fly home, maybe it's not worth pursuing something with him. Not if he can't make it to ten days without losing six letters in his last name.

CHAPTER 32

*H*AYDEN

WHEN WE ARRIVE IN ISTANBUL, we have a few hours to kill before Zoey and Anders need to be back at the airport.

Once we got home from the bar, I couldn't stop myself from fucking Bree all night. As if I could untangle the mess in my head by losing myself in her. But no matter how many times I sank into her body, this sense of urgency never left. It's like I can feel the end of us drawing near.

I thought we were both giving hints we're ready to continue our relationship after we return to the US. But as our deadline looms, I'm doubting if we're right for each other. If the cracks that are forming can be mended or not.

It started last night when Bree betrayed my trust with Anders. She promised she wouldn't do it again, and I have to believe her. Even if it's hard to. Even if eventually Anders is going to ask about it. The other crack is how brutally efficient she is in cutting people out of her life. She openly admitted I'm different from the other men she hooks up with. That must mean she isn't using her letter removal system on me. Not since Princes' Islands anyway. I may joke about it, but it hurts to even consider she's judging everything I do and weighing it against an imaginary scale.

Doubts are flying in left and right, but I don't want to succumb to them. The countdown until our farewell is on. And it's like a noose around my neck. Pulling tighter with every second that passes.

Tomorrow we're supposed to take the flight back to the US.

Tomorrow, we're supposed to say goodbye for good.

Unless I'm brave enough to ignore all the doubts and ask her for something no one has ever given me—to continue an "us" after meeting abroad.

Everything I've been ignoring for the past ten days is coming to a head. Major decisions need to be made, and it feels like no matter which way I turn, if I don't handle all of this with care, I'll lose something. My family's opinion of me on one side, my sanity and Bree on the other.

"Would it be okay if we see that dog you came here for, Bree?" Zoey asks once the van pulls out of the Istanbul airport.

Bree tenses for a split second before smothering her reaction with a smile. "Sure."

To say I'm surprised is an understatement. I expected

her to brush off the request or redirect it. I give her a confused look and she shrugs.

"It'll be the last time I see him anyway, since we're leaving tomorrow," Bree says. "Might as well say goodbye now."

I nod and pull up Bilet's Instagram feed. He's been spotted on the same tram line we first met him on.

I give the information to our driver, and he takes us there.

On the way, my phone buzzes in my pocket. I glance at it. Adrien, again. Since answering his call last night, he's been blowing up my phone. Insisting I fly straight from here to Singapore. Trying to convince me to take the deal.

I hit ignore and focus on anything else but him. Zoey's face is glued to the window, and it reminds me of Bree when we first arrived.

"Not sure you're close enough to see everything," I tease.

"Fuck off," Anders says. "This trip is the first time she's left the US."

"Really?" I ask.

"Yeah," Zoey says sadly. Anders wraps an arm around her shoulders, as if protecting her from some imaginary threat.

"Well, what a way to pop your travel cherry," Bree says. "And you got an engagement too."

Zoey laughs. Bree has a small smile on her face, as if making Zoey happy made her day.

"And," I say, "you've got the best tour guide in the country to impart some wisdom on you while we drive."

"You keep saying that, but I've yet to see these so-called skills," Anders says.

"Oh yeah? Well, Istanbul was founded in the 7th century BC. And it's had three names over the years."

"Thanks, Wikipedia," Bree says, laughing.

"Could you be a tour guide for any of the other countries you've lived in?" Zoey asks.

"Definitely not," I say. "I never cared about any of the other places we lived in before. Not until here. There was an instant connection between me and the city."

"I get that. I had it with Italy," Anders says.

"What about Theo?" Bree asks. "What city or country did he connect to?"

"Portland," Anders and I say at the same time.

"That's unexpected," Bree says. "I thought you were going to say something exotic."

"Theo never wanted to travel and always craved stability," I say. "So he connected to the one place our parents chose to settle."

"It probably helps that Ruby lives there," Anders adds.

"And Ruby is?" Bree asks.

"The love of Theo's life and my best friend," Zoey says.

"Hey, I thought I was your best friend," says Anders.

"You are." Zoey pats him on the arm in a placating way.

Bree laughs and I grin.

"I've got to meet this Ruby person," Bree says. "She sounds cool."

"She is," we all say in unison.

We chat for the rest of the drive, but Bree gets quieter and quieter the closer we get to Taksim. I ask our driver to pull off when we're a couple of streets away from our destination.

Zoey and Anders are lost in their own world as we approach the red tram.

I stay by Bree's side and ask, "Are you okay with this?"

"Sure."

It's a lie, but I don't call her out. Not in front of the others. I pay for everyone's ticket and Zoey and Anders walk up the steps first. Zoey's bouncing in place, she's so excited. Anders has a fond look on his face as he watches her. And Bree… Bree's clasping her hands behind her back.

Bilet is in the back of the tram this time. We shuffle forward every time the door opens and people get off.

When Bilet finally comes into view, Zoey squeals. "Oh, my stars. Isn't he adorable?"

She takes out her phone and snaps a few pictures of him.

When she finishes, Anders guides her into a seat.

Bree finds a seat in front of a boy who is sitting across from Bilet. He looks to be in his teens, has his head on the window, but his gaze is on the dog.

"Can you ask him if he's here for Bilet?" Bree says, nodding to the boy.

I do as she asks, and the boy lifts his head from the window.

"Do you speak English?" Bree asks him.

"A little," he says.

"I'm here for Bilet too," Bree says. "Do you mind if I ask what your reasoning is?"

"Being here, around him, is the only time I can be myself."

Damn. He said it so sadly, like he has to put on an act all day long and is tired of pretending. Never knew I could relate to a kid so hard, but that's exactly how I feel in my own life.

The boy looks Bree over. "What about you?"

"I'm trying to understand why people love dogs," she says.

"And?" the boy asks. "Did you find out why?"

"Maybe," Bree says. "Everyone I've met has a different reason. Some say it's for the unconditional love, others for social reasons, and another found a new purpose in life through dogs. But I think yours is the one that resonates with me the most. The lack of judgment in an animal."

The boy nods but doesn't say anything else. Bree's lost in her own world as we continue the ride. Anders and Zoey watched the entire exchange, but they haven't said anything. Maybe they're picking up on how important of a moment this is for Bree.

Bree nods to herself, as if coming to a decision.

"Can I get by?" she asks me.

I stand and let her out of the seat. She walks slowly over to Bilet. He lifts his face from his paws and stares at her. Bree stares back, and they're both locked in this moment together. I take my phone out and snap some photos.

Bree lifts a shaky hand in front of her, and Bilet sniffs it. She flinches and curls her hand into a fist, but she doesn't back away. Bilet nuzzles her hand, and she squeezes her eyes shut. Her entire body is tense, but holy shit.

She's doing it.

She's allowing a dog to touch her.

Not just any dog, but Bilet. The dog she came for.

After a few more seconds, Bree takes an unsteady step back. I grip her shoulders and turn her to face me.

"You did it," I say in awe.

"I didn't imagine it?"

I laugh. "Not at all."

She starts with a small smile, but it grows with every second into the most beautiful smile I've ever seen. It's the type that lights her up from the inside until it's so bright, it's blinding.

I snap a picture of it and brush my lips across hers.

"You're amazing," I say. "I'm so proud of you."

"I can't believe I did it."

"I can. You're the bravest person I know."

"Let's get out of here," she says.

We get off at the stop, and Zoey immediately hugs Bree.

"I'm not sure why touching the dog is a big deal," Zoey says. "But I can see it is. I'm proud of you too."

"Thank you," Bree says. "I'm deathly afraid of dogs and it's the first one I've touched in ages."

"This is huge," Zoey says. "We should celebrate, but I can't drink anymore alcohol. How about we celebrate with some Turkish tea? Those glasses were just too cute."

"We've only got time for one drink before we have to catch our flight," Anders says.

We race to the nearest café and order tea for everyone, even Zoey.

"To overcoming our fears," I say, lifting my glass in the air.

We all cheers and take a sip.

"I think we're going to need to get a dog," Zoey tells Anders.

"We work all the time," he says. "How will we care for a dog?"

"Good point. But one day..."

"If you really want one," Anders says, "I'm sure we can find a way. You know it's my life's goal to make you happy."

Zoey melts, literally melts, into him at those words. Maybe I should take notes from Anders on how to woo a woman, especially if his grumpy ass gets that kind of reaction from Zoey.

Bree even swoons at my brother's words. Fucking hell, what world am I in where my brother's got game?

Anders checks his watch. "We've got to go."

Zoey sighs and pulls me into a hug.

"Happy looks good on you," she whispers in my ear. "Thanks for letting us crash your time with Bree."

"It wasn't a hardship. Not when I like you more than Anders."

She laughs and squeezes me tighter. "Don't be a stranger, yeah?"

"I promise."

Anders claps me on the back.

"I don't think I've ever seen you so happy before," he says.

"It's the city."

"Hmm. Or more like the company."

"That helps too," I say. "And taking a vacation for the first time in ages."

"We need to talk about NomNom when you get back. Don't sign anything with Adrien until you talk to Theo and me first."

"That's not necessary."

"I think it is," he says.

"Fine." I say it just to placate him, but I don't need to consult with him about my future.

Bree hugs them both and they each say something to her. Bree's face gives nothing away, and I'm left guessing what in the world could be so important to tell her that I couldn't overhear.

CHAPTER 33

REE

"Well, well, well. Look who finally called." Jules glares at me through the video. "I was this close"—she pinches her fingers together—"to calling Hayden and making sure you were alive."

"Oops," I say, putting my foundation on.

"Oh no, you don't get to go radio silent for days in a foreign country and scare me half to death and say 'oops' in response." The vein in her forehead pulses, indicating how mad she really is.

"I didn't mean to lose touch. I was just busy having the best sex of my life, spending my days on a boat, and meeting part of his family."

Jules's eyes widen. "You met the family?"

"Just the brother and his fiancée, but yeah."

"We'll circle back around to that in one moment. Just

316

promise you'll at least message once a day from now on. You, Mom, and my kids are all I have."

"I..." I swallow past the building tears that are clogging my throat. "You're right. I'm sorry and I promise."

"Good, now tell me all about this brother of his." That's the best thing about Jules. She doesn't hold a grudge. She's able to move on easily after an apology. I've never been more grateful for that than now, especially when I feel like the worst sister ever for worrying her.

I fill her in on what we've been up to and how much fun I've had.

"You liked them," she says.

"Yeah, they're cool. And they like me too."

"How do you know?"

"They told me before they left that I'm welcome to visit them anytime, even without Hayden."

"Wow," Jules says, "that's big."

"Right? I made... a friend?" How long has it been since I've made one? Ten years? More?

"Sounds like you made two to me."

"And... I let a dog sniff my hand."

Jules literally falls out of her chair, and the video only shows the floor. She snatches her phone back up and says, "Say that again. I think I misheard you."

"A dog touched my hand."

"Ahhhhh," she screams. "I'm so proud of you. This is huge. I can't believe you did it. Were you scared?"

"Yeah, but Hayden was with me, so I figured if I lost my hand, then he'd take me to a hospital."

Jules snorts. "At least Hayden's got that going for him."

"Yeah... at least."

"So... are you going to see each other when you return home?"

"We haven't talked about that."

"But you're flying tomorrow."

I blow out a long breath. "I know."

"Well, what do you want?"

"Let's put it this way. Even though he's lost some of his letters, this is the first time I've wanted to add letters to someone's name for all the amazing things they do for me. The good outweighs the bad."

"O.M.G." Jules breathes. "It's finally happened."

"What?"

"My baby sister is in love."

"No, I'm not," I say.

"Uh-huh and what would you call wanting to add a letter to someone's name for the first time in... ever?"

"That I like him more than anyone else."

"Exactly."

"But it's not love," I insist.

"Tell me this. How many letters would Hayden Watson have in his name right now if you added letters to his name?"

"I don't know... maybe fifty?"

"He's only got twelve letters in his name. Even my name is only Jules in your phone."

"Because I don't play this game with you or Mom," I say.

"Thank you, because I'd probably be blocked every other day. But don't you see? It's worth a shot."

"I don't know..." I hedge, too scared to believe her words. Not when there's a nagging voice in the back of my head reminding me he lost five letters already. That it's only been nine days, that's almost a letter every other day.

"If he was with another woman, how would you feel?"

"Fucking feral," I say honestly.

"Well then, that's your answer. Talk to him. Maybe he's feeling the same way."

"But he pretty much hinted that he doesn't see a future with me."

"How certain are you of that though?" she asks. "Because if it's anything less than one hundred percent, then it's worth having a conversation about it. I don't want you two to throw away something special because you don't just talk to each other."

"That's actually good advice," I say. We're supposed to be honest with each other, and we should have a conversation about this. I should be honest with him about my feelings. That I'd like to see where this goes. Even if I'm fucking terrified.

"Of course, it is," Jules huffs. "I gave it."

I grin. "I'll let you know how it goes before I leave for the airport tomorrow."

"Can't wait. Good luck and I love you."

"Love you too."

THE WAITER BRINGS us to the window and seats us at the only empty table in the entire restaurant. Dim lights give off a romantic feeling, and the scent of mint and rosemary fills the air. The Turkish paintings on the wall just add to the whole experience.

The waiter speaks English and explains the menu and concept of the restaurant. We can order at our table, but most people go to the counter where all the freshly made specials are displayed and order directly from the chef.

Hayden and I glance at each other for a split second before saying, "Let's do the specials."

Our waiter guides us to the protective glass, and it all looks delicious. There's everything from stuffed grape leaves to green beans and spinach, to meats. We each point out different items we'd like to try. Hayden talks to the chef for a minute before translating.

"The chef has some fish that was caught this morning. He says he can bake it for us. Is that okay?"

"Definitely," I say.

When we return to our table, Hayden reaches for my hands on the top of the table.

"Did you have fun over the past ten days?" he asks.

"Yeah, this might be one of the best trips I've ever had."

"Same," he says.

"We make a good team," I say, trying to figure out where he's coming from. To make confessing my feelings not as scary.

"That we do."

"Truth or truth time?" I ask.

Okay, I can do it. I can ask him.

"Hit me with it."

"I like you."

"I like you too," he says, squeezing my hand in his.

"And…" I take a deep breath. "I'd—"

The server comes with our wines, and I place my hands in my lap.

"What were you going to say?" he asks.

"It's not important now." I'm totally losing my nerve here. Who knew it'd be so hard to talk about how I feel when it comes to my heart?

"Everything you say is important," he says.

"Okay, fine. I'm wondering what will happen when we return home." I give him a meaningful look, trying to convey everything I'm having a hard time saying.

"Well, work is going to take up all my time for the next two months..."

"And after that?" I ask, holding my breath. I don't mind waiting for two months. That's nothing if I get Hayden at the end of it.

"I'm not sure what I'll do about Adrien's offer."

"You can't seriously be considering it?" I ask, disappointed he didn't pick up on what I was really asking. Disappointed he's wanting to continue with a job he hates.

"It's a lot of money, and it's only a year."

"What was the point of figuring out our future if you were just going to throw it out the window and stay with what you're comfortable with? Especially when you're unhappy."

"The point was to figure out what I really wanted."

"And do you really want to work on NomNom for another year?" I ask.

"I'm still undecided about what to do, okay?" he says. "Can we talk about this on the flight tomorrow instead? I'm not in the right headspace to think about what to do with Adrien right now."

"Fine," I say, understanding he's overwhelmed. Now isn't the time to talk about our future. I can wait until the flight to get answers about us. "I still think you should open a restaurant with all your favorite dishes from around the world."

"Only if you join me." He says it playfully, and I can't tell if he's joking or if he means it.

"That'd only work if I owned the majority of the restaurant," I say.

"That can be arranged," he says. "And you could make all the art for it. Something for each dish's country."

That actually sounds dreamy.

"Perfect, but there's one condition. No potatoes are allowed on the menu."

Hayden laughs. "I wouldn't dream of it."

When the food arrives, it's so delicious, every dish could be added to our imaginary restaurant's menu. And that's saying something when I've had some of the best food of my life while here.

"I know why I lost my letters," he says.

"Enlighten me." I grin, covering my concern that he's only down to a *W* for his last name.

"It was because of that one time I purposely poured an entire bottle of mint extract in the cookies I baked for my family's annual Christmas bake-off."

"Did they eat it?"

"They had to try a bite. It was the funniest thing to twelve-year-old me."

I smile. "I can imagine."

"But you know what's next?"

"Yeah, yeah. I lost another letter," I say. "Bring it on. What did I do this time?"

"You're too compassionate."

"And you're full of shit."

We laugh and the dinner passes by so quickly. But when we're done, all I want to do is go back to his house. I could try to squeeze every second remaining here outside, enjoying the city to the max. But I can't seem to spend enough time with Hayden.

I never got a clear answer if we're going to be together after tomorrow or not.

Tonight just might be our last night together.

CHAPTER 34

*H*AYDEN

"Want to swim?" Bree asks when we arrive back at the house in Bebek.

After dinner, she wanted to come home. I'm so glad she doesn't want to see any more of the city. Not when I just want her.

"Good idea," I say.

"You mean it's a brilliant idea?"

"No, a brilliant idea would be if you wore *the* bathing suit."

"Hmm." She taps her chin with her fingers. "I'm having a hard time remembering which one you mean."

"Smartass. Come on. Put a man out of his misery, why don't you?"

Her expression shutters for a beat before she covers it with a grin. "Maybe I should autograph it and get it framed for you. That way, you can hang it on your wall as a reminder of the best sex of your life."

"Hmm." I'd rather I have her instead of a memento of our time together. At dinner she brought up what'll happen after we return home, but I thought she meant about my choice with NomNom. I realized far too late that she was probably asking about us. And I missed the chance to tell her how I feel. That I want an *us*. That she's important to me.

Bree gives me a lingering look before disappearing up the stairs. I grab my swim trunks and dive into the pool. The cool water is a nice balance to the warm night.

The sliding glass door snicks open and I turn to Bree.

She's breathtaking.

All her creamy skin and curves are on display. And that top... that fucking top should win an award or something.

"Come here, beautiful," I say, patting the edge of the pool.

She saunters toward me with all the confidence in the world. It's just one of the things I love about her.

I still.

Love?

I don't have time to think about that as she sits down and dangles her legs and feet inside.

"Why do you want me on the edge?" she asks.

"I need to have a good look at this bathing suit," I say, spreading her legs.

The bottoms are wedged between her pussy lips.

I groan at the sight. "Touch your breasts."

She immediately does as I requested, cupping her

perfect tits before squeezing them together. She runs her fingers over the edge of the tiny triangles that barely cover her nipples. Teasing me with glimpses of them.

I fist my hands, refusing to interrupt her fun. Once I touch her, it'll be game over. I don't think I'll ever be able to stop.

She trails a hand down to her stomach and pulls on the edge of her bottoms, giving me an even better view of her gorgeous pussy lips. She keeps one hand on her breast and the other teases the edges of her pussy.

"Take off your swim trunks," she says.

I remove them in a blink.

"Touch yourself."

She stares at me as I fist my cock under the water. Shifting her bottoms to the side, I get the perfect view of her pink pussy. And it's dripping for me.

I lean forward and lick her wetness, moaning at her taste. The taste that I'll dream about the rest of my life.

She lifts her hips into my mouth, as if she can't help herself, before pulling away.

"Ah, ah, ah," she says. "No touching. Or licking."

"And why not? I want to feast on you."

She moans softly and says, "But I want to play first."

"Play later."

"But—"

I grip her hips and pull her pussy to my mouth. Using one thumb to keep her bathing suit to the side, I use the other to tease her entrance as I lick, suck, and nip at her clit.

"You ruined my plans," she pants, gripping my hair with one of her hands. "I wanted to go down on you."

"Baby, we've got all night." I grin. "You can do whatever you want to me later. But first, let me eat my favorite meal."

She clenches around my thumb and nods.

"Oh fine, give me an orgasm," she huffs.

"I plan on it. How many do you think you can handle tonight?"

"What if we don't count and just lose ourselves in one another?"

"Why?" I ask, genuinely curious. I thought she liked having me count them out, wringing all the pleasure I can from her body.

"Because I want both of us to be so high on pleasure that we're not coherent enough to count."

"You're so perfect for me," I say.

I lick her clit and then blow on it.

Shivers go through her body and then I feast.

Feast on her like she's the last meal I'll ever eat.

Bree passed out an hour ago in my arms after fucking all night. There's desperation in both of us every time we join. We can't keep our hands to ourselves, and even if we try to take it slow, we can't.

I'm exhausted. But I'm too afraid to close my eyes, too afraid I'll miss out on a single moment with her. I've woken her up regularly throughout the night, and now the sun's rays are starting to lighten the room.

Ten days have come and gone in the blink of an eye. I wanted my time with Bree to be memorable. To be able to look back on this trip and remember it forever, and we've achieved that… and more.

We've still got some hours before we need to leave for the airport, and I plan on making her breakfast in bed and telling her I want a future with her while she eats.

My dick hardens inside her just thinking about calling her mine.

I brush the hair from her face and whisper, "Baby?"

She stirs, and I move my hips experimentally.

"Huh?" she asks, still sounding half asleep.

"I need you."

She opens an eye. "You're insatiable."

"Only with you."

I gently push her fully onto her back and kiss her slowly, dreamily, as if we have all the time in the world. I rock into her in the same slow rhythm of our kiss.

I hold her face as if she's precious, as if she means something to me. Because she does. I keep up this slow rhythm the entire time, and it's life changing. Like our bodies are rewiring themselves and making room for the other in our souls.

It's powerful, all-consuming, addicting.

Once we both come down from our highs, she snuggles into my side.

"We're going to have to get ready soon," I say. "But I'd like to make you breakfast in bed."

"With tea?"

I grin. "Of course."

"I'll call Jules now, then. She's still awake and was mad I went a few days without talking to her."

"Sounds good."

I head to the kitchen and make tea. When I bring it back up, I hear Bree and Jules's conversation.

I pause by the door.

"And? Did you tell him yet?" Jules asks.

"Not yet, but I will."

"You can do it. You love him. He'd be stupid if he doesn't love you back."

My heart charges like a bull within my chest at her words. She loves me, as I love her.

"I know, I'm just worried," Bree says. "He lost five letters in ten days... shouldn't he have lost none if he was the one?"

A cold, sinking sensation settles into the pit of my stomach, like an anchor dragging me into the depths of despair.

Bree's been removing letters from me this entire time? Even after Princes' Islands? I knew I lost two for some still unknown reason in the beginning. But how the fuck did I lose three more between then and now?

She said I was different, and I stupidly thought that meant she wasn't using her system on me. A system she still hasn't explained. And while I was falling in love with her, she was cutting me out of her life, one letter at a time.

I only have twelve letters to my name, now seven. Which means I only have seven chances before she ghosts me. And I don't even know what I did wrong to begin with. I don't even know how to prevent the loss of my other letters.

Sticky, suffocating panic consumes me.

I'm disposable to her too. She tells Jules she loves me,

but she's just waiting to leave me. It's not even a risk that may materialize. It's a certainty.

She's just like everyone else I've met while abroad. I'm such a fool to think she was different.

When she hangs up with Jules, I push the door open.

"Hey," Bree says, smiling when she sees me.

"Five letters?" I choke out.

"What are you talking about?"

"I lost five letters?"

"I… yeah."

"Why?" I place the tea on the side table. "Explain why you're still continuing to remove my letters. Why would you do that to me?"

"It's not like that. I use the letters to ensure I'm not settling," she says. "I'm scared to miss a red flag."

"Not every man is your dad."

"Don't you dare bring him into this," she says through clenched teeth. "I told you about him in confidence and not to be used as a weapon in an argument."

"Fine," I say, the rage building inside me. "Do you understand how this makes me feel? You're going to ghost me based on some unknown criteria. I'll wake up with my calls blocked, just like you did to the guy you were with before you got on the flight. I can't live my life with an axe over my head, ready to be swung at a moment's notice. I can't deal with that and all the other pressures I'm under."

"You're putting that pressure on yourself. No one is forcing you to work for Adrien."

"Not this again." I throw my hands up. "My job isn't the problem."

"It is. It's the cause of all your problems."

"It's not," I say. "But your letter removal system is the cause of all of *our* problems."

"That's not true." She lifts her chin high in the air, refusing to admit it.

"I can't be with you if you continue to remove my letters."

"Are you giving me an ultimatum right now?" she demands.

"Please," I beg, my voice breaking. "For me, please don't use it."

"But I need it... I'm sorry," she whispers. "I—"

"Then this is the end of us," I say, outraged that she'd choose a silly system over me. "I hope you're happy. You're throwing us away because you're too fucking stubborn to admit you're wrong. You're too stubborn to change your ways."

"And you're the one giving me an ultimatum. I'm trying to change. But what are you doing? You're exactly in the same place you were when I first met you. If our love can fall apart within ten days, maybe you're not worth it."

You're not worth it.

Her words are a variation of what I've felt my entire life. They spin an inferno of rage that starts in my stomach and extends to my entire body. She's dug her nails into an open wound, pressing into it with all her strength. My past plays on repeat in my head, but this time the person hurting me is in front of me.

For the first time in my life, I have a chance to say everything I've always wanted to say when people rejected me, failed me, ghosted me, hurt my feelings and broke my heart.

I finally get to hurt them as much as they've hurt me. And luckily for me, I know just where to strike to cause the most damage.

"I agree. I could never be in a relationship with you," I say the words carelessly, after only one thing from her—pain. "You're too messed up for me."

CHAPTER 35

REE

I SUCK IN A SHARP BREATH. He did not just go there. He did not just throw my greatest fear in my face.

That's not okay. On so many levels. Life is too short to waste it on a man who doesn't want me.

I clench my hands into fists, my nails digging into my palms. The sting centers me. All the words I could say back to him, to hurt him just as deeply as he's just hurt me, bubble to the surface. But I stuff them down.

There's no point in saying them. Not when it doesn't matter. I'll never see him again.

His face morphs from anger to horror. I hurry out of his room and into mine, slamming the door shut behind me. I stuff all of my belongings into my backpack, because I need out of here, ASAP. As long as I have my electronic devices and passport, I don't care about the rest. I throw on my travel clothes and it takes minutes, max.

I fling the door open, and Hayden's standing right there with a towel around his waist. As if he was too afraid to get fully dressed and miss me leaving him.

He says, "I'm so—"

"No. I don't want to hear another word out of your mouth. You've said enough."

"But where are you going? Our flight isn't for another few hours."

"I'm leaving."

"Bree, I'm sorry. I didn't mean what I said. It came out all wrong."

I rush down the stairs, refusing to listen. "No, you said exactly how you felt." Isn't that what people say in anger, the truth?

"But—"

"What's the point of talking more?" I ask. "We're finished and will never see each other again."

I'm out the door and marching down the driveway as fast as I can.

"Bree, wait."

I ignore him. I need to get as far away as possible from him. The sound of his feet hitting the dirt follows me, but he doesn't have a right to follow me. Not when he's wounded me so much.

How stupid was I to tell him anything about myself?

"Bree," he yells.

But I don't stop. I pick up my pace from a speed walk to a jog and then to a sprint until I'm skidding and slipping down the hill and into Bebek.

A yellow taxi is idling on the corner, and I push myself to go faster to catch it.

I bang on the window and dive inside.

"Airport," I demand, looking out the back window to see Hayden running this way.

"Which one?" the driver asks.

"The biggest one there is." How the hell can I even think about the name of an airport when my heart is breaking? "Please, just start driving."

With the towel still around his waist, Hayden waves his arms to get the taxi driver's attention. Thankfully, the driver pulls away from the curb.

Sinking into a seat that smells like cigarettes, I will the tears away. Tears won't do me any good now. I need to create a callous around my heart. Time has to be good enough to solidify it, because this callous needs to be a thick bitch and enough to last the journey home.

There is no way in hell I could endure sitting next to him on the flight. Nope, I don't need to torture myself with that.

At the airport, I change my flight to an earlier one.

In Amsterdam, I shoot Jules a quick message telling her it didn't go well and what time my flight will arrive.

In Boston, I block Hayden's number and remove all the letters in his name. Out of everything, this moment breaks my heart. Even though I was ready to add back his letters and more, it's the beginning of our downfall. All because I couldn't give it up.

It's like my safety net. It's what I use to make sure I don't end up like my mom, with someone who didn't really love her. It was stupid to say that I'd choose it over him, but I was scared and triggered and lashed out.

And now we're done.

When I trudge through the Seattle airport after too many hours awake on a plane, I'm dead on my feet. Less than an hour to go and I'll be home. At least I don't have to wait for any luggage, not when my trusty backpack is all I have.

I shoot a message to Jules once I'm in my Uber to let her know I've landed and I'm on the way home.

Just a little longer until I can break down.

When I open the door to my studio apartment, the stale air tickles my nose. I open the windows, trying to freshen up the place, but the traffic noises are too jarring, the view from my window too boring. Nothing like Bebek.

Nope, I refuse to think about Istanbul.

About Hayden.

I quickly shower and collapse onto my bed. I thought I'd be too tired to think. That my superpower of sleep would overtake me once I got home. But I haven't been able to sleep on the entire journey here. That's never happened before.

My brain can't shut off. It's running a highlights reel of Turkey… and Hayden.

Stupid brain.

I need a distraction.

I could visit Jules, help with the kids. She'd love that, but I don't feel like fun Aunty Bree at the moment. More like just-got-my-heart-ripped-out Aunty Bree. The kids don't need that in their lives. They'd pick up on my emotional state faster than I can say chocolate.

I could go for a walk, clear my head. But I'm too tired for that.

This is the time when having a friend would be helpful. When I could call someone and talk to them about my guy issues.

I grab my phone and scroll through my contacts. There's only a handful, and no one except for Jules and Mom would care anyway.

My finger hovers over Mom's name. Before I can talk myself out of it, I call her.

She answers on the second ring.

"Hi, darling, are you okay?" she asks.

"What makes you think something's wrong?" And how do moms always know something's wrong? Maybe that's why I called her in the first place, so I don't have to pretend to be okay when I'm not.

"Well, for one, because you're calling and not texting. But also, because I know you and can hear it in your voice."

"I'm so fucking angry," I whisper. "All the fucking time."

"About what?"

"Everything."

"Oh, darling, I know," she says. "You've had a hard go at it this year."

"No. I haven't. You have, and I'm making it all about me."

"We all deal with trauma in different ways. Your scars

are invisible to the naked eye, but it doesn't make them less traumatic than mine."

"When did you get so wise?" I ask.

She snorts. "I'm a mom. I was born wise."

"You should put that on a shirt."

"If only I was internet savvy."

We laugh for a moment together.

Damn, it feels good to talk to her. I've missed her so much.

"I'm sorry," I say. "For disappearing, for being the worst daughter alive, for being the cause of your injuries."

"Oh, darling," she chokes out before sniffling. "Don't you *ever* be sorry. I'd do it again a million times over if it meant you were safe."

"How could you say that?"

"How can I not?" she asks. "That's what you do when you love someone."

She says it so simply, but it's like my world rocks on its axis. Love. Such a simple word, but one that packs so much meaning.

I knew Jules and Mom loved me, but I guess I never realized the extent of it. Not when all I could focus on when I was growing up was that my father didn't love me enough to stick around. But by focusing on him, I conveniently ignored the fact that I had two people who loved me so much that they filled all the holes my father made when he left.

And I took it all for granted.

I'm still taking their love for granted. I haven't been reciprocating properly. Mom and Jules keep giving to me, and I keep taking.

"Maybe you've forgotten," she says, "but you saved me. You fought for me. If you didn't stop the dog when you did, who knows how much more damage he would've caused?"

"I... I did?"

Normally my flashbacks consist of blood, screaming, and my mom. I don't focus on anything else.

Not the desperation I felt watching her get mauled.

Not me picking up a heavy stick.

Not the crunch when I used it.

I've spent many months purposely blocking out the fact that I killed a living thing. And what's worse is that I'd do it again in a heartbeat if it meant saving her.

"You did," she says. "And I never thanked you properly."

"You don't have to thank me."

"Then you don't have to feel guilty."

"Well, you've got me there."

She laughs. "I've missed you."

"I've missed you too. Do you want to meet for lunch tomorrow?"

"I'd... I'd love that."

We hang up shortly after solidifying our plans. A weight that's been sitting on my chest, that's been my constant companion over the past months, lifts. Just a little. Just enough where I can imagine myself healed and not carrying around this constant pain.

Building on this feeling, I call the mobile number of the therapist I ditched more times than I can count.

"Hello, Bree," she answers. It's after hours, but she still answers.

"Hi. I... I'm sorry for not meeting with you all those times. But I'm ready now. If you... if you'll still help me."

"When would you like to come in?"

"Now?" I ask.

She laughs. "Sounds like you want to get started immediately."

"I do."

"How about I squeeze you in tomorrow morning at eight?"

"You'd do that for me?"

"Of course. I know it's scary, but I'm here to help you."

"Okay... see you then."

I'm impressed with myself. With how much I've accomplished with two quick calls. I pace my apartment, looking for more things to do. Should I do a summer cleaning? Go through my clothes?

I cross my studio apartment, and I'm in front of my closet door before I can finish that thought. But the closet isn't full of my clothes. No, all my clothes are inside a dresser next to my bed. The closet is where I store all my paint supplies. I may not be the tidiest person in the world, but the one thing I make sure is organized to a T are my supplies.

I roll out the tarp to keep the floors stain free. A tie of my apron, a mixing of colors, a scattering of paper on the tarp and I'm ready. I paint without consciously thinking about it. Like a faucet turns on in my brain and the art streams out of me and onto the paper.

It's a form of meditation, where I feel and do without correction or judgment.

Hours pass, and I continue.

I don't break for anything.

Before I know it, three paintings lay on the ground.

The first is full of blacks and reds. In the middle of the abstract painting is an eye that's fractured, exploding outward in geometric shapes. Shades of red, gray, and black make up the eye. It's angry and raw. The attack.

Another paper is full of turquoise, green, and tan, streaked and scattered across the canvas. An abstract view from Princes' Island. Of happiness and laughter and beauty.

My heart clenches at the memories of Hayden. Of him making that day so special.

But the last is the one I can barely look at. If it wasn't still wet, I'd stuff it in the closet. Never to be seen again.

It's of two hands with rumpled sheets underneath it. It's a reminder of Hayden and me having sex. My hand is stretched as if I'm in the middle of climaxing. His curls around mine, holding on as if I'm his lifeline. I don't know how a picture of two hands can be passionate, but it is. It's one of my best works and yet it's the most painful to look at.

It's more painful than the one of the attack.

I spin away from it, leaving it on the floor, while I head for the shower. Where my tears can mix with the water, and I can pretend I'm not crying over a man.

CHAPTER 36

HAYDEN

REGRET HAS BEEN my constant companion on the journey home. I can't believe I said those words to her. But they came out of my mouth before I even had a chance to think. It was like someone else was in charge of my mouth and my body.

And now I've lost her.

I tried calling her multiple times, but it went straight to voicemail each and every time.

I don't know how we went wrong so quickly. How everything we built together could have crumbled within minutes.

When the plane's boarding was complete, I asked the flight attendant if I could walk back to economy. I wanted to switch my seats with the person next to Bree so that I could sit with her.

They let me, but it wasn't until I walked by the very last row that it finally hit.

She wasn't on board. She changed her flight.

It's clear she's done with me, and she's not willing to work it out. She wasn't willing to hear me out when she was packing, but I thought when we were both calmer, we could talk.

But I was wrong.

When I land in Seattle, I call Bree five times. Each one goes straight to voicemail. Shit, I'm probably blocked. I must've lost all my letters with my careless words to her.

In Portland, my phone rings. I jerk my phone out of my pocket, hope filling my chest.

Hope it's Bree.

But it's not.

It's Adrien.

I direct him to voicemail, but he calls again. And again.

Annoyed with his bullshit, I answer. "What?"

"Where are you? I'm at the airport to pick you up."

"I'm not in Singapore. I'm in the US."

"What? We talked about this—"

"No, you talked. I never agreed to come directly from Istanbul."

"You—" he begins, but I tune out the rest of what he's saying.

I'm so tired of dealing with Adrien and his bullshit. Enough is enough. Bree didn't deserve what I said to her. I was triggered, and I hurt her. But Adrien? Now he's someone deserving of my anger. And I'm done.

I've been so worried about telling my family about my job, but it all pales in comparison to losing Bree. I don't even care about NomNom. Not when I've just lost something far more important.

"Adrien," I say, interrupting him, "I quit."

The second I say the words, it's like a weight lifts from my shoulders. It's what I've wanted to say to him for far too long. But I was too scared about what it meant for my identity and my role within my family.

It's ironic how sometimes it takes a monumental event to see everything with perfect clarity. Bree leaving me and how I treated her is becoming that event. But it's only in the aftermath, once the dust has settled, that clarity occurs. And it's too late by then, everything's already been lost.

Adrien's silent for a good ten seconds.

"If this is a negotiation tactic, it's not going to work," he says. "We offered you the maximum we could."

"It's not a tactic. I'm serious. I quit. Effective immediately."

He huffs out a laugh. "You have to give at least two weeks' notice according to your contract."

"Okay," I say, "take this as my two weeks' notice. I'm also going to be on sick leave for the next two weeks."

"You can't do that," he shouts.

"I can. I'm burnt out and the stress of everything is affecting my mental health."

"You spoiled—"

I hang up and stare at the black screen in relief.

Finally, I'm done with him.

* * *

COLD WATER SPLASHES ME AWAKE.

"What the fuck?" I yell and sit up.

Theo and Anders are standing next to my bed with their arms crossed, both of their faces serious.

"That's what you get when you don't respond to any of our messages," Anders says.

"I've been busy." I say, lying back down on the damp bed.

I couldn't reply, not when I'm just sad... all the fucking time. It's been two days since I've arrived home, and I have done nothing but sleep and pine for Bree.

My suitcase from Turkey is in the corner of my room, still mostly packed. The only thing I've unpacked are Bree's drawings. I saved every single one over the ten days we were together and have been sleeping with them next to me every night.

Oh no, the drawings.

I lift them from the bedside table and inspect each and every one. Luckily no water splashed on them. I breathe out a sigh of relief and move to the other side of the bed and lie back down, still clutching the drawings.

It's the only thing that makes me feel a little better, to have a piece of her near me.

"I never should've given you a key," I say. "Go away and let me sleep."

"I've never seen you like this," Theo says.

"I'm sick," I say, and maybe that's the truth. I've barely left my bed since coming home.

"Yeah, love sick," Anders says.

"Fuck you." I glare at him.

"Get up, we're taking you out," Theo says.

"No, I'm good here."

"If you don't get up, I'm going to carry you out of here," Anders says seriously.

With a heavy sigh, I find the energy to get out of bed. Barely.

I don't change or shower. I just put on my shoes and leave. Anders and Theo keep shooting me looks as we pile into Anders's truck.

I don't ask where we're going, I don't care. Not when I just want to go back to bed and not face the real world. The world where everything is falling apart, and Bree's not by my side.

Anders parks next to a hiking trail I used to love, but today, there's no joy in nature for me to find. When we're a few minutes in, Theo guides us to some tree stumps to sit on.

He passes me a protein bar and a bottle of water.

I chug the water but leave the bar untouched.

"You need to eat," Theo says.

"Why?" I ask. "Are you trying to fatten me up before you're going to kill me in the middle of the woods?" The joke falls flat.

Anders and Theo exchange another look and they both frown.

"I've never seen you so... sad," Anders says. "What happened?"

It's all too raw. I can barely admit it to myself. That we're never going to be together. So, I blurt out the other thing bothering me. The thing Bree pushed me to tell them.

"I told Adrien I quit."

"Why?" Anders asks. "I thought you liked working with him?"

"I hated it." I glare at them. "And I hate you didn't notice."

"I thought something was up, but I didn't know it was this serious," Anders says.

"Every time we asked how you were, you said you were great," Theo says. "How could we have known?"

"I don't know. I expected you to know," I say. "Even without me saying anything."

"That's irrational," Anders says. "You lied to us, so we couldn't have known."

Shit, he's right. It *is* irrational.

"Why did you lie?" Theo asks.

"We needed the money. It was part of the deal, of our payout." I glance at Theo. "And just so you know, Adrien will be on a warpath."

"First, we have lawyers for a reason," Theo says. "It'll be fine. But second, who cares about money? Nothing is more important than you and your health."

"I still don't get why you didn't tell us sooner," Anders says.

I scrub my hand over my face. "I was a fuckup until we started NomNom together. But with our company, I was able to contribute to this family. I don't want to go back to being a fuckup."

"We never thought you were a fuckup," Anders says. "Or else we wouldn't have brought you into the business."

"Yeah, sure."

"Seriously," Theo says. "Not sure why you think of

yourself as a fuckup. You're the most competent person I know."

"I barely graduated high school, let alone college," I say. "I never had good grades. I was more focused on having fun and partying."

"So what?" Anders says. "It's not like that hurt you. We all have enough money to last us multiple lifetimes because of you."

He's right, but I've been clinging to this idea of seeing something through to the end as a test for myself. I've had to leave everyone I've ever met while growing up when my dad's next job came around. Sure, the flip side is they never followed me, but I left them first. I didn't want to leave NomNom like I had to leave all those places and people. I've been insistent on seeing it through until the end because it's something I never got to experience.

Fucking hell.

That's why I've clung to this job for so long.

That's why I couldn't stand to give it up when Bree kept pushing me to be honest.

"Are you okay?" Theo asks. "You look like you're straining there."

"Shh," I say, "I'm having an epiphany over here."

"Care to share with the class?" Anders asks.

"Oh, just playing out some childhood trauma with NomNom."

Anders frowns and Theo nods.

"We all grew up abnormally," Theo says. "On one side, it was fantastic, but on the other... it leaves behind insecurity and a lack of stability. Why do you think I'm so attached to Portland? Why do you think Anders pushed Zoey away?"

"Look at us and our problems," I say, sighing.

"We should start a club," Theo says.

"Slow down there," I say. "I wouldn't go that far."

They laugh and I can picture Bree joking that she should put that on a shirt and sell it online. My stomach clenches at the thought of her. She was right. I just had to talk to my brothers to clear the air.

"There's something else I messed up," I say.

"No surprise there," Theo jokes, but I don't react.

They both turn serious, waiting.

"With Bree. We had a horrible fight. I was ready to try with her, but then I got triggered and she got triggered and I said something that hurt her."

"What did you say?" Theo asks. "No, don't give me that look. I need to know on a scale of one to ten what we're dealing with."

"I said I could never have a relationship with her because she's too messed up," I mumble.

Anders winces and Theo grimaces.

"Okay, so we're dealing with level one hundred there," Theo says.

"Do you love her?" Anders asks.

"Yes," I say without hesitation.

"Then get her back," Anders says. "Make it up to her somehow."

"You don't get it," I say. "She cuts people out of her life if they hurt her. There's no way she'd take me back."

"When has that ever stopped you from going after what you want?" Theo asks.

"He's right," Anders says. "Make her listen. You don't want to go the rest of your life wondering what if."

They're right.

I just need the best idea in the world to get her attention.

CHAPTER 37

REE

My first therapy session wasn't as scary as I made it out to be.

Sure, it sucked to talk to a stranger about the most traumatic moment in my life, but I guess my little stint with Hayden helped. Because I got through it.

It also helped that my therapist, Nicole, only sneaked a peek under the lid on the box of my traumatic memories. One specific memory jumped out relating to the attack, mostly about the lead up to it and my guilt over insisting we "jog" a specific route. The route that eventually led to disaster.

We worked through my guilt, or at least started to. Luckily, I didn't have to go through the entire event at once. That would've been too overwhelming, and it's the thing I feared most about therapy. Turns out I didn't need to worry about it.

When we have about ten minutes left in our first session, Nicole asks me, "How often do you make your last-minute trips?"

"Since the attack, a couple of times a month."

"And before that?

"Any time I had a breakup. I used it to get some breathing room since I was a teenager."

"Why do you think it's increased since the attack?" she asks.

"Because it's fun?" I say, avoiding the question.

Nicole looks at me over her tortoise-shell glasses and raises an eyebrow. She doesn't say anything and just keeps staring at me expectantly.

"Or not," I say, and she huffs out a laugh.

"It's completely normal to have a strong desire to travel and explore. However, in your case, it seems like you've been using travel to cope with difficult emotions. Feeling the need to avoid your mom is completely normal. As is the need to avoid Seattle and the memories here."

With each syllable she utters, it's as if she's granting me permission to feel what I feel, to release the pent-up emotions without the weight of guilt. Her words become the key that unlocks the floodgates of my thoughts, setting them free in a turbulent rush.

"I just… it's complicated." My voice trembles and tears glisten in my eyes, reflecting the turmoil within. "It's like there are these warring feelings inside me. On one side, there's this overwhelming urge to escape, to distance myself from my mom. It's like I'm running from the pain, the heartache, the helplessness. But on the other side, guilt gnaws at my soul. It's a relentless reminder that I owe her everything, that I should be there for her, unwavering and selfless."

A heavy sigh escapes my quivering lips as I struggle to find the words to convey the storm raging in my heart. "Every time I travel, it's like I'm leaving a part of my humanity behind. I'm enjoying the life I have, taking trips, spending money, living as if her suffering is just a distant echo. But it's not. It's there. It's real, and it's a constant, agonizing presence in my life."

My throat tightens, and I can hardly speak, the words choking me. "I'm doing nothing to support her. I should save every penny, every ounce of my energy for her treatment, for her comfort, for her happiness. And yet, I prioritize my own desires, my own freedom, over her pain." I whisper brokenly, "I'm so selfish."

Nicole passes me a box of tissues, and I use one to wipe at my face.

"Thank you for sharing your feelings," she says. "Your inner conflict is entirely understandable. Balancing personal desires and caregiving responsibilities can be overwhelming. But it's crucial to recognize that taking care of yourself doesn't make you selfish. Together, we'll work through your trauma while also finding a balance on how to support your mom and pursue your dreams without overwhelming guilt."

I nod and blow my nose. That's exactly what I want.

"Let's pick up here when we meet next time." Nicole glances at the clock.

"Do you have availability tomorrow?"

"I love how excited you are to start your healing journey, but it's best to have a few days between appointments to allow time to process everything."

"Oh, fine."

"Don't worry." Nicole smiles. "We'll get through everything in time."

* * *

I MEET Mom at her condo. It's a small two bedroom, but she loves it. I think it has more to do with the neighborhood and how she can walk everywhere. She loves to be outside. Even after the attack, she refused to stay indoors and hide. She's way stronger than me.

Mom engulfs me in a hug the moment she opens the door. And I hold her tight.

We remain in her doorway, hugging. Neither of us makes a move to pull away. Not until we hear Jules call from the bottom of the stairs.

"Sorry I'm late," she says.

There's nothing new to that. It's difficult for Jules to keep on top of everything when she's single parenting two kids with a full-time job. She runs up the stairs and smiles when she sees Mom and me.

"I've got forty-five minutes and then need to get back to work," Jules says, before pulling me into a hug and kissing my hair.

Mom leads us to the kitchen where there's a variety of sandwich meat and fixings on the counter. I watch as Mom goes to the cabinet and takes out some plates. Her face was once smooth, but now the right side is a landscape of intersecting lines and ridges, mapping out the battle where flesh met fang.

Her left arm remains bent slightly and her movements on that side are jerky, no longer fluid. She needs more surgery to repair the damage, but we didn't have the money to pay for it. She didn't have health insurance since she was only working part time.

Jules and my own savings were nowhere close to get her the care she needed. And even if we saved every penny we had since January, it still wouldn't be close to enough.

"What kind do you want?" I ask Mom.

"Turkey and cheese would be great."

I prepare her sandwich first, remembering Hayden's dad making his mom's plate first. I'm not sure Mom ever had that kind of treatment, but I plan to rectify that.

Jules keeps shooting me looks.

"What?" I ask.

"How are you doing with… everything?" Jules glances at Mom and doesn't elaborate. She's been messaging me nonstop since I landed, checking in on me since I told her everything fell apart with Hayden.

"Well, I went to therapy this morning," I say, deflecting the real question she's asking.

Both Jules and Mom stop what they're doing and stare at me in shock.

They speak at the same time.

"You did?" Mom asks.

"How was it?" Jules asks.

I laugh. "It was okay and yeah, it's about damn time."

"I'm so proud of you," Jules says.

"Me too," Mom says.

"Thanks." I finish up the toppings on my sandwich and nod toward the table. "Shall we?"

I carry Mom's sandwich for her, and we all sit down. It all feels so normal, and not at all like this isn't the first time we're all together in months. It's comforting, and I didn't realize how much I missed this. Just being with the people I love.

"Tell me more about Istanbul," Mom says, taking a bite of her food.

"Well…" I debate how much I should say, but then I quickly throw away that thought. I need them and their support. I was stupid to push them away when I needed them the most. But not anymore. I refuse to make the same mistake twice.

I can't deal with the trauma from the attack alone.

I can't deal with Hayden breaking my heart alone.

"It was amazing and fun and horrible all at the same time," I say.

"What? Why?" Mom asks.

"Because I met a man."

Jules gives me a sympathetic look before saying, "She got her heart broken."

"What kind of asshole would do that to you?" Mom seethes.

"Apparently Hayden. I thought… I was starting to think he was the one." I choke out the last words.

"I did too," Jules says softly.

"You met him?" Mom asks Jules.

"Only on video," Jules says. "And by accident."

"Well, he's stupid to have let you go," Mom says, wrapping her good arm around my shoulder and kissing my hair.

A small huff of laughter bursts out of me. It's the most typical mom thing she could've said. It feels good to have them in my corner.

We spend the rest of the lunch going over the trip and everything I experienced. I don't diminish what Hayden and I had before it all fell apart.

I need them to understand that I may look okay on the outside, but on the inside, I'm completely shattered.

And I need help to glue the pieces back together.

CHAPTER 38

$\mathcal{H}$AYDEN

My mom was so excited when I told her I'm in love. But then she promptly gave me a lecture when I told her in the next sentence that I messed it all up.

I suffered through the lecture before we agreed on a family brainstorm session. I fiddle with the place settings on the dining room table while I wait for everyone to arrive. Mom rolls out a huge whiteboard and places it at the head of the table.

"What's that?" I ask.

"And here I thought you were smarter than that," Mom says.

"I meant, why do you have a whiteboard? What is it, the year 1999?"

Mom swats my shoulder. "This is a very serious

meeting we're about to have, and I refuse to have technology mess it up for us."

"Mom—"

"Zip it. You'll thank me later."

She pops the top off the black marker and writes MISSION WIN BREE BACK at the top of the board.

Maybe it wasn't the best idea to get the family involved.

Soon after, everyone arrives. Anders and Zoey, Theo, Ruby, and my dad. Ruby immediately grabs the green marker and writes "because Hayden fucked up" under Mom's title.

Theo grabs the blue marker and draws a stick figure of what I'm assuming is me given the tears on the face and the arrow through the heart.

Zoey laughs and pours me an entire tumbler of whiskey. "Here. I think you're going to need this to make it through tonight."

"Thanks." I take it and chug half in one go.

Anders has a bowl of popcorn in front of him, as if he's watching a movie. What an asshole.

Once we all settle around the table, Mom stands in front of the whiteboard.

"Thank you all for coming to this emergency family meeting," she says. "We will not leave here until we have a concrete idea on how to win Bree back."

"Is this all really necessary?" I ask.

"Did you screw up?" Theo asks.

"You know I did."

"Then we need to ensure you don't screw up again," Anders says. "Not when this is a matter of life and death."

"Since when did you become so dramatic?" Ruby rolls her eyes at Anders.

"I blame you," Anders says. "But it's the truth. It's a matter of Hayden living the rest of his life happy or wishing he were dead. That's how I'd feel if Zoey wasn't in my life."

We all look at Zoey, who's staring at Anders like he's her reason for living. Dramatics aside, Anders has a point. I can't imagine my life without Bree in it.

"Fine," I say. "But no more jokes. I need us to be serious for once."

Everyone nods and I relax a little.

"Tell us about Bree. Her likes and dislikes," Zoey says.

Mom has a marker in hand, ready to write what I say.

"She hates potatoes, she loves art and painting, she's scared of dogs—"

"Do you think she'd like it if you commissioned an art piece for her?" Ruby asks, interrupting me.

Mom writes that idea down with a star next to it. Zoey adds a few words to the list, like loves to travel, kind, and fun.

"What about taking her on her dream vacation?" Dad proposes. "Or a trip around the world."

Mom writes the idea down and we brainstorm for another hour. Everyone is excited to help, and they all give good ideas. But it all hinges on her talking to me first. I need to get her attention first. To do something so big, Bree can't ignore it even if she wanted to.

I zone out for a moment, thinking about what's important to her. And it all comes back to one thing.

"I've got the best idea," I say. "Quick, take a picture of the whiteboard so we don't lose what we wrote."

Dad takes a picture and I erase it all.

"Bree and her mom were involved in a dog attack. It permanently scarred her mom," I say. "I'm going to help her. Even if Bree doesn't want me anymore, it's the least I can do. For her. For them."

"I don't see Bree accepting money from you," Anders says.

"But she would if you created a charity and had her mom be the first person benefiting from it," Ruby interjects.

"That's brilliant," I say.

"And you're surprised, why?" she asks.

Theo covers his laugh with a cough, and she glares at him.

"What I meant to say is Ruby, you're a majestic queen who has only wise things to say. Your beauty and talent are unparalleled."

"That's better," she says, smirking.

"Would Bree like public displays, or is she more private?" Mom asks.

"Public, we joked about that once. That I should...." I trail off. Sure, we were joking in Bodrum about grand gestures, but what if part of her really wanted it? I'm probably grasping at straws, but the longer I think about it, the more the idea sounds like the best idea ever.

"Don't leave us hanging," Theo says.

"I've got the perfect way to win her back."

I tell them about our conversation. We spend the rest

of the night ironing out the details and splitting up the workload.

I hope Bree's ready, because she's in for a surprise.

CHAPTER 39

REE

"BREE, you won't believe what happened," Mom says the second I walk through her door.

I've come over every day for lunch for the past month. It's been fun reconnecting with her. We haven't gone into details about the attack or how I acted afterwards, but my therapist, Nicole, recommends we do some sessions together and work through it. Our first joint session is set for next week.

"What?" I ask, coming into the kitchen.

Mom is almost bouncing on her toes, a ball of energy. I smile along with her, caught up in her excitement about whatever happened.

"My doctor called this morning. They applied for me to be part of a charity. One that helps people like me, people permanently scarred from animal attacks."

"But we looked into that after the attack and there were no options." I spent days calling around, trying to find some organization to help, but there was nothing. I called plastic surgeons to see if they'd do something pro bono. Again, nothing. This sounds like a scam. And I don't want to break her heart, but I've got to be sure.

"I guess a new one just started, and… I got in."

"You did?" I ask.

"Yes, and that means I'm going to have access to all the best surgeons in the world. My arm might function more normally." She begins to cry.

My heart squeezes at her admission. I pull her into a hug and say, "You're beautiful. No matter what."

"You have to say that." She sniffles.

"Trust me, I don't. What's the charity called?"

"It's called Pawsitivity Recovery Foundation."

I take my phone out and open Google, typing in the name. Videos of Hayden fill my screen. I'm so shocked at seeing his face that I almost drop my phone.

"What's wrong?" Mom asks.

"It's… that's… Hayden." I turn my phone to her.

"You mean the douche from Turkey?"

I nod and Mom grabs my phone. She clicks on the first video of Hayden and it plays.

"Thank you for gathering today to celebrate the launch of the Pawsitivity Recovery Foundation," Hayden says on the screen. "My journey began with a powerful encounter— meeting the love of my life. She survived a dog attack, and after witnessing her resilience, strength, and bravery, I was moved to create this foundation."

Mom glances at me, but I can't say anything, too eager

to hear the rest of his words. He made this foundation after meeting me. What does that mean?

"The Pawsitivity Recovery Foundation is built on the belief that no one should endure the aftermath of such attacks alone. Our mission is clear: to provide free reconstructive surgery to those in need in the aftermath of an animal attack. We want to rewrite their stories of pain and offer them a chance for healing, empowerment, and renewal. The story behind this foundation is one of love, courage, and the conviction that we can transform pain into strength. We aim to make a difference in the lives of survivors, helping them regain their confidence and reshape their future. Thank you for joining us on this journey of compassion and transformation. Together, let's be the healing hands that change lives."

The audience claps and Hayden smiles charmingly into the camera before the video ends.

"So... he's cute," Mom says.

I snort. "Yeah... he's something alright."

"These aren't the actions of someone who's a complete douche."

"I'm so confused."

"Maybe he wants to say he's sorry," Mom says, grabbing her own phone. "Let's call Jules."

"That's not necessary. She's working."

"No, it's her lunch break."

Mom dials Jules even though I protest. She answers on the first ring and Mom puts her on speakerphone.

"Hey," Jules says. "What's up?"

"Bree's going to send you a video and I want you to

watch it," Mom says and motions for me to actually send it.

"That isn't weird at all," Jules says.

I roll my eyes and send her the video we just watched.

Jules is silent as she watches it and then says, "Holy shit."

"He loves her," Mom says, full of confidence.

"I think you're right," Jules says.

"Are we all forgetting," I say, "that he said he could never be with me because I'm too messed up?"

"And guess who got into the charity?" Mom continues talking as if I didn't say anything. She waits a beat before saying, "Me."

"You did?" Jules whispers, her voice thick with tears.

"I did."

"Put me on video," Jules says.

Mom passes me the phone to do that. Jules has a serious expression on her face, so at odds with the tears pooling in her eyes.

"Bree," she says. "These aren't the actions of someone who doesn't love you."

"But he hurt me. Took my biggest insecurity and threw it in my face."

"I get that," she says. "And you couldn't let go of your letter removal thing. It sounds like you both made mistakes during that fight. All I'm saying is maybe you should talk to him. If nothing else, to gain closure from it all."

"I'll think about it." I resigned myself to a life without Hayden. It's too much to reconsider everything after one video. They're asking me to change how I feel about him, to erase the hurt he caused, between one second and the next.

That's not possible.

The callous I placed around my heart might be too thick to let him back into my life. Even if he's offering Mom something as precious as this, I'm not sure I can get over what he said. What he did.

We say bye to Jules, and I go through the motions of lunch with Mom. But I'm not really here, not in any way that counts. I'm more numb than anything, frozen and unable to process what's happened in the past hour.

I make it back to my apartment, not remembering the drive. My iPad ends up in my hands without conscious thought. I type in the foundation name in my search engine. There's video after video, website after website, all featuring Hayden.

There's a link to his social media at the bottom of every webpage I visit, and it's bigger than the typical icon size. Curious, I click on it, and I'm taken to a TikTok page. Zoey and Hayden are in all of them. I click on the pinned post and Zoey smiles on the screen.

"We need your help," she says. "If you haven't heard, Hayden here needs to get his girl back. In honor of his fuckup, we made a special drink here at A Cup of Zodiac. It's called A Cup of Wanderlust. The drink is inspired by a place that's dear to both of them. It has Turkish coffee as its base and is infused with cardamon, rose water syrup, with powdered sugar around the rim of the cup. It's perfect for all the Zodiac signs dreaming of a different life. Whether that's the desire to travel or win back someone they've lost, come and get it. Wanderlust will only be on the menu for this week."

Hayden nods and says, "And for the entire week, I'll be waiting at A Cup of Zodiac, desperate to make my grand romantic gesture and right my past wrongs. B, if you're listening, please come and let me explain. I didn't mean it, and I'm so sorry. For everyone else watching this video, your mission, should you choose to accept it, is to spread the news far and wide. It's time to see if persistence pays off or if I'm just setting up shop for a week-long rejection party."

The video was posted yesterday, and it's already at three million views. There are thousands of comments of people guessing what he did to upset me, guessing who I am, and saying they'll happily date Hayden if the mysterious "B" doesn't.

I click on another video and it's Hayden and Zoey holding up a shirt with #WanderlustRekindled. Below the hashtag is a stylized heart that's outline is dotted and in the flight pattern of a paper plane. There's a pawprint at the start of the heart, while the plane is at the end of it.

"To help raise money for my new charity," Hayden says, "and to get the love of my life back, we're selling these limited-edition T-shirts. I met B while traveling to my favorite country and our shared love of travel connected us. This hashtag represents that, and I hope you will all like it."

"And," Zoey says, "anyone who visits A Cup of Zodiac wearing this shirt will get a free gluten-free donut with their order."

"What more can we want?" Hayden smirks into the camera.

That smirk makes me pause.

It reminds me of Bodrum and when we were discussing—

Holy shit. He's doing everything he said he would when we joked about it in Bodrum.

I can't help but be impressed with his determination. That he did all of this just to get my attention.

And fuck him, because he's got it.

CHAPTER 40

$\mathcal{H}$AYDEN

IT'S BEEN three days since Bree's mom got the news about being part of the charity.

Three days of me waiting like a fool at A Cup of Zodiac.

Three days of people coming in to take photos of me. They're mostly of me alone at a table in the corner with a sad face. It's pathetic, but I don't care. Not when it increases the chance of Bree seeing it. Of her deciding to come.

Not if it brings her to me, even if every day my hope that she'll show shrinks.

I really thought it'd be enough. That she'd come and at least hear me out. But perhaps... perhaps I hurt her too much.

Almost everyone in the coffee shop is wearing the shirts Ruby had made. Anders drew the picture on it and I'm not going to lie. They did a great job.

But everywhere I turn, I'm reminded of my mistake.

If plan A doesn't work... I don't know what I'm going to do. We didn't discuss a backup plan at the emergency family meeting.

Thirty minutes before closing, Zoey comes to my table and drops off a drink.

"It has alcohol. Looks like you need it," she says.

I sigh. "What if she doesn't show?"

"She will." Zoey squeezes my shoulder and heads back to the counter with Athena, the chef, and Ruby.

They whisper all together and keep glancing over.

I sigh again and take a sip of the drink. The hot chocolate is amazing with a dash of Bailey's and cinnamon. But I can't enjoy it. Not when Bree doesn't show... again.

* * *

THERE'S ten minutes until A Cup of Zodiac closes on day six, and there's still no sign of Bree. I wish time would speed up, just to get this day over with.

The past ten TikToks we posted went viral. The shirts sold out and a new shipment arrives tomorrow. Everything is going well. Everything except the purpose of this —to win Bree back.

For the past five days, I've started every single day hopeful. Hopeful that today will be that day. That she'd show.

Last night I realized if she hasn't shown up by now, that she's not going to. My grand gesture was all for naught.

Today I woke up with my hope buried under the weight of despair, like a diamond lost beneath the rubble of a shattered dream.

Tomorrow is the last day, and I don't even want to show up.

Not when there'll be a crowd of people to witness my failure. Every photo taken tomorrow will be a painful reminder that I lost the best thing in my life. All because of fear.

I sigh as Zoey finally flips the sign over to closed. But when her hand touches the lock, the door flies open, only to bounce back shut when it hits Zoey's foot.

Zoey steps aside quickly and Bree pushes inside with all the confidence in the world. Like she didn't leave me hanging for days. Like she didn't arrive at the last possible second.

"Hey," Bree says to Zoey.

"You came," Zoey whispers.

Bree strides to the counter, not even looking around the place.

Her oversized turquoise shirt perfectly offsets her red hair and creamy skin. She's radiant and it's like a knife to the chest. It doesn't seem like the weeks we've spent apart ravaged her like they did me.

Zoey's right behind her as Bree asks, "Can I have one of those Wanderlust drinks you're going on about in your videos?"

"You saw them?" I ask, standing so fast my chair topples over.

Bree glances at me and lifts her shoulder in response. Whatever that means.

"I'm not here for you," Bree says. "I'm here for Zoey."

"It's good to see you," Zoey says and prepares her drink.

Ruby snickers, and I glare at her. She has the decency to turn her back before laughing fully. Anders pulls Ruby to the far side of the shop and talks to her in low tones.

I stand there frozen, not sure what to do. I've imagined this conversation going in so many directions for the past month, and this was not on the list of possibilities.

That she'd show up... but not for me.

What does it mean? Either way, I refuse to have us part again without talking. I hurry to Bree's side.

"Make that two Wanderlusts, please," I say to Zoey.

Bree glances at me out of the corner of her eye.

"Thank you for coming," I say to Bree.

"You made it hard to ignore you."

"Good." I grin. "That was the plan."

Zoey hands us each a drink and says, "I'm going to just..." She points to where Ruby and Anders are and makes her way over to them.

"Do you want to sit?" I ask.

"Fine."

I pull a chair out for her, but she bypasses it and takes a different one.

Shit, this isn't going well already.

"I'm not sure why you even went through all that

effort," Bree says. "You made it clear how you felt in Istanbul."

"No, I didn't. I fucked up and planned to explain to you on the plane what happened. But you never showed. You deserve an explanation and an apology about what happened."

"Go on."

"As a child, I learned no one would follow me, or keep in contact with me, because I always had to leave because of my dad's job. I felt disposable to them, and when I found out you were still removing my letters, it felt like history was repeating itself. That you'd eventually cut me out of your life like they did to me."

She remains silent and stares at me as if weighing my words, weighing the truth in them.

"But then when you said I don't deserve your love," I say, "it triggered all the fear and rejection from my entire life. I lashed out at you, trying to make you hurt like I was hurt. I didn't mean a word I said to you because I was talking about myself. Not you, never you."

Bree takes a small sip of Wanderlust and nods. "Thank you for explaining what happened."

I wait for her to say more, but she remains silent.

"Perhaps I'm not being clear," I say. "From the first moment we sat next to each other on that flight, it was as if my wandering soul found its destination. I discovered my true north and my forever home with you. I love you, Bree."

"But how do we make this work?" she asks. "We live in two different cities. You're in Singapore nonstop..."

My heart leaps at her words. They're not a thank you

and see you never. They're full of possibilities. My buried hope rises from the rubble, ready to fill me to the brim.

"Well, I have some ideas for that, but I've got to know where you stand first. Do you forgive me?"

She stares at me for a beat, and I brace myself for her answer. I try to convince myself that I'll be fine if the answer is no, but I know I won't be.

"I started therapy to work through everything," she says.

That's the last thing I expected her to say.

"I'm so fucking proud of you," I say.

She flashes me a small smile before saying, "And I've talked about you in the sessions."

"That doesn't sound good."

"It's not." She grins. "Because my therapist helped me work through my feelings about what happened between us."

"And?" I ask. I can't take the suspense. It's like my entire soul is waiting for her next words.

"I realize I triggered you with my careless words. I'd never choose letters over you. I'm sorry for saying that and that you don't deserve my love. I was just terrified and hurt, like you were when you said what you said." She takes a deep breath and lets it out slowly. "I forgive you. And I love you."

Hope sparks in my veins and a flood of warmth fills my chest. She loves me. She loves *me*. But she's not smiling, not like I expected her to do after admitting that.

"Why do I feel like there's a 'but' coming?" I ask.

"Because I don't see how we're going to work out in the long run. What happens if you get scared and push me away again? I want to be with you, but I'm also terrified of getting hurt again."

"I get that. I do. And I know nothing I say will change how you feel. Only my actions will prove that to you. Just so you know, I quit my job. So, I'm ready to do anything to make this work. I can move to Seattle tomorrow if that's what you want. We can go off and travel the world together if that makes you happy. We can buy multiple houses anywhere you want and change where we live every few months, enjoying the best weather every time."

"You've thought about this."

"Thought?" I say with a huff. "If you mean obsessing over every possibility and find a solution to it, then yes."

"Really?"

"Of course," I say. "I want to prove to you with my actions that you're my priority. And I think it's time I see a therapist myself, to work through my abandonment issues."

"That's a good idea."

"And someone really smart gave me the best idea in the world."

"And who is this really smart person?" she asks coyly.

"You, it's always you. And if you'll join me, I'd love to travel, make a list of our favorite dishes, and learn how to cook them."

Her eyes widen. "I… you want to open that restaurant with your favorite food?"

"No, I want to open it with *our* favorite food."

"But the menu is going to be insanely long."

"Then maybe we need a few different places."

"You're serious?" she asks.

"Yes."

I cup her face in my hands. I can't take not touching her anymore. It's been too long.

"Okay," she whispers. "Let's do it."

She closes the gap between us and kisses me softly, tentatively. As if reacquainting herself with me. Savoring me, as if we have all the time in the world.

And we do.

Clapping sounds from behind us.

We break apart and Theo is standing in the doorway of A Cup of Zodiac with a grin on his face, his phone in hand, and the #WanderlustReKindled shirt over his suit. He looks ridiculous but Zoey, Anders, and Ruby all come over and high five each other.

Bree gives me a confused look and I laugh.

"It was a team effort to win you back," I explain.

"Yeah," Ruby says, "and FYI, if you didn't show tomorrow, then I would've hunted you down in Seattle."

That's the first I'm hearing of this plan, but by the looks on everyone's faces, it seems like they were all aware and on board.

"I've never had a fan club before," Bree says. "Want me to sign your shirt?"

"How about my chest?" Ruby grins.

Theo's head whips so fast in Ruby's direction that I'm surprised he didn't pull a muscle. He looks at Ruby with so much passion and expectation, it's a miracle they're both still clothed. They've really got to work out the tension between the two of them.

"I'd be honored." Bree laughs.

Ruby jogs to the counter, grabs a sharpie, and hands it to Bree.

"Welcome to the tribe," Ruby says to Bree.

And nothing has ever sounded so good, so right.

Because I hope Bree will become part of the family sooner than she thinks.

EPILOGUE

REE

FIVE MONTHS LATER

Hayden insisted on blindfolding me. He's so dramatic, but he wanted to show me something. We've been in the car long enough for me to get anxious, but traffic in Istanbul is always hit or miss, so I don't have any idea where we could be.

The past five months have been the best of my life. Every month, we've spent two weeks traveling somewhere new, one week in Portland, and one week in Seattle. We decide our new city or country to visit by picking a piece of paper from a bowl, and we take turns pulling them out.

That's how we ended up back in Istanbul.

It was a pleasant surprise. But today's been cold and rainy. Hayden's been grumpy about it, but it doesn't matter. We've never let something like weather get us down before, so there's no point in doing it now.

"Will you give me a hint?" I ask for the millionth time.

"We're going somewhere cold."

"Oh, I've got it. We'll be skydiving naked and freezing our important bits off."

"Close." He nuzzles my neck. "But I'm quite fond of all your important bits."

"So then we must be driving go-karts down the busiest street, dodging pedestrians like a video game."

"Closer," he says, laughing.

The car stops and Hayden says, "Wait here."

I'm dying to take the blindfold off, but I also love surprises. So, I hold off. Barely.

He guides me out of the car.

There's nothing that gives away where we are, just the normal city noises and traffic surrounding us.

"Hop on my back," he says, guiding my hands to his shoulders.

I hop on with a laugh.

He grips my legs and I lean in and kiss his neck.

"Love you," I say.

"I love you too."

He squeezes my legs and walks. It feels like we're walking up some stairs, and it's not just one or two. It's many. When he finally stops, he has a short conversation in Turkish with someone. It's a man, but I can't glean anything from the conversation to give any hint where we are. Or what we're doing here. Or why I'm blindfolded.

He walks up a few more steps and says, "I'll let you down now, but be careful. We're on some stairs."

His voice echoes around us.

"Can I take the blindfold off?" I ask, sliding down his back. He stabilizes me the second my feet touch the ground.

"Yes."

I whip it off and look around. We're inside a circular structure, like a tower. It's dim inside, but the steps leading upward have LED lights illuminating the pathway.

"Keep walking up," Hayden says.

"Where are we?" I trail my hand over the rough walls. They're a mosaic of large rocks in cement. There's brick colored rock lining the ceiling and a couple of small windows that look like old lookout areas.

"The Galata Tower."

I pause mid-step and look back at him. "Seriously?" I ask, recalling our conversation on the yacht so many months ago. "But you're scared of heights."

"Remember when I said I wouldn't let anything get in the way? I also meant that I'd face my fear when I met the right person."

"How could I forget?" I was jealous at the time of the faceless woman who he would make this trip with. The trip that means he wants to marry them, be with them forever.

"Good, then you know what this means."

I swallow hard, trying to cover my reaction to his statement. To his declaration. To the idea that he wants me. Forever.

"Should I make you carry me the entire way?" I joke.

"If you wish."

"Race you to the top?"

He grins. "I wouldn't expect anything else."

"On the count of three. One, two—"

I break off and sprint up the stairs, thankful for the waterproof boots I'm wearing to keep me from slipping on the stone steps.

Hayden laughs and is right on my heels, so close I feel his heat. But the steps are narrow and there's no way he'll be able to pass me.

I cackle at the realization that I'm going to win. But then Hayden moves like a ninja, scooping me up in his arms for the last few steps. He doesn't even break his pace and runs up them with me in his arms.

"I was totally going to win," I gasp, trying to get oxygen back into my lungs.

"Yup, but I always pictured taking these last steps together, with you in my arms, and our love illuminating the path ahead."

I melt, honest to stars melt, at his words.

We burst into a room, a restaurant of sorts. There are balloons and flowers everywhere, as well as a bunch of people.

I do a double take.

Wait, I recognize everyone.

Our families?

Hayden's smile is bright when he sets me down. Jules, her kids, and Mom stay where they are but wave at me. Mom uses her injured arm more freely after her surgeries. All thanks to Hayden and his generosity. Hundreds of people have contacted the charity for a chance at recovery, and Hayden's accepted every single one.

Zoey, Anders, Theo, his parents, and Ruby are also here. They whistle and clap when they see us.

I spin back to Hayden. "What's going on?"

"Surprise."

I laugh. "An amazing surprise at that, but why is everyone here?"

"Because I wanted them to witness my declaration of love and our engagement."

"Eng—"

I break off when he kneels on one knee and takes out a black velvet box.

"Amidst life's uncertainties, one truth has remained unwavering: you, Bree, are my North Star. My guiding light through every uncharted horizon. With you, every step I've taken is a step closer to the home my heart has yearned for, a home I've found within the shelter of your love. You are my compass, my destination, and my endless adventure. I can't wait to continue to find joy in the simplest pleasures and create memories that will forever shine in our hearts. Will you be my partner in all of life's travels and my refuge, my heart's truest home?"

I swallow hard, past the lump of emotion clogging my throat. But I want to say something in front of our families. It's time they all heard how much I love him.

"With you," I say, "I've found my forever joy, and in your arms, my truest home. With every beat of my heart, it whispers your name. So, yes, a thousand times yes, to a lifetime of love, laughter, and endless adventures together."

Hayden sweeps me into his arms. We gaze in each other's eyes, a million unsaid words sparking between us.

Our lips meet in a kiss that echoes across the world, through eternity. A promise of our souls intertwining.

Our family cheers and the pop of a champagne bottle sounds in the room.

"You didn't even see the ring," Jules shouts.

I pull back and laugh. Leave it to her to remind me of that.

Hayden opens the box and what's inside causes my breath to catch.

A huge heart-shaped diamond is nestled in the center. The band gracefully splits into three distinct paths that all hug the showstopping stone. A mixture of turquoise and diamond stones line the bands. It's the most unique ring I've ever seen.

Hayden lifts the ring and slides it onto my finger.

"Turquoise has been known to give travelers good luck and protection," he says before showing me the inside of the band and the coordinate engraved there. "It's for Istanbul. The place that brought us together and connected us."

"Oh my," I breathe, unable to look away from it. "It's perfect."

He slides the ring onto my finger and kisses me again. Our family descends upon us, and his is the most perfect proposal in the world. I wouldn't want it any other way.

Hayden taught me how to face my fears and how to fall in love with someone. It's something I didn't think was possible, but he proved me wrong.

He taught me that true love is a thread in life that never fades. It's the color that enriches every hue in the tapestry of our lives.

Love is the story etched into the universe; a tale written with every heartbeat.

And I'm lucky enough to have found it.

With Hayden.

And with me.

THANK YOU FOR READING

Thank you for reading my book. I know it's extra effort to write a review, but I'd be forever grateful if you could leave one on Amazon and/or Goodreads.

I do this all for you, my readers, to bring you joy and the ability to escape life's problems for a few hours. Thank you for your continued support.

Buckle up, because Theo and Ruby's much-awaited story is next.

ACKNOWLEDGMENTS

From the very beginning, the idea of crafting a novel rooted in Turkey held a special allure for me. With my husband being Turkish, and our shared connection to the beautiful country, it felt like a natural and deeply meaningful choice.

This particular narrative was conceived during my time residing in the vibrant city of Istanbul. While living in there, I was struck by the abundant presence of stray cats and dogs in the streets. What truly astounded me, however, was the remarkable care bestowed upon these animals—individuals going out of their way to provide sustenance and shelter. This stark contrast in treatment, compared to other countries, served as a poignant inspiration for me.

During my childhood, I harbored a profound fear of dogs, rooted in traumatic experiences of my own from aggressive canines. Through the character of Bree, I sought to convey these visceral emotions and illuminate the perspective of those who don't inherently possess an affinity for animals—a perspective often overlooked by those who assume everyone shares their love for them. Over time, I managed to confront and, to a large extent, conquer my fear, though I remain cautious when encountering unfamiliar dogs.

This story owes its existence to my husband, who graciously opened the doors to his culture and homeland. Your role as my own personal tour guide, revealing the intricacies of your beautiful country, has been invaluable. I'm grateful for your unwavering support and love.

Thank you to my brother-in-law, whose insights and recommendations about the city enriched the narrative with its non-touristy charm. Your contributions have been instrumental in bringing Istanbul to life within these pages.

To my mom: In the garden of life, you've been my unwavering sunshine, nurturing my dreams with your boundless love and unwavering belief. Your support is the cornerstone upon which my journey is built, and your encouragement, the wind beneath my wings. You've cheered for me from the sidelines of every chapter, making me believe in myself even when doubt threatened to creep in. Thank you for being the best mom I could've ever asked for. I love you.

To my sister: From the very beginning, you've been my partner-in-crime, my confidante, and my biggest cheer-leader. You've celebrated my victories as if they were your own, and your belief in me has been a constant reminder of the heights I can reach. I couldn't have done this without you, and I can't thank you enough for being your awesome self. I love you.

To my writing friends Gayle, Sandy, and Lisa: Your invaluable insights, creative guidance, and unwavering encouragement have been my cornerstone of this crazy self-publishing journey. I'm so grateful we all found our way into each other's lives. Thank you all for your support!

To Lizzie: Seriously, what would I do without you? You are not only an exceptional editor but a dear friend. Your blend of humor, astute commentary, profound insights, unwavering support, and invaluable feedback is a constellation of gifts I thank the stars for each day. Justice for Gerald!

And finally, to my readers. Without you, none of this would be possible.

MORE FROM ALEXIS GORGUN

A CUP OF ZODIAC (BOOK 1)

From author Alexis Gorgun comes a steamy, laugh-out-loud romantic comedy series. Indulge in this modern twist on Bridget Jones's Diary.

Zoey Phillips made one rule when she fled to Portland —no more relationships.

Too bad she didn't account for a tattooed, bearded, and grumpy coffee shop owner called Anders Watson. The reviews all agree that he hates people, especially those who change his drinks menu.

She's forced to apply for a job at Anders's coffee shop after her disastrous decisions lead her to rely on a horoscope app for everything.

But the app didn't warn her that Anders would hate her on the spot and refuse to hire her. It also didn't tell her that she'd make the worst first impression in the history of first impressions. Or that those are the exact reasons she'd get the job.

With the stars on her side, her luck has got to turn around sometime soon.

Could her escape to Portland be the key to turning around her relationship with money, family and romance?

ABOUT THE AUTHOR

Alexis Gorgun writes laugh-out-loud, steamy stories that'll tug on your heartstrings.

Every book will introduce you to a sassy heroine who will inspire you and a stubborn man they will fall for. You'll experience moments that'll make you throw your book across the room.

Learn and grow with real characters facing real challenges. They aren't afraid to cuss, and they will stumble as they navigate life.

But here's the guarantee: every story will make you earn your happily ever after.